LIMBO

LIMBO

A novel about Jamaica

by

ESTHER FIGUEROA

ARCADE PUBLISHING
NEW YORK

Arcade Publishing books may be purchased in bulk at special discounts for sales promotion, corporate gifts, fund-raising, or educational purposes. Special editions can also be created to specifications. For details, contact the Special Sales Department, Arcade Publishing, 307 West 36th Street, 11th Floor, New York, NY 10018 or info@skyhorsepublishing.com.

Arcade Publishing® is a registered trademark of Skyhorse Publishing, Inc.®, a Delaware corporation.

Visit our website at www.arcadepub.com.

10 9 8 7 6 5 4 3 2 1

Library of Congress Cataloging-in-Publication Data is available on file.

ISBN: 978-1-62872-319-9

Printed in the United States of America

DISCLAIMER

This is a work of fiction. All characters are fictitious and the invention of the author. None is identical with any person living or dead. Real places, actualities, incidents, and policies that appear in this novel are based on documentation, research, and/or personal experience but are used fictitiously. Though I would wish otherwise, the International Institute for Environmental Sciences and Advocacy does not exist, nor does MIT have anything to do with this Institute, nor do any named foundations or public individuals. This is a satire. It is meant to make you laugh lest you weep.

We are lost, but only so punished
That without hope, we live on in desire.

Dante Alighieri
La Divina Commedia

...
And limbo stick is the silence in front of me
limbo

limbo
limbo like me
limbo
limbo like me
...
knees spread wide
and the water is hiding

limbo
limbo like me

knees spread wide
and the dark ground is under me
...
sun coming up
and the drummers are praising me

out of the dark
and the dumb gods are raising me
...

Edward Kamau Brathwaite
Limbo

TO

John Maxwell

(1934–2010)

and

Diana McCaulay

Chapter One

Flora Smith is checking her math, tallying the money she needs to meet next month's payroll, stop the roof from falling in, pay the rent, and keep projects going. She scrutinizes the subtotals then re-adds the numbers, starting at the bottom if she previously started at the top, but stubbornly the bottom-line remains the same. Her office extension is ringing, but she ignores it. Her cell phone is off. Math requires her complete concentration. Doris, one of her staff, waves a hand in front of Flora's face and mouths, "Mr. Krenshaw on the phone for you. Says he's been calling you on your cell but no answer."

Flora is about to tell Doris that Mr. Krenshaw can leave a message, but he is one of the richest men in the Caribbean, and she has these nagging figures in front of her, so she picks up her phone.

"Malcolm, I heard you on the radio this morning. I was very impressed. You sound so passionate."

"Flora, why you don't answer you damn phone? Been calling you all morning."

"Malcolm my dear, it's that time of the month when I have to reconcile my books, and during such time, much like you during carnival, I don't answer my phone."

"So what you think about this damn disaster?"

Flora bites her tongue and does not ask which damn disaster. She can think of many disasters of which his personal tragedy is not anywhere near the top of the list. Instead she consoles, her voice a calming purr, "What a ting ee? How dem coulda do you such a ting?" Then she adds the purely rhetorical question, "You know who did it?" Flora is pretty sure she knows who did it, and she knows Malcolm knows; the question is, would anyone actually identify who had done it and would there be any consequences? The answer is most likely no. Jamaica is a small island; everything might be known, but everything is off the record. You might end up at an event with someone you had named, and when confronted, what would you say to them? You would of course say, "Nah man, wasn't me."

"Well, we have some ideas, have some leads. Damn truck driver who had first said where he had taken the sand now refuses to speak. Tell me (*Oh, oh,* she thinks, *he's actually going to ask me for a favor*), is it possible to trace where sand comes from? You know, like stealing a . . . a . . .."

Flora, who has a doctorate in earth sciences, her specialty mineralogy, interrupts his linguistic labor, "Yes, you can. Sand has DNA just like you and me."

"You mean if we get a sample . . ."

"You can compare it to a sample from somewhere else and see if they match? Yes."

Malcolm sighs. "Flora, you can do that?"

"There are government agencies to do this sort of thing."

"Yes, but I don't trust them."

It is Flora's turn to sigh.

"Tomorrow morning. We doing some investigating. I want you to come and lend your expertise. Will send the jet for you. Will only take a few hours of your time, and you'll be back in two twos."

"LEND, Malcolm? I cannot LEND. I have to raise three million JA dollars by the end of this month, or I have to lay off two of my staff, and I will have to close the office because I can't pay the rent. And either way I have to close the office because the roof is collapsing. Seems to me that our last request to you for a donation was met with a form letter saying SO VERY SORRY!"

"Flora! Flora, calm the hell down. When did you request money from me? I don't recall seeing any request from you."

"Well, let's see, how about every year for the last ten years?"

"Okay. Okay. How much you need?"

Flora looks at her columns. "I need one point three for the roof. I need one point five for salaries. I need a hundred thousand for rent and another hundred thousand for utilities and such."

"Alright. I will have my assistant Leslie-Ann call you and make arrangements. She will have a check waiting for you at the airport tomorrow. Okay?"

The sleek corporate jet holds eight, but there are only four people on board. When Flora asks for Malcolm, Leslie-Ann informs her that Malcolm and his partners flew over the night before. In addition to Flora, Executive Director and CEO of Environment First, there are three members of the news media: two print journalists who specialize in environmental matters—Milton "Milt the Lion" Brown and Natasha Silo—and Mark McKensie, Jamaica's leading radio talk-show host. The day is unusually clear. There is a high-pressure trough ahead of a tropical wave that no doubt will be more than waving when it arrives. There are no clouds, and it is already blazing hot at 7:30 in the morning. Flora is very well acquainted with her fellow travelers, and they exchange lively speculation as to who, what, where, and when, as well as deep skepticism as to how something of this scale could have happened unnoticed, and why a multi-million dollar property would go unmonitored.

Having left Kingston, as they head north over the core of the island, Flora takes note of the scars, gouges, and disfigurement of the hills mined for bauxite, and the craters, pits, sludge lakes, and discarded bauxite roads. Milton, sitting across from her, eagerly photographs the ravages as they fly by. He is the senior statesman of journalism, whose stories are always peppered with names dropped of all the prime ministers and leading figures he has known, stories always begun many decades before, to remind in case any one had not noticed, that he is the most senior, most knowledgeable, and most capable person among them. Milton and Flora, long-time co-conspirators, have been working together to stop the building of an alumina refinery in St. Ann, and some weeks before had been soundly booed and ridiculed at a public hearing packed with workers from the bauxite company. As they pass over the refinery site that is already being cleared for construction, they look at each other, shake their heads, and laugh.

At the end of that meeting, a friend very highly placed in the Jamaican government took Flora aside and warned her about her safety. He told her that she needed to be aware that the bauxite company is owned by one of Russia's most dangerous oligarchs, and she needed to be careful. She performed her usual Iron Lady routine and acted both outraged and unafraid, but on the drive home, she found herself shaking uncontrollably. And when home, went straight to bed, continuing to shiver no matter how many covers she burrowed under. She could not sleep. Hadn't there been a Russian journalist who had been forced into hiding because he dared to write about a bauxite oligarch? Was it the same oligarch or a different one? Who could keep track of the various oligarchs? But, really, what can they do to her? She has no horse to decapitate and place by her pillow. She has no pets at all (unless you count the croaking lizards living behind her paintings), so animal torture is off the list. She has no children, currently no husband, and her ex-husbands have disowned her. She is an only child, and her parents are already dead, so she has no family they could hold hostage. They will have to come directly after her. Would they kill her outright or make it look like an accident? For a while, she tried to remind herself to be like a pilot and examine her car before she got in, but she had no idea what she was to look for and stopped stooping down to look for bombs, because the last time she had ripped the seam of her pants. The constant checking under the bonnet to see if various cables were intact led to her hands getting dirty, thus her clothes getting soiled and her face smeared with grease. She has given up on vigilance.

❂

The jet taxies to a halt in Montego Bay, and they get out into a rush of heat rising off the tarmac. They are met by resort developer Quincy Gold, who Flora thinks of as Young Gold even though he isn't particularly young anymore and who, to his face, she calls Junior Gold. He has certainly taken to looking like his father, with the protruding belly and fattening jowls of the successful businessman, but his voice betrays him, never reaching his father's commanding bass, but still sounding like the petulant teenager she'd known when she'd been one of his father's legion of mistresses. Flora runs her hand through her hair as she smiles at Quincy and asks how his father is doing. He shrugs, "The old man? The doctor says he should stop smoking, stop drinking, get some exercise, but no one can tell him anything!" Feeling sorry for Young Gold, Flora gives him a hug and links her arm in his as they walk in the direction of the waiting helicopters.

❂

Flora recognizes that her weakness for men has led her to some not-so-smart decisions. Senior Gold was one of her more tawdry moments between husband one and husband two. Being a devout heterosexual has led to complications. There were the husbands of other women and then there were her husbands. The first till-death-do-us-part lasted five years, which more than exhausted Flora's capacity for domestic fidelity. The second lasted only three years, but had felt like a decade, they were so hopelessly unsuited and spent most of their marriage trying to separate. Now men her age are not the least interested in her romantically. Their gaze only registers younger women, and she has become invisible to them. Her eager young men are lots of fun, cute, and hard and keep her thinking thoughts more appropriate to her teenage years, but they ultimately bore her as they had when she was a teenager.

What to do? She has no answers. Having given up on marriage, Flora lived for two years in unwedded bliss with her last man, until he had abruptly rung wedding bells with the daughter of a prominent politician and left her to wonder what she had done wrong this time. Flora had gone through a brief period she calls her "Oprah Phase" where she hoarded self-help books: *Smart Women Stupid Choices*, *Ten Steps to Reclaiming Your Inner Power*, *The 14 Secrets to Successful Self Fulfillment*. She had founded an environmental organization out of nothing and has been making it work for fifteen years when most nonprofits don't last five, and this in a place where the environment isn't on anybody's radar. So isn't this a great achievement? Isn't this enough? If it had ever been enough, she now has very grave doubts.

As they approach the helicopters fronted by a smattering of men standing waiting, Malcolm walks toward them, warmly greeting Flora as he removes her arm from Quincy's and leads her discretely to the side.

"Flora! So happy you could make it. You are looking especially delicious this morning. Did Leslie-Ann take care of you?"

Flora pats his arm and tries not to inhale his cologne. "She did. Thanks, Malcolm. We can talk more about that later."

Malcolm, looking anxiously toward the helicopters, mumbles, "Yeah man no problem." As the helicopter blades begin to whir, he points Flora back in that direction. "We better get going. We can talk on the way over."

Yeah, sure, thinks Flora. Anyone who has ever been on a helicopter knows you can't talk above the din. In her handbag is an envelope with a check for fifty thousand Jamaican dollars with a promise of another fifty thousand to come soon. Cheap bastard! He has given her less than a thousand US dollars. And the insult of the "rest to come" was dependent on what, her solving his problems? But Flora is not perturbed, he needs her expertise, and he will pay for it. The bill she will send for her technical services and lab work will go a long way to guaranteeing that the Environment First office stays open with a brand new roof.

CHAPTER ONE

The two helicopters rise into the air and fly along the shore, first heading east to Trelawny from Montego Bay. The helicopter door is open so a television news cameraman can record, and Milton is also snapping away. The noise is deafening; communication takes the form of pointing. Flora is admiring the singular length and beauty of a white sand beach when Milton gesticulates with great urgency. The helicopter swoops down low so they can get a close-up and then rises above so they can fully grasp the scope of the destruction. She had seen photographs of the site, but they do not adequately capture the dimensions of the damage. The once exquisite beach has been turned into a large-scale mining pit that is filling with slimy water. There is a makeshift road with big tire tracks where the trucks hauled out the sand.

Tears wet Flora's face. She has absolutely no connection to this location other than her objection to it being the projected site of a huge hotel, casino, and luxury condominium development, but every molecule in her body hurts when she sees her island being abused. Her shoulders begin to heave. After they land, she sits with her face in her hands, weeping. The others go ahead. She knows they think her overemotional, but too bad. That is one thing she has no intention of changing.

Flora gets a grip, blows her nose, dries her face, and grabs her sampling equipment. When she makes it to where everyone has gathered at the side of the mine, Malcolm is in full stride talking to two television cameras. Flora takes note of who was in the second helicopter: in addition to the cameraman from the other TV station, there are the Bent brothers, sons of the richest hotelier in the Caribbean (they are referred to in the press as entrepreneurs and investors in the development); Matt Cohen, the Warren Buffett of the Bahamas (before Warren started to give his wealth away); and Sheldon Day, pit-bull attorney to the wealthy who is usually snarling at her (Environment First sued one of his hotel clients for dumping sewage into the ocean), but today is smiling benignly at her.

"As you can see, this is the utter criminal undoing of a ten-billion-dollar absolutely unique, highest quality, seven-star development that would have brought needed employment, development, and pride to this area." Malcolm's voice is cracking with anguish, "Instead, because of the theft of our sand, we are left with a despoiled environment and an impaired ability to continue with our project. Those who have committed this criminal act must be held accountable. They must be punished. They will be punished. I will see to that." Malcolm shakes his fist at the camera as he says these last lines, and Young Gold and the Bent brothers break into applause. Flora avoids eye contact with Milton so as not to lose her composure. He's whispering something to Natasha Silo, and Flora can easily imagine his droll remarks. Malcolm had been very forgiving when other people's sand was stolen. He'd told Flora to "ease up nuh man" and that "everybody do it." She's looking forward to sharing a beer with Milton and having a good laugh. Malcolm and the rest of these developers' sudden conversion into zealous environmentalists is beyond ludicrous.

As Malcolm leads the group on various photo ops, Flora goes off to collect sand. It really is a large, well-situated property. If it was worth so much, why hadn't they protected it? Flora is absorbed in her work and relieved to be alone. She looks out for fossils and observes the various geological substrata. She thinks about the millions of years and intricate biological processes that went into making this piece of the Earth, to making the sand. It is irreplaceable. Sand formation is slow, and now even slower with the depletion of sand-producing fish due to overfishing, destruction of fish nurseries by shoreline development, degradation of the coral reefs by algae-producing pollution, and global-warmed bleaching. In addition, rising sea levels and bad development practices cause shoreline erosion. Developers are desperate for sand. They have to get sand from somewhere, and that means stealing it from another beach, shipping it in from some other tropical location, or making "sand" from crushed rocks. Malcolm's resort development will have to acquire sand, but there is little likelihood that once deposited the new sand will stay put. Flora takes samples from a range of sites, labels them carefully, and photographs each sampling area. She hasn't been outdoors doing fieldwork in a long time, and it gives her fulfillment in a way that overseeing staff or persuading policy makers never does.

Back in the helicopter, they fly west over the likely culprits. The first is Conquistador Bay & Village, a cluster of high-rise luxury hotel-condominiums and villas, which despite the ads and brochures depicting a romantic beach broader than any in Jamaica, has no beach whatsoever, and is in the process of blasting the rocky shoreline and attempting to engineer a beach. Flora doesn't need to take samples because the Conquistador has already handed over evidence to the government's environmental agency, saying they had legitimately bought sand from a certified company. Malcolm used his close connection to the Prime Minister to get her some of that sand for testing.

The next hotel is part of the very successful Vista Mar chain, of which there are four on the island with another two planned. Flora can't understand why they would need sand since they already have a beach, and that is the very thesis the Vista Mar Pine Grove argued when absolutely denying taking any sand. But as they fly low over the shore, Flora immediately sees dissimilar coloration and texture of sand on one end, and guesses they already have an erosion problem and added new sand to compensate. Luckily for Flora, that side of the beach has no security guards. To not blast the area she will sample, the helicopter deposits her at a distance. Running, she quickly shovels sand from three locations into three small buckets then waves for the helicopter to come and get her. She hasn't had so much excitement since the previous year when she and Milton drove all over empty bauxite roads videotaping the failed reclamation efforts. No one stopped them, but driving by a few months later, the entrance they had used was blocked with concrete slabs, and had a very large No Entry sign posted, replacing the smaller one they had ignored.

The last hotel is the Calypso, the largest in Jamaica yet still expanding. Located on what had been a sugar plantation spreading out onto a rocky point, a truly picturesque setting but with a dearth of beaches for the 3,000-room resort. There had been a few small, delicate coves, but they did not satisfy the grandiose aspirations of the hotelier, so shoreline was pulverized, sea walls built, and tons of sand deposited. As Flora flies over, she sees gangs of workers spread out frantically raking sand; they stop long enough to shout obscenities at the helicopters and fling their arms in the Jamaican sign language that signifies "go weh." Since most Jamaicans lack steady employment, the opportunity to work brings great loyalty to the one who is keeping them from hunger, at least until they start to feel exploited, and then they burn the place down. But this is simply an unexpected day's work for people who are financially vulnerable, and they aren't about to have anyone box food out of their mouths. Flora can't get samples. The site is too big, and the situation too threatening. They will have to figure out something else. She can only hope that the raking will not defeat her sampling methodology.

The jet back to Kingston is full. Malcolm sits beside Flora, spoiling her fun. She is unable to share notes with Milton, and her plan of shooting the breeze over a beer is dashed as Malcolm takes them all out for a late lunch—the media always ready for free food. Flora can barely stay awake after the unusually heavy meal. When working, she is used to eating granola bars or peanuts with raisins and calling it lunch. She and Malcolm discuss the Calypso sampling problem, and he is unfazed. He has already paid someone to sneak in during the night to get what she needs. She explains that, given the raking, said person would have to take sand from a variety of sections, digging deep as well as scooping exposed sand. She doubts he will be able to label anything and worries over sample contamination. Flora reassures Malcolm that she will do some preliminary testing at the lab that night. And he promises that if she sends his company the bill for the roof they will "take care of it."

CHAPTER ONE

Flora drives home on autopilot; it takes less than ten minutes, and she has no recollection of any part of the journey. She walks in the house, goes straight into the bathroom, and sticks her head under the shower thinking the water could never be cold enough. And then she turns the fan on full blast and flops naked on her bed. When she wakes, it is dark, and she curses the thought of having to go anywhere. It is now deliciously cool, and there is her favorite sound: rain falling. She turns off the fan and slides under the covers to listen to the raindrops on the leaves outside her window.

All the lights in the department are on. Graduate students apparently like to work at night. It's been six years since Flora was in the faculty of Earth Sciences, but she is still called "Prof." She enjoys being an occasional guest lecturer but refuses to return to the university despite being pestered to do so every year. She is frequently invited to speak to obscure groups like architects, retired teachers, and bird watchers with maybe three people in the room interested in what she has to say. She is a celebrity fixture on all the talk shows. Not hard to be a celebrity in a place that is small and has hardly any environmentalists.

Flora waves at Derek, her favorite grad student, who still has not managed to finish his dissertation. He is the department darling. In addition to being brilliant, he doesn't mind doing his professors' work, is a very competent teacher being paid graduate student rates, and is a wiz in the lab. What's not to like?

"Hey Prof," he grins, "I know why you here."

"Is that so?" He bounds into the lab behind her. Flora rubs her temples. "That being the case, how about you help me?"

"Sure ting." They walk outside into what has become a drizzle and get the remaining samples out of her car. Another of Derek's attributes are his muscles. Flora's are feeling sore, so she lets him carry most of the gear.

"Okay. Sample One of Site A. Compare with Sample One of Site B." Flora focuses the microscope, switches the slides back and forth, then moves for Derek to take a look.

"Look the same to me, Prof."

"Me too."

Flora goes through each batch quickly. She will examine them more carefully on a specialized imaging machine that takes isolates and then do chemical analysis. The more tests she does, the higher her bill to Malcolm and associates.

"Derek, don't you have your own work to do?"

He laughs, "I waiting on Prof Maraj to get back to me on my last chapter. He's had the thing for almost a year now." Flora rolls her eyes. Maraj is notorious.

"Well, let me know if I can help." Maybe there is some test she hasn't thought of that Derek can perform and get paid for. There is that new infrared spectrographic imaging technology that the geology guys working for the oil prospectors have. That would probably cost more than Derek's wages for the semester.

She locks the samples in her locker and leaves Derek in the laboratory. Her feet wet from a puddle she hadn't noticed, Flora stands by her car and calls Malcolm. He doesn't answer, so she leaves a message. "Malcolm, the samples match. Their sand is your sand. This is preliminary testing. I will follow up with tests that can stand up in court. Night, night."

Chapter Two

In the middle of a vivid dream set in Prague, Flora stands outside a cathedral whose bells are ringing a mournful toll that gradually becomes her phone ringing. There is no way she is getting out of bed, so she flails her left arm along her bedside table in hope of encountering a phone. Her mouth feels like a dry sponge, and she is convinced that aliens landed and operated on her brain during the night. Brain, what brain? The phone stops ringing as soon as she finds it. Fuck! Flora opens one eye and uncovers the digital clock; she can't sleep with it winking at her. Eleven sixteen. Wow. She managed to sleep over five, maybe six hours. She can't quite remember what time she made it home.

The phone rings again. It is Sandy, one of her board members and a persistent busybody.

"So are you alone?"

"Huh?" Flora cannot get her voice working.

"Was just wondering if you had company in bed with you given the way you and that young man were going at it on the dance floor."

Flora sits up and looks with great alarm at her bed, half expecting to find some young man in it. None. Should she check under the bed?

"No, I'm alone." The effort of speaking makes Flora cough.

"You okay?"

"Oh yeah, just waking up, was in the middle of a dream in Prague. I've never been there!"

"Sounds lovely."

Flora can think of not a word to say.

"Just called to say congrats. A fabulous time was had by all and a very successful fundraiser. Everyone was there! Doesn't hurt that you were on the front page of all the newspapers yesterday."

Yesterday? Flora remains speechless.

"Well, darling I have to rush, but just wanted to say how great I think everything went."

Really couldn't wait to tell me that, huh? She forces herself to speak, "Thanks, Hon. See you at the board meeting on Monday."

On the toilet, peeing, Flora begins to recall fragments from the night before. Covering her face in horror, she laughs so hard she wants to throw up.

❁

Last night was Environment First's bi-annual fundraiser. Sandy is correct. Flora had been front page, on television and on all the radio talk shows that day (well, if not always in person, she was the subject.) Because of her expertise, what one editorial called her "sound science," she as sole witness (in typical Jamaican fashion all the actual eye-witnesses had disappeared, leaving only the "expert witness") had convinced the judge with her dazzling scientific evidence. She had delivered a half-hour deposition accompanied by a stunning PowerPoint presentation, Derek's handiwork for which she had paid him handsomely with Malcolm's money. The multimillion dollar case was going to trial with a fairly obvious outcome unless the defendants wanted to settle fat sums of money out of court. Malcolm had already shown his gratitude: the environmentally friendly materials for a shiny new roof at Environment First's *Eco Yard* had been delivered.

CHAPTER TWO

The attendance at the fundraiser was not only double what was typical, but they had raised easily ten times more than they usually did. And this was not counting the earlier generosity of Malcolm's partners. Oh yes, Flora was whistling a happy tune, so happy that she kept visiting the bartender for his delicious rum punches. All beverages were provided by Jamaica Rum Ltd., the CEO of which was a previous board member, and the food catered by Mystic Blue Mountain Catering, owned by a daughter of a loyal donor.

In the waning hours, Flora found herself on the dance floor with Jerome, a dive master at one of the north coast high-end boutique hotels. There exists a group of well-heeled, very bored middle-aged women who pass around their young men like so much candy, and she had heard rhapsodic talk of Jerome. Her friend Miranda had encountered him when taking guests out for a spin on her husband's yacht and had insisted on individual dive lessons that had started in her pool. Miranda never actually bothered with certification but claimed to have learned all sorts of useful things. Flora started out dancing with any and everyone, but Jerome stayed close at hand and became her exclusive partner when the DJ started playing slow music. In retrospect, Flora was relieved that most people had departed, especially people that mattered, because who wanted to witness a fully grown woman grinding on the dance floor with a guy young enough to be her son?

Flora goes into the kitchen and pours herself a long glass of coconut water, followed by fresh-squeezed orange juice and then filtered tap water. She massages her face and scalp and says out loud, "Did I really do that?" as she tries to remember what they had actually done when they left the gala and drove to where Jerome was staying. She had not gone inside, she was sure of that. He had not invited her. They had stayed in her car in the driveway making out. She had not brought him home, she isn't sure why, but now is very grateful.

She should not have been driving at all. "This has got to stop!" This insane indulgence in risky behavior has to stop. But she's told herself this numerous times before and still has these humiliating lapses. Maybe she needs to track down and capture husband number three. Maybe she should go online and find her ideal match, her soulmate. Or maybe she should just go over to her friend Petra's house and buy some of the sex toys she is always pushing, "Better than any man! After this you will want no man! Trust me."

The morning after always fills Flora with self-loathing and menacing voices in her head calling her a slut—her father's voice the loudest and most insistent, a stinging slap across her face. No way is she calling Jerome to get his version of their dalliance. Instead, she calls her best friend, Lilac, who listens to her ranting and blubbering and assures her that, yes, she can still show her face. No, it had not looked so bad. She and Jerome are very good dancers, and they were just two people enjoying themselves. And, anyway, those who might have noticed are all people who love and respect her. So she is not to worry. And, yes, Lilac is coming right over and will make them lunch.

Lilac arrives promptly with three bags of provisions. She knows better than to expect anything resembling fresh food at Flora's. Flora snoops in the bags as Lilac places them on the counter. Lilac swipes her away, "Behave youself bad pickney! I am making us something delectable." Delectable? That was guaranteed. Flora knows she isn't to interfere so sits on a bar stool and watches her friend go to work, Lilac's long, graceful fingers professionally slicing and dicing. And as she has repeatedly done over the years, Flora puzzles as to why she just doesn't marry Lilac. She'd be well fed, she'd be loved and fussed over, and since Lilac is a mother of adult children, she'd have children and grandchildren without the responsibilities of raising them. She and Lilac have known each other since kindergarten, and no one else knows her every flaw and still manages to love her.

CHAPTER TWO

Lilac adds diced sweet peppers while whipping the eggs she seasoned with onions, garlic, nutmeg, thyme, pimento, and cilantro. She is making an ackee and brie omelette. This she serves with fried breadfruit chips, and a heaping of mixed greens with beetroot and blood orange slices, dribbled with a lime and mustard vinaigrette. Dessert is chilled lychee fruit. Their beverage is a smoothie of mango, banana, and papaya blended with home-made passion fruit juice.

Flora lies on her living room floor on a Guatemalan throw rug she bought at a global warming conference, rubbing her stomach and moaning in ecstasy. "Laad av mercy you kill me! Me cyan move!" Lilac, with all five foot ten of her stretched out on the hand sculpted guango-wood couch, shows no sign of distress, most likely already thinking of what she will prepare for dinner. Flora soaks in Lilac's calming beauty, her smooth rich black skin, her slender elegance, and thinks of her friend's quick intelligence and uncomplicated savvy. Lilac has not one drop of Drama Queen in her DNA.

Lilac opens her eyes, meets Flora's gaze with a wicked smile, "Pretty Browning get youself ina trouble wid man again!"

Flora sighs, "Lilac Samuels, you clearly do not love me. If you did you would not reference my most recent humiliation! And, anyway, I am not in trouble. I have no plans to see Jerome again!"

Lilac rolls her eyes and laughs, "I do so love you. Come here, bad pickney." Lilac moves over to make room for Flora who crawls over to the couch. As she has done since they were girls, Lilac gently strokes Flora's arms and shoulders with the tips of her cool fingers and plays in Flora's curly hair, once a lush brown with blonde and red tones when in the sun, now auburn with gray streaks.

Flora purrs, "You putting me to sleep."

"So tell me this: is who tief di sand?"

"Me cyan seh."

"What you mean you cyan seh! Remember Bunny, my assistant at Chez Michel?"

For ten years, Lilac had been in charge of the kitchen at the most expensive restaurant on the north coast. Flora does not remember Bunny but nods her head anyway.

"He is now chef at one of the New Vista Mar restaurants—would you believe it pretends to serve Mexican food? Anyway him seh him friend drive one of the sand truck dem. And one next friend in a fishing boat one night see all sorts of tings agwan."

Flora is noncommittal. "E'heh?"

Lilac stops her caresses. "Well, Bunny tell mi seh whole heap of Big Man involve, including politician and police and maybe some of the landowner demself. Is true?"

Flora takes Lilac's hand and replaces it where it had been, the tender soft inside of her right arm, "Don't this is Jamaica? So what you think? Cho! But mus!"

Lilac's fingers expertly resume their path up and down Flora's arm, "The trial not going go through den!"

"Well, I have done my bit. If it turns out I am the only uncorrupt person on this island, well then, so be it." Flora closes her eyes, snuggles into her friend's body and falls asleep.

Chapter Three

Underwater but not wet, Flora is at the newest north coast attraction, Sea Fun World. She, along with a few tourists and Susie Jenkins (the newspaper reporter who covers north coast tourism, and writes bubbly, enthusiastic stories repeating every word the minister, the tourist board, or anyone in the tourist sector breathes), are walking along a submerged concrete walkway with a wall of glass that allows them to remain dry while admiring the marine life. A diver swims into view, scatters feed from his bag, and where before there was nothing to look at, now there is a swarm of Sergeant-Major fish.

Flora is trying to avoid a panic attack. She dislikes small confined spaces (once the blush of lust was off, her second husband had taken to calling her Mrs. Neurotica and Madame Hysterica because of her occasional displays of terror). Perspiration pours down her armpits, as she both hallucinates that the diver is Jerome and that the plate glass is cracking. To distract herself, Flora searches the tableaux to find some marine life other than the cockroaches of the deep. She notices a school of tiny reef fish and wonders if someone imported them, maybe dumped out their aquarium. The reef itself appears to be fake, which reminds her that Nigel, one of the co-owners of Sea Fun World, builds reefs. He had gone from being chairman of the board of the Marine Conservation Park to being the leading expert and proponent of artificial reefs. The Minister of Tourism had proclaimed that Jamaica would be a leading dive site within a year, and despite the waters being overfished and inner reefs dead and dying, the answer had been, as always, "no problem mon!" We'll take all those tires we don't burn, and those rotting cars, and hey if you have some crashed planes, they are good, sunken boats will also do—anything. Just dump it in the sea and presto: new reef!

Flora tries to steady her hand as she gulps from her glistening glass of ginger beer. She had thought of ordering a Red Stripe but managed to stave off that impulse. She sits at an outdoor table in the Sea Fun World Happy Dolphin Restaurant (yes, there is a carved smiling dolphin over the entrance and photos and paintings of prancing dolphins everywhere; the insignia on the staff's polo shirts is the same smiling dolphin that is over the entrance) with Susie, who is doing an exclusive on the attraction, and Madge Murray, the owner who wants Flora to endorse Sea Fun World as a shining example of Jamaican eco-tourism. Flora's jaw hurts from the phony smile on her face as she listens to Susie wax on about how educational the experience was and Madge boast about the license they have gotten to have captive dolphins in their World.

"It's just such a spiritual healing thing to be with the dolphins. You can just see the transformed looks on people's faces once they have been with the dolphins. And we have the best trainer. He used to be at Disney. He got tired of the hectic lifestyle, was looking for a place to chill, and we're really lucky to have him." Susie takes notes, even though her tape recorder also records Madge's every gasp. Flora is guessing why the best trainer would end up in Jamaica. Coke burn out? Easier to feed his weed habit? Or was he just plain fired?

"Now Flora, I know in the past you've objected to captive dolphins, but we are going to have the most state-of-the-art facilities.

They are going to be actually better off than living in the wild." Madge beams at Flora, who hides the fact that she can no longer smile by taking another gulp, except her glass holds no more ginger beer, and she ends up with a choking mouthful of ice. Oh yes, Massa! Thank you, Mistress! Weren't the slaves better off on the plantations than in the wilds of Africa? Wasn't that a defense of the slave traders? Madge waves a waiter over and tells him to refill Miss Flora's ginger beer. He bows while taking her glass. Flora tries to stop her eyes from following his ass but when she shuts them has an unsettling flash of Jerome and immediately reopens her eyes.

"So Madge, how many divers do you have?" Flora's smile is back on. Madge looks baffled by this non sequitur. "Divers?" Madge's smile now looks shaky and strained.

"Oh, you know, at Fun Sea World I know you do all the water sports—jet skis, water-skiing, sailing, snorkeling, diving. . ."

"Oh yeah, we do have the Full Fun Package!" Madge indicates some brochures that are on the table, from which Susie is busy copying pertinent information. Madge hands a diving brochure to Flora, who is convinced the featured photo is Jerome.

"Who is your dive master?"

"Oh, we have several."

Flora cannot help herself, "Do you know Jerome Fontaine?" A dreamy look crosses Madge's face as she turns and looks out to sea. The silence is an eternity, so that even Susie notices. Looking up from her notes and brochures she clears her throat, returning Madge from her reverie.

"Jerome? Yes, Jerome is quite a diver." Madge turns back to Flora, their eyes meet for a defiant moment, and then they both flush and look away.

Okay, so who hasn't he fucked? And why did that make her want him more? She, the petulant child who wants to make sure she gets her bag of goodies at the end of the birthday party. Not to be left out. No, not her. The waiter brings Flora a fresh glass of ginger beer, and then they are surrounded by two other waiters and a waitress, each bringing them lunch though not remembering who had ordered what. She watches the irritation on Madge's face. Yep, so impossible to get good help—isn't that the main topic at tiresome get-togethers?

Hell would freeze before she gave Environment First's stamp of approval for this fraudulent marine petting zoo. Flora watches as Susie tells Madge how tasty her curried shrimp is and realizes they don't need her stamp of anything. It will be written up in the *Sunday Edition* as the newest, greatest thing to happen to Jamaica. Having poured too much ketchup onto her fries, too much mustard onto her soggy veggie-burger, Flora eats quickly, trying not to taste what she is eating. She will stop in Ocho Rios, eat a real meal at her favorite Indian restaurant (she closes her eyes and imagines dipping crisp, fragrant garlic nan into steaming mung bean dhal), then she will head home to Kingston, the long tedious drive through the hills, inevitably stuck behind some belching, horn-blowing truck, and into the filthy, traffic-ridden, ever-expanding megalopolis that is her hometown. It will be dark by the time she arrives. How she hates the tourism-industry–infested north coast. She really has to learn to say no!

Chapter Four

Monday morning, the usual staff meeting, the usual inane administrative problems. There is a conflict over who gets to take leave when, everyone wanting to take leave over the same two weeks. Last Flora checked, a year had 365 days, give or take a day. Why did her entire staff desire the same fourteen days? Flora has been fuming since Sunday morning when she opened the *Sunday Edition* to find—as expected—a huge feature on Sea Fun World—but unexpected—a photograph of herself looking quite goofy peering through the glass at the pretend reef placed beside rhapsodies about the dolphins soon to be at the attraction, her photo and a photo of frolicking dolphins with splashing, smiling children. She has a throbbing headache. Her attorney said she could not sue. She had screamed, "Why the fuck not?" not hearing a word he said in reply, then spent the morning pacing up and down cursing. She had penned her rebuttal to send to the Editor but stupidly first sent it to her board, and they were hemming and hawing and suggesting she remove what Sandy called her "more provocative statements."

Flora gets on the intercom. "Keisha, I asked for the folder on captive dolphins, you brought me the folder on sewage spills!" Her tone is ice. She is ready to punch someone, something, anything.

Flora stares at the feature for the millionth time. She knows the content by heart, but what she is obsessively drawn to is her photo; in addition to looking goofy, she looks exactly like her mother. Oh god, she has become a paler version of her mother!

Keisha, abjectly apologizing, brings the correct folder. Flora leafs through, looking at documents they acquired via the Access to Information Act, as well as some successful snooping. Madge is involved in several dolphin attractions. One already in Jamaica, one in the Cayman Islands, two in Mexico, and two in Florida. Why did she want another in Jamaica? Answer: Because they are so lucrative. All those people who grew up watching Flipper, and the New Age types looking to commune with nature so they can find mystical healing, and humans just like to see animals do tricks. The cruise-ship hordes have to be entertained, and why not bus them to some safe, packaged fantasy where they will be occupied for a few hours before going back on the ship for their fifth meal for the day. You get to cuddle and kiss dolphins, feed and swim with sharks and stingrays, feeling really daring and extreme, except the stingrays' barbs have been removed and the sharks are tame, so not to worry. That the animals get diseases from the human petting, that many die when captured and transported, that they are bored and depressed and swim round and round in their pens till they kill themselves is not in the glossy brochure or the pretty website.

Flora also has disturbing videos, surreptitious footage of the transfer of dolphins when—oops—they dropped them (yes, dolphins do bounce when dropped), of dolphin babies being taken from their mothers (a lot of screaming there if you get the sound frequency right). She thinks maybe she should get some PETA types to fly down, dress up in smiling dolphin costumes, and liberate all those Flippers. It would certainly beat anything she could manage to say or do. She had recently overheard the head of a competing environmental organization dismissing her as ineffectual to a potential donor, "She's lost her touch. No one is listening to her anymore," he said, flicking a wayward dreadlock, then stuffing his mouth with a tasty morsel being passed around by a black servant wearing white gloves.

The phone is ringing, but no one picks up. Where is her staff? She grabs the phone, "Eco Yard, may I help you?" Her tone of voice is more "Eco Yard, may I help you drop dead?" She is so distracted by her fantasies of how to destroy Madge and her animal torture masquerading as wholesome entertainment that it takes her a while to recognize the tentative voice on the line.

"Malcolm! What happen? You not sounding so good. You okay?" Usually Mr. Positive, he sounds downright depressed.

"Flora, you hear the news?"

Oh god, what now? "Uh, what news, Malcolm? You worrying me!"

"I just got a call from a friend in the PM's office informing me (he did not need to add, of course, "off the record") that our stolen sand case is being reassigned."

"Come again?"

"They are taking Mason off the case."

"But they can't do that. He's the most senior judge on the Supreme Court!"

"He is apparently retiring."

"Retiring? He is neither of the age nor in ill health. Malcolm who's behind this? I thought you and the PM were friends!" She did not say what was closer to the truth: I thought you bought the PM his successful election.

"Bwoy, Flora, me did think so, but you see what him did me with the new Conquistador construction?" The PM, claiming extensive breaches of the country's environmental laws, had demanded a stop to construction on the Conquistador near one of Malcolm's hotels, and there had been a big media splash about the Rule of Law, but then silence. Nothing. Nada. Despite the government environmental agency's technical staff all saying, "very bad idea, don't do it," the permits for the Conquistador expansion had gone through, and a new eighteen-story wing was underway with plans for a golf course and casino, all on an unstable coastline with underwater springs and caves. And then the King and Queen of Spain had arrived to give the Prime Minister a special Spanish Royal Honor, pinned a medal on his chest, made him a Gentleman of Seville or some such.

Flora's mind races: what do they have on Mason to force him to give up his job? She wonders if he is in the rather extensive pornographic collection of upstanding Jamaican men cavorting with ghetto boys that had fallen into the wrong hands when the collection's owner, along with the ambassador of a very prominent nation, had been brutally murdered by two of said boys.

"Malcolm, I am truly sorry."

"I feel damn bad. I mean you did such a good job."

"I'll talk to Mase and see what I can find out for you, okay?"

"Thanks Flora, you are more than worth your weight in gold!" Flora hangs up the phone. Did that mean she was fat? How much does he think she weighs? Maybe she needs to go to the gym more regularly, but nothing bores her more. Maybe she should go back to walking around the dam, but then she'd run into people she is avoiding. Maybe she should get a stationary bike, or rowing machine, or elliptical, or whatever the latest contraption is. But she had not so long ago thrown away (well, donated to a good cause) various exercise equipment that she hardly used, so she knows better than to waste money on such ventures. "Worth my weight in gold?" She should check out the current value of gold and find out her worth! Malcolm was definitely out of practice if he thought that was a way to compliment a woman!

Flora's cell phone rings. She is surprised that it had not rung while she was on the office-line with Malcolm, because inescapably tragedies come in threes, calls in as many phones that you have at hand—these are life's hard-earned lessons. Flora looks at her phone, which reads Private Number, and foolishly, not heeding the advice of the popular song, "Bad Man don't answer private number," answers her cell phone. Her stomach clenches and then flips, her mouth goes dry, her temples start to pound again, "Prof? Prof, you hearing me?" Since when does Jerome call her Prof?

Chapter Five

Flora stares at herself in the bathroom mirror: does she really look like her mother? Is that so bad? Her mother had been a great beauty in her day. But hadn't that day long since passed? Her mother was one of the first "lady" doctors on the island, so why fixate on her mother's looks instead of her exceptional intellect and accomplishments? In what century is she living?

Jerome insisted he was in town for just a short time and needed to come over immediately to show her something. She almost giggled at the visual conjured by his choice of words, but his tone conveyed nothing sexual, no double entendre, no Jamaican lyrics. He didn't say she's been on his mind and he must see her again. He made no reference to their night of lust (or whatever it was, she is starting to wonder!). He offered no excuse for not getting in touch earlier. And . . . he called her Prof. Was he ever in her department? Certainly not when she was a professor. What is going on? She had suggested they meet at a nearby cafe, but he said he needed a DVD player or computer. She can't cope with him coming to her office. She'll have to send her staff away on some errand. She doesn't want to face Lilac after all her denials that she would see Jerome again, but maybe she should beg Lilac to come over and protect her.

Flora slams the bathroom door in disgust and returns to her office. She resists the need to call Lilac and confess. She checks the DVD player to make sure it is properly connected to the television screen and that all the various remotes are handy. Confirming that everything is in order, she sits at her desk to check her email, but keeps imagining Madge and Jerome in a watery embrace among several hypersexual dolphins. She decides she clearly needs therapy and wonders who she could go to who doesn't know her, when she hears behind her footsteps on the wooden floor and then Keisha's voice, "Prof? Mister Fontaine to see you." Mr. Fontaine? The two of them could have gone to high school together!

Flora swivels in her chair to face them. "Thanks, Keisha." As Keisha leaves, Flora turns to Jerome, managing not to blush. "So, Jerome, what you got for me?" She points to the DVD player. "It's all set up." Jerome puts his stylish shoulder bag on the conference table and searches through it. Who gave it to him, and where did she buy it? Hong Kong? Milan? New York? He pulls out a disc in a paper sleeve, smiles while showing it to her, then nervously looks around the room, "Can we close the door?" Flora shakes her head "no," walks over, and hands Jerome the DVD remote. While he inserts the disc, she turns the volume down in case he is worried about incriminating himself. The DVD menu appears, and he scrolls down the chapter listings. "Wow, you shoot underwater footage?" He nods while clicking on the chapter of choice: "Marine Conservation Park." He sits on the edge of the table, and she stands behind him, close but not too close.

At first she can't make out the footage. It looks like a generic Jamaican reef with algae and no fish. Then the scene changes to a healthier portion of the reef, and she sees a diver, someone she knows all too well, breaking coral from the reef and putting the pieces into a bag. "Bumbaclaat! What the rass is he doing?" Jerome says nothing, his eyes glued to the screen. "When did you shoot this?"

"Last week. I have plenty more. You won't believe what I have." He sounds like he is going to cry. "Years of footage, just put it together over the weekend."

Flora closes the gap between them, wraps her arms around him, and repeats like a mantra, "It's okay, it's okay." She rocks him slightly and nuzzles his neck. She has no idea what is okay. Nothing is okay, but she can't think of anything else to say. The person who is breaking the coral is about to get his doctorate in marine conservation. He is also Mr. Artificial Reef and Madge's Sea Fun World partner, Nigel. She had heard rumors, but now she has evidence.

"Jerome, sweetheart, can I make a copy?" He sighs, and she holds him tighter, gently rubbing his back and neck.

"I made this for you."

"What you want me to do with it?"

He turns around to face her pulling her into him. "Don't know. Take a look and we can talk, okay?" Flora touches the tears on his face and then pulls away.

Chapter Six

Flora tries all his phone numbers for the nth time but can't get Mason. She is starting to worry. The first time she called the Supreme Court, his secretary said His Honor was in session. When Flora called again, someone else answered and said His Honor was gone for the day. Mason's cell phone goes straight to voice mail. His home phone just rings. His boyfriend Kevin's phone stays busy. What the hell? She texts Malcolm, "cyan fine M."

In her distress, Flora stops at the supermarket before heading home and buys a vulgar assortment of chips and ice cream. She needs company to indulge, so invites Lilac over, but Lilac has promised her daughter she'd babysit. It's her anniversary.

"Bring Punky over here. Aunty want to see her. Tell Shelly just drop Punky off on their way to wherever they are celebrating the romantic moment, and we will look after baby." Lilac is silent. "Is what you fraid? Me not going kill the pickney! Okay, so I have no child of my own but me practice pon yours and them survive, don't?"

"Barely!"

"Me take no credit for their trauma. That credit go to that eedyat father you inflict on the darling little creatures." Flora can hold out no longer and puts a handful of kettle-cooked salt and malt vinegar flavored potato chips in her mouth and crunches away.

"What you eating?" Ahah, the way to get Lilac's attention!

"I have treats for you." Flora crunches some more as emphasis, "Got you your favorite ice cream. (Crunch.) Your favorite chips. Your favorite dips. (Crunch, crunch.) Got you your favorite wine." She can hear Lilac salivating. "Need I go on?"

"Yes, go on."

"Got you strawberries!"

"Ripe?"

"Flown in this very morning." Poor Lilac, Flora has her licked. "Spend the night, no one is in the office tomorrow, so me not going in till late."

❂

Flora picks the juiciest strawberries for Lilac, cuts them into slivers, the red juice running down her fingers. She scoops Dulce de Leche ice cream into a parfait dish lined with strawberries and then scatters more berries on top and puts the glass back in the freezer. As children, they poured condensed and evaporated milk on their ice cream. Anything was an excuse for condensed milk. They vied for novel ways to consume their favorite food. Smashed ripe bananas spread on toast and topped with condensed milk was a favorite.

Flora savagely stabs at the sealed bag of lime and chili flavored blue corn chips that will not open. She arranges the chips on a platter and pours salsa fresca into a bowl she'd bought in Peru. She lays out crispy pita bits, hummus, and a mix of fragrant olives on a silver platter that had been a wedding present when she was married to Husband Number Two. Hmm, these flavors don't really combine that well, but each is delicious. She opens the Merlot to breathe, and the Prosecco is already well chilled. What else?

She hears a car drive up and goes to open the door. Shelly carries such an abundance of things you'd think the child was staying for the week. Behind her follows Devon with Punky fast asleep in her car seat. Shelly, though tall as her mother, wears heels, towering over Flora she bends at the waist so they can kiss. "Shelly, you are not allowed to get any more beautiful! This is an order." Flora kisses Devon on his cheek. "Oh my god! Look at the angel!" Devon walks quickly inside so Flora cannot molest their child.

"Aunty, don't you dare wake her up!" Shelly warns in a stage whisper as she drops her various baby wares on the couch. "Where's Mummy?"

"Don't panic, she's on her way." She has a feeling Shelly and Devon will not leave the house until Lilac arrives and there is a responsible adult in sight! Flora escorts them to a quiet corner of the living room. "See Aunty set up a comfy place for our cutie-pie pumpkin Punky." She has laid out an area with baby blankets and a quilt Flora's maternal grandmother made for Flora's mother when she was a baby, and she has carefully placed cushions and soft barriers to protect the child from ever having to touch anything hard. The parents visibly relax.

"Oh thanks, Flora, this is great." Devon unstraps the car seat and gently shifts the three-year-old into her nest. Thankfully, she remains fast asleep. The parents relax some more.

"So can I offer you two a drink, shall we toast to your special moment—four years, huh?"

The two look at each other, should they?

"Where you going for din?"

"Norma's." They actually answer in unison!

"Oh yes, I've had a few anniversaries there myself, but don't let that spoil your evening!"

Lilac walks in, "Oh good, you reach already." Flora watches the parents rush to greet Lilac like an answer to their prayers. Flora pours sparkling wine into four slender glasses they clink together.

She sips and then offers the toast, "To happiness." They smile at each other and echo, "To happiness."

⚬

"Ice cream first?"

"E'heh."

Lilac checks on her granddaughter while Flora takes their ice cream out of the fridge.

"Here you go." Flora hands Lilac the parfait glass.

"Cooya! Rahtid!" Flora watches with pleasure as Lilac dips her spoon to taste the caramel covered vanilla ice cream (like condensed milk only better) and then the strawberries. Lilac closes her eyes with each spoonful, savoring the textbook combination of cold, sweet, and slightly sour. "Perfecto, baby girl! Take a bow, take a bow, take a bowwowwow."

Flora pours melted fudge onto her combo of chocolate brownie and Belgian chocolate ice cream. The warm fudge starts to congeal, just like when they used to pour evaporated milk on their ice cream. Lilac watches the chocolate orgy in astonishment. "Get enough chocolate?" Flora nods her head, takes a chunk of brownie, swirls it in fudge, and then plunks it in her mouth. "Rough day?" Flora nods again. "Still don't recover from what evil Madge do to you ina di paper?" Flora shakes her head no, then pauses in her eating long enough to ask, "Your day?"

"You know the party this weekend? The Social Event of the Year you boycotting cuz too many of you ex going be gather in one place?" Flora giggles. "Well them call today and add one next fifty to the already three hundred we suppose to be catering for."

"Shit! So that makes it three hundred and fifty of Senior Gold's Very Special Friends. Didn't know he had any friends last time I checked!" Flora refills their glasses. "Last one, then we take a breather and switch to red okay? So how you going manage?"

"Oh, extra fifty people no biggie, have to over-cater these things anyway, cyan have food run out no, no, no. Anyway, Shelly and Devon have things under control. I am retiring." Flora ridicules the notion of retirement and takes their empty dishes to the sink. They walk over to where Punky now on her back is squirming.

"You think she going wake up?" Flora wants to tickle Punky's exposed belly and kiss her loudly everywhere.

"Could very well. But let's pray is when her parents put her in the car!" Lilac arranges the cushions closer around Punky, who quiets down.

Flora brings out the chip and dip course along with a bowl of tabouli salad. What is the exact type of indigestion one can expect after ingesting large amounts of chocolate, olives, and salsa? Well, Lilac can eat anything without ill effect, and Flora eats like this on a regular basis, so pass the chips.

Punky did wake upon the arrival of her parents, unfortunate considering they probably wanted to go home and straight to bed. After they depart, Flora refuses Lilac's efforts to tidy up and instead insists it is past their bedtime. Flora sits on her bed flossing her teeth while Lilac takes a shower. She wonders if Jerome is safely home and has a flash of guilt that she has not been able to bring herself to watch his compilation DVD. She cannot face any more horrors. She needs a break. One night of silliness please. She goes into the bathroom and cleans her teeth again—that much chocolate will surely rot them. Lilac comes up behind her, checks her flawless teeth, and then yawns, which causes Flora to yawn as well.

They settle in bed.

"That was nice, Sweet-pea. Thanks for changing your family's plans for me!"

"Thanks for my treats!"

"Any time." They lie listening to the sounds of the night: a dog barking, a car alarm going off, moments of thick silence.

"Bad pickney?"

"E'heh?"

"You have something to tell me, don't?"

Chapter Seven

Flora parks her car alone in the lot. The Environment First office is still and empty. Her staff is at a two-day capacity-building retreat sponsored by a UN agency that did not know what else to do with leftover funds. She wonders what touchy-feely exercises they will bring back this time, new and better ways to remember names? "Hi, I'm Flora, I'm fun, formidable, and fuckable." Flora walks pensively from room to room, trailing her fingers over things, observing—as if for the first time—her empire. Her eyes roam the walls crammed with colorful posters and photographs. No Mission Statement. No Vision Statement. In the early days, there had been a board retreat where they spent a day drafting such things; she can't remember that mission or vision, but she knows how every item of equipment and every piece of furniture was begged, cajoled, donated. She remembers every harebrained idea from the beginning and that cascading optimism, the belief that if people just knew, if they were better informed, they would demand change, they would become "the change they wanted to see"—that hackneyed slogan people use to sign off their emails. As far as she could see, the trickle had not become a torrent, had not become a huge churning body of actualized anything. Everyone wanted her to solve something—why hadn't she saved such and such special place; did she know the dump was on fire yet again, why couldn't she stop the burning; why hadn't she sued the government for X, Y, or Z? Over time, she has become bone-achingly exhausted.

Flora sits at her desk but cannot bring herself to turn on her computer. She studies the objects in her room. Her university degrees are framed and displayed on the wall: Geography—Columbia University, Biochemistry—UWI Mona, Mineralogy—MIT. It had been a joke, but no one got the joke. They admire her display of higher education. There are photos of her with various famous people. One with Al Gore, who had been the keynote at one of the annual conferences she has to attend, says, "Flora keep up the good work! Al." Now that is creative!

Flora spins around in her chair till she's dizzy then retraces her steps through the office and back outside. She walks around the yard remembering which tree fell in which hurricane and the losing battles she's had with her respectable neighbors over not having the border hedges chopped down. She is somehow adding to the security risk of the neighborhood by wanting there to be anything more than manicured grass. She sits on the uncomfortable stone bench and admires the shiny new roof. Not bad, not bad at all. This house had once been crumbling. This organization had once never existed. Could she survive without it? Without *Eco Yard* she wouldn't be coming to the office at all, she'd be working from home. Would she be able to get out of bed? Would she have to go back to the university? Who would she be if she were not the founder, CEO, and Executive Director of Environment First? She has no answers to these questions, which is why she keeps coming to work.

Late morning, starting to feel very hungry, Flora heads to her car. Breakfast had been a pot of ginger tea that Lilac had sensibly brewed. As they sipped on the steaming antidote to their excess, Flora knew Lilac was waiting for her confession. She couldn't bother with any foreplay and simply handed Lilac the DVD. While Lilac pondered what she was holding, Flora explained, "It's from Jerome. He stopped by the office yesterday and dropped it off."

"What is it?" Thank you Massa God! Lilac had once again proven herself to be a superior being among mere mortals. Anyone else would have jumped up and down shrieking, "Jerome? Oh my god, you saw Jerome?" and demanded details.

"It's a compilation of awful footage he's been shooting over the past few years. Me cyan bring myself to watch it."

"Well me sure as hell don't want to. Miss Flora you're on your own." Lilac handed back the DVD, and Flora flung it on the couch.

"Yep. Alone again, naturally."

Flora is pulling out of the parking lot when a silver BMW zips in and slams on the brakes. She's about to start some serious cussing when she recognizes the driver.

"Kevin, you scared the living shit out of me!"

"Honey, I'm so sorry, I didn't expect anyone to be coming up the driveway. Where you going?"

"I'm foraging for food. What you doing here?"

"I'm actually on my way to the airport." Flora opens her mouth to speak, but Kevin puts his hand up, and she closes her mouth. "Don't ask! I know you've been trying to reach Mason, and I'm sure you're worried. Let's just say he is safe but not in Jamaica." He again puts up his hand, and Flora swallows her questions. "We will be in touch. Your boy says he'll be in touch as soon as things calm down a bit, and he's really, really sorry. Okay?"

"Thanks, Kevvy. I love you. Glad my boy is safe. Tell Mase I love him. Please."

Kevin wraps his arms around Flora and kisses her on the top of her head. "We love you too, Florita, we love you too."

CHAPTER SEVEN

Flora watches as Kevin backs out into traffic. She sits on the hood of her car and stares into space. If there was something she intended to do she has lost track. Mason is gone. Flora reverses to her parking space. Food? Why bother eat? She goes into her office and turns on the television and DVD player, remembering the curve of Jerome's back and the smell of his hair. She leans on the table and hits play. Who cares, start at the top. Sometimes it's hard to get too bothered when the choice is between shit and excrement.

Chapter Eight

The images from Jerome's DVD have invaded her brain, and whether open or closed, her eyes obsessively replay the most repulsive scenes. She has no idea what she is supposed to do with this Dantesque gift. Which circle of hell is reserved for those who have done irreparable damage? What should be their eternal damnation? For those who explode, claw at, dig out the Earth's insides, let them forever inhale cascading debris. For those who discharge sewage into the ocean, let them drink it. For those who study the dying reefs and do nothing to stop or protest their death, let their bodies become food for little nibbling fish. For those who enslave animals for entertainment, let them join the devil's circus. For those who enrich themselves through lies and silences, let them listen to a ceaseless, blaring, tuneless chorus singing of the consequences of their actions. Let them be driven mad.

Flora gives up on sleep, gets her laptop, and Googles Dante's *Inferno*. She takes an illustrated virtual tour of hell. There seems to be some quirky justice to Dante's scheme. It is gratifying that the gluttonous who did nothing but create garbage now wallow in it, that frauds and hypocrites are in the innermost circle of hell. She can imagine the great satisfaction Dante reaped in conjuring this world and writing it into rhyming verse. She takes the inferno test scoring low on fraud, high on lust and violence, and very high on heresy. The test sends Flora to Limbo, which she decides ain't so bad, really. She is with virtuous Pagans, great philosophers and authors, unbaptised children, and others unfit to enter the kingdom of heaven. She is in the company of Homer, Virgil, Socrates, Aristotle, and Plato—imagine the arguments they could have!

In truth, I found myself on the edge
Of the abyss of the valley of tears
That gathers the din of unending crying.

Limbo is a place of sorrow, but without punishment, without torment.

Here, as far as I could tell listening,
No lamentations, only the sighs
That caused the air to everlasting tremble.

She sighs, turns off the computer, and curls up under her sheets. She imagines she is in a cool, dark cave, outside the wind is blowing, and it is raining torrents, but inside she is dry and safe and loved. She says goodnight to everyone she loves, first the dead, starting with her mother, then the living, ending with Punky. And at last she is able to fall asleep.

Flora drives through the banana fields at the bottom of Junction Road and turns on to the new highway. Under perpetual construction, the section she is on was finished the last time she drove on it but is now completely dug up to lay pipes. A sign says Expect Delays. But there are no delays, because no one is working. Instead, her car lurches from one sudden detour to another. As she passes the banana chip factory, she wonders, as she always does, whether one can stop and get freshly made chips, warm and lightly salted, as opposed to stale and heavily salted as she frequently encounters them in stores. She really must give up her chip habit—so much plastic. She has taken a vow to cut down on buying anything in plastic. She provides her own bags at the market and supermarket, which inevitably requires much coaching, cajoling, and reassuring market people and supermarket baggers that she is not insulting them by turning down their clear- or scandal-bagged hospitality. Enraged that all the beaches and waterways are strewn and clogged with plastic bottles, she no longer buys drinks that come in plastic bottles. One small step for . . .? One giant step for . . .? She can't remember whom the small step is for . . . Jamaica? But the giant step is not for mankind, but nature.

Flora turns onto a side road that immediately deteriorates into a pot-holed mess. She is thankful for such bad roads. It delays the inevitable destruction of the land and the replacement of trees with houses and hotels. If she had the money she would buy all the land along this lonely stretch of coast, as it has not yet been overcome with construction. She passes a small inlet with a sweeping view of Annotto Bay, miles of Portland coastline, and the Blue Mountains rising above the Rio Grande valley, mountain stacked upon mountain—sky, mountain, valley, river, sea—perfection.

Flora turns the car into the overgrown entrance of what was once a house but is now only steps to a concrete foundation. She walks across and sits on the sea wall looking out at the expanse of sea and land—this island-in-the-sun that fills her heart to bursting—this island she loves more than she has ever loved anyone. To the left of her is a large, piercingly white hotel perched for all the world to see on the best spot with the best view. It is locally owned and has no visitors, but there it proudly stands, a token to ego fulfillment and the possibilities of private property. Flora does not come from a land-owning family; her land-owning desires were defeated before they ever began.

CHAPTER EIGHT

The road is now a track, first dirt, then grass with ruts caused by tire lines that she tries to match, but her car is too small. The track is getting narrower and narrower, and soon she won't be able to turn around or go forward. She isn't quite sure where she is going. She has passed cute little guesthouses: one owned by a German woman, another by an Italian, another by an American. They had all come in the 70s as tourists, bought land and set up businesses. These pioneering white women had bought Jamaican land for pennies while Jamaican whites were fleeing the island.

Flora had been away at college in New York for the last, worst years of the 70s, what some call Jamaica's Civil War, but she remembers the frenzy of anxiety reported by family and friends and what she herself witnessed before she left: the empty food shelves, the screaming headlines of rape, inexplicable gruesome murders of doctors, everywhere foliage angrily denuded for "security reasons." The home in which she grew up had been surrounded by trees: mango, orange, grapefruit, lime, cherry, paw paw, soursop, sweetsop, almond, guava, poinciana, cotton, guango. She had come home one Christmas and found all but the old cotton tree cut down. Her father, who was the professor of tropical agriculture, had not objected. The thick hedges of hibiscus, alamanda, and mock orange all gone, only the ram goat roses outside the kitchen window remained. When Flora returned to Jamaica after college, the immigration officer stamping her passport had given her a sharp look and said, "Miss, you heading in the wrong direction!"

The last shack Flora passes is owned by a Rasta named Jah Truth. He has his name painted above his fruit stand. This district was once part of a slave plantation extending thousands of acres. Over 200 years after emancipation, seeking to change the trajectory of that history, a group of Rastas had settled small lots.

Flora abandons her car, grabs her backpack, climbs over a gate, and heads through a field in the direction of the rumbling sea, sure she will get grass lice, as she wades through thigh-high grass.

She passes three horses sheltering under wind-blown trees that all lean in the same direction. The horses are minded by a Napoleonic mule who keeps trying to mount them, male and female; getting nowhere he persists.

At the last of the trees, she comes to the edge of the cliff. Below is a small beach in a sheltered cove, with water splashing gently against coral heads, rock outcrops, and tiny limestone islets. She searches for fish in the dark patches of reef. The sea shifts color as clouds cover and uncover the sun—lighter then darker, transparent then opaque—all in vibrant shades of blue and green. Flora wants to stay, to never leave. Imagine looking at this every day! Wondering how to get to the beach, she looks for a way down. Above the beach on a rocky point is a weathered wooden house with a small veranda looking out over the cove; on the veranda is a man who waves at her. She waves back as if they are neighbors.

Chapter Nine

Jerome, tell me you don't own this place!"

"I don't own it."

"No really, how you lucky so, ee?"

Flora had climbed the uneven rock steps up to the house. The point juts out over the cove, and as she climbed, she imagined the spray smashing against it in rough weather. She walked along the stone walkway bordered with aloe plants, inhaling deeply the sea smell of freedom. Now standing on the veranda, straight ahead, she can see far beyond the cove to the horizon with its long line of clouds. To the right, she can see the curves of the St. Mary coast. Jerome comes from behind and presses himself into her, kissing her neck as he reaches for her breasts. He is wearing surfer shorts and nothing else. He smells of sweat and salt and sand. Flora wants to lick the sea off him. She strokes his arms and leans back into him. She imagines them kissing and knows how that will end—she decides better to wait and slips out of his embrace.

"Sorry, but I want to go in the water. It's usually not this calm, right?"

Jerome frowns and Flora laughs, "Good things come to those who wait!"

He takes her hand, and they walk down to the other side of the house and into a room tucked under a ledge. Flora is impressed by the order. Carefully arranged in geometric precision is diving and snorkeling gear. Two kayaks and surfboards of varying sizes are stacked neatly against the back wall. Three off-road bicycles hang from the ceiling. Wetsuits are dangling in a corner. Everything is clean.

Jerome goes over to a box of snorkeling equipment and chooses a pair of fins for her. "These should fit you." Flora tries them, and they do indeed fit. She is starting to think this young man will definitely not bore her. They walk down the side of the cliff to the beach, which is more pebbles than sand. The water shushes over the pebbles, and they click together, a sound that always fills Flora with joy. "Hey Jerome, you don't mind if I move in? Me cyan cook but me have other talents." Jerome laughs. Reefs to dive, rocks and islands to swim to, before her a watery playground she would never tire of. "So who own this place?"

"My aunt. She know you."

Damn, they probably went to school together. "She does? Did we go to school together?"

"Yep. Ingrid Small."

"Oh my God! Ingrid! Scandal bag! Didn't she run off with some Rastaman before it was fashionable to do such things?" Jerome nods. "So this is where she came! Turn out she was way smarter than the rest of us." Flora, holding her fins, wades into the water and closes her eyes to better feel the water rise and fall around her calves. She opens her eyes and looks at her legs. She is so pale. She is letting down her mother's brown-skinned family. The last time she was at a beach was months before when she went to Lime Cay with a visiting friend, but she had spent most of the time in the shade daydreaming. She could change her life. She could spend her days outside instead of in her office. Ingrid had left them, silly schoolgirls, behind, found this jewel, and what had Flora done? One conventional safe thing after another! College . . . work, marriage . . . work, university . . . work, marriage . . . work.

Jerome stands beside her in the water. "You can swim good?"

"Don't worry, me won't drown." She puts her arm around him and rubs her foot against his leg. "Show me your favorite places."

He points at the crescent-shaped islet that she had admired from the cliff. "We swim there first and work our way back. Okay?" She puts on her snorkeling gear and they slip into the water, fins propelling them forward, masks magnifying the view.

Flora is swimming against the current. She figures this is good because she will have it with her on the way back when she could use the help. Below her, Jerome swims in and out of holes, lies still on the sea floor contemplating something she cannot see. She can only make quick forays below the surface, one gasp and down, and then gradual expending of air, and she's back on the surface. He, on the other hand, does not seem to need to breathe. She sees a mixture of corals; some seem healthy. She sees schools of fish but can't name them. She notices a ray moving elegantly through the water. She wishes for a turtle. She pulls the mask off her face and swims on her back, looking at the sky and the land, watching as the point and Jerome's home begin to recede.

The sea is rougher on the outside of the islet, and she imagines waves crashing over it. Jerome gestures for her to follow and guides them to the front of the crescent, to a small landing between jagged rocks. You have to time the swell so it brings you in, but Flora is slower than Jerome and does not make it in with him. On her third try, he grabs and pulls her in and they scramble up onto the part of the island that is smooth enough to walk on. There is no shade but the sun is low, about an hour away from setting, and the breeze is cool. Jerome takes her to where there are holes in the rock floor, and they stand watching the sea rush in, rush out, revealing, and then concealing. Black crabs scurry away from them.

"I spent a night out here once."

"You not scared a big wave come and get you?"

"Was calm. A few days after full moon. I was night diving."

"All by youself?"

"Just me."

"And some sharks."

"Me, some sharks, some big ass eels, that's true. Was a rare coral bloom."

"Didn't you get stung?"

"Oh yeah, plenty times. Was worth it. Here look." Jerome shows her some fine scars along the inside of his right arm and down his side. Flora tries to think of marks on her body that engraved something monumental in her life. Marks, not cellulite, muscle atrophy, skin blotching. No children—no birthing stretch marks. No athletic feats—no torn ligaments, no scars. There was the time Husband Number Two in a jealous rage beat her senseless, but there is nothing to show for that or any of his other acts of violence. At least nothing etched on her skin. Flora examines Jerome's skin. It is riddled with stories.

"And what's this?" She traces an indentation in his left bicep.

"I got shot."

"You too lie!"

"No, is true. Some drug-ists steal the boat me was working on."

"How dem never kill you?"

"Well, them try. But I dive deeper and hold my breath better than them can shoot."

"Them kill someone else though, don't?"

"Yep, them kill my boss and the boat captain."

"Rass Jerome. Come here. No more stories for now. I fraid what you going to tell me next!" Jerome stretches out on his stomach with his head on Flora's lap. She caresses and rubs his head, neck, and shoulders. He murmurs his appreciation. How many lives does Jerome the cat have? Yet she does not fear for him. She comforts herself that he will land on his feet no matter from what height he falls.

CHAPTER NINE

The light fades, soon the clouds will turn pink, the sea violet and then black. "Jerome, time fi head back, unlike you me don't want see no shark." In reply, he moves his face down to her crotch, spreading her legs enough to ease away her swimsuit. "Jerome, hold off, do." He ignores her. "Boogie, please." Flora bends over and whispers a detailed message into his ear. He jumps up, grabs his fins and mask, and dives into the water, leaving her to follow suit, a little less expertly or gracefully.

They stumble out onto the pebbled beach and head up the path to the house. The pinks in the sky have turned purple and the air cold. But the water from the cistern is warm from sunning itself all day, and it warms them, as Flora rinses Jerome at the outdoor shower. First splashes of fresh water, then she soaps his skin, lingering at all his most sensitive areas. She licks his armpits while slowly soaping his ass.

Flora turns on the shower and rinses away the soap. She turns off the water and holds him lightly, her breasts brushing against his chest, then releases him, holding him at arm's length, appraising his nakedness. "Touch yourself, I want to watch you." He trembles under her gaze as he strokes himself. "Ahah, you're a lefty." She puts her left hand on his and mirrors his movements, she replaces his hand with hers and then makes her way from his nipples down his torso to his belly button; his stomach muscles in spasm. She knows the moment she gets her mouth on him he will come. And he does. She smiles knowing she has met one of her promises. She has promised him much, but the night is young, and so is he.

Chapter Ten

Flora gets up and opens the curtains. The sea is in a tumult, and she wonders if it is high tide or bad weather. She goes onto the veranda to look. The cove is churning, the wind a steady blast. Flora worries about the horses. Are they tethered or free? Dark clouds are threatening. Terrific. It will rain, the road will flood, and she will be marooned. She smells smoke and looks down to find Jerome roasting breadfruit outside the kitchen door. She blows him a kiss and goes back into bed.

She touches her body. She is aching in all sorts of strange places. Flora decides if she is to continue this gymnastic sex life, she needs to take up yoga, that and maybe marathon running and sleeping twelve hours a day. Clearly, she must retire. She cannot continue to run an environmental organization and have a sex life. It's one or the other.

Though she'd rather stay in bed all day, she gets up and carefully makes the bed. She checks around the room to make sure she has not strewn things about. She does not want to bring mess into Jerome's tidiness. She walks through the house examining his life, enjoying the intimacies that are revealed by private spaces. Did he get his aesthetic from Ingrid? How much of this house is her and not him? There are two landscapes by Esperanza Carboni; one is the cove and islet, the other a crumbled piece of sugar mill in dense forest, ficus roots growing out of its walls. Flora had thought she owned Esperanza's finest pieces, but these two are even better. She is amazed that the salt air hasn't damaged them. There had been a wild rumor that Ingrid and Espie were lovers and had raised their children together with the same Rastaman. She admires Ingrid's eyes, which smile at her from a silver-framed black and white Carboni photograph, and decides that in all likelihood it is neither wild nor rumor. As if in confirmation, the color photograph hanging beside Ingrid is a domestic scene of five children and three adults. She is trying to remember the Rasta's name. He is standing between the two women. No one is looking at the camera. She thinks one of the children is Jerome. He looks about three. She senses there is great tragedy in this grouping. She tries to remember bits of gossip from years past.

Flora stands in admiration at an intricately hand-painted floor-to-ceiling bookcase and is intimidated by its content. Does Jerome really read books in French and Italian? She searches, and sure enough there is *La Divina Commedia*, a bi-lingual version. She turns to Inferno—Canto IV—the poet visiting Limbo:

"Per tai difetti, non per altro rio,	*"For such defects, and for no other fault,*
semo perduti, e sol di tanto offesi	*We are lost, but only so punished*
che sanza speme vivemo in disio."	*That without hope, we live on in desire."*
Gran duol mi prese al cor quando lo 'ntesi,	*Great sorrow pressed my heart when I heard him,*
però che gente di molto valore	*Because some people of great value*
conobbi che 'n quel limbo eran sospesi.	*I knew in that Limbo were suspended.*

Flora repeats out loud, "Semo perduti. Se-mo per-du-ti." We . . . are . . . lost.

She goes into the kitchen where on the stove three pans are cooking—callaloo, ackee, plantain. Jerome is in deep concentration peeling the blackened skin off the roasted breadfruit.

"Cho Jerome, marry me nuh? Me is desperate for a husband and cyan think of no better choice than you."

Jerome chuckles and keeps at his task. "You have a dowry? What you bringing me?"

"My brilliant mind. My impeccable character. My outstanding reputation and expansive connections. And of course the best sex you will ever have."

Jerome looks up with a wide grin. He strokes his chin, "Really?"

"E'heh. And well I am apparently known to your family, so there is no need for go betweens or dilly dallying."

While Jerome puts the food on the table, Flora slices a long alligator pear. Its flesh is her favorite shade of green. "Is Espie around?"

"Nope, she's in Rome with Trevor, her youngest. He's at university. She splits her time between there and here."

"Who running the guest house then?"

"Pearl. She is very much in charge!"

Flora walks over to the family photograph and beckons Jerome, "Come show me."

"After we eat, food going get cold."

"Come nuh? Please."

"This Pearl, she's the eldest girl. That's me. That's Tallawah." Jerome pauses, and his voice falters. Flora puts her hand over his heart. "That's Aisha and there's Paolo. Trevor not in the picture because him never born yet."

Flora points at the adult male, "Trying to remember his name, Knowledge?"

Jerome nods, "He did really name Delroy Watson but name himself Ras Knowledge."

"Don't Tallawah die soon after that photo?"

Jerome nods, and his eyes fill with tears.

"What happen, him get sick?"

"No, he and some other boys climbing a tree, him slip, bruk him neck."

"Shit Jerome, were you there?"

"No, was with my grandparents in Mobay. I used to go between Mobay, here, and Kingston. And later to my dad in Paris."

"Of course! Ambassador Fontaine is you father! He's now with the UN, right?"

"Yeah for a while now. He's in Geneva."

Flora is afraid to ask about Jerome's mother. She remembers that one of Ingrid's sisters died tragically young but can't remember how. Was it a car crash or brain tumor? And wasn't she Lilac's good friend? Was it Cathy or Liz? She is afraid the sister is Jerome's mother. She is sorry she started this whole process of revelation. She is ruining their light morning together. Their meal is waiting. But she can't stop now. She takes a deep breath. "What happen to you uncle, Ras Knowledge?"

"Ingrid and Espie were in Kingston, I forget why. There was no phone. He had diabetes. Cut himself with his machete one day when him was clearing some land to plant. It get infect bad. Him catch high high fever then fall into a coma. Die few days later. Ingrid and Espie mek it back just before him dead."

"Jerome sweetie, I am sooo sorry." She takes Jerome by the hand and leads him to the table. "I'm sorry to bring up such sad memories."

He releases her hand, gives her a hug, and goes into the kitchen to get utensils. "Nah man, am fine really. Just long time me don't talk about any of this. I don't mind. Is how we get to know each other, right?"

"Right."

"So Prof." He pretends to have a microphone in his hand, which he holds out toward her, "Professor Smith, please tell us, your fascinated audience, about your exciting life."

Flora laughs while she shares food onto their plates. "Exciting? Is who fool you seh my life exciting?" Onto two large ceramic plates with scenes of Venice she piles finely chopped callaloo; ackee cooked with onions, garlic, sweet pepper, and tomatoes; fat chunks of fried plantain; and thinly sliced roasted breadfruit. "Well, the first Professor Smith was an Englishman of course." She forks pear slices onto their plates, hands one to Jerome, and sits down beside him. "Bon appetit." They clink forks. One by one, she tastes everything on her plate. "Wow. Everything is so delicious!" She could eat the entire breadfruit by herself.

Jerome pokes her, "Go on. No stalling."

"But me have to eat, cyan eat and talk. Try wait." Flora savors several more bites then continues, "Okay, so my grandfather was a botanist at Kew Gardens in their tropical plant section. Used to be sent by the British government to gather specimens in the colonies and what not, and he end up station at Hope Gardens."

"Way cool! You knew him?"

"Well, him was pretty old by the time me come along. But I remember a little old white man who live up in the hills past Newcastle who like to fuss over him roses and grow strawberries." Flora piles their plates again. "My dad grew up at Hope Gardens, went to JC, used to walk over to school. His mother left and went back to England when he was about seven. Guess she was sick of Jamaica. She just left and never came back. You bored yet?"

"Hell no. Continue please." Jerome strokes her hand in encouragement.

"Well my father, the second Professor Smith, was a leading expert on tropical agriculture. He was sent round the Commonwealth advising governments on improving soil yields, that sort of thing, but his specialty was tropical plant diseases. My mother was a doctor. She look after sick people. My father look after sick plants. Guess I should have been a vet."

Suddenly, there is a resounding clap of thunder. "Bumbaclaat!" They shout in unison. Outside, the light is doused as they watch the squall race in from the cove and slam against the window. The rain sheets down. Flora knows if she is to get home she has to leave immediately. The road will start flooding within minutes, and her car will not make it. The thought of being marooned had been so enticing, but in cruel reality she has two attorney meetings the next day, one to sue the government over ongoing sewage negligence, the other because they are being sued by Madge for defamation—Environment First, trying to block the importation of dolphins, has just disseminated a press release claiming that dolphins were dying in Madge's care—clearly their little tete-a-tete at Sea Fun World the other day had not brought them any closer. She also remembers, the day after she is supposed to be present at some panel the Prime Minister has convened on renewable energy. It is bullshit, but there is some grant money involved that she wants to apply for. And she is late on a paper for a publication on the evils of extractive industries. Her paper is on the false and failed reclamation efforts of the bauxite industry—the same topic of her dissertation and her book, "The Bauxite Blight—Extraction, Destruction and Development." It's a topic of which she never tires. Flora muses that, yet again, she is choosing work over pleasure. Apparently she has puritanical issues that need resolving—but not right now.

"Jerome sweetie, sorry but I gotta nyam and run weh or my car will be washed away in the deluge." She runs into the bedroom to grab her backpack and find her car keys. Jerome, who always keeps his keys hanging on a nail by the door to the garage, is waiting in his jeep with the engine running when Flora rushes in. They kiss a long kiss of regret, then he puts the jeep into four-wheel drive, and they race onto the field. Flora looks out for the horses, but as they careen over the grass, she can see nothing but rain.

Chapter Eleven

Flora is exhausted and irritated. Her first legal appointment was postponed at the last minute till the afternoon, and she has been waiting for almost an hour for her second appointment. Lawyers apparently have taken up the habits of doctors. She is sitting in the ostentatious reception area at Crown, Battle and Harding. It is furnished in masculine shades of dark wood. There is a large Albert Huie painting of Kingston Harbour. She is grateful it is not one of his lurid nudes. Would not do to have "Miss Mahogany" spread naked behind the carefully coiffed receptionist. The room is sprinkled with art works that should be in the National Gallery. The only law office more lavish is Barnett, Lindo, Sharp, Hackman and Associates. Husband Number Two had been a partner there until he ascended to the Court of Appeal. She has not set foot in that place in many years but heard it now boasts a large water feature to add to its signature exotic orchids.

Flora rubs her sore left shoulder—always a sign of stress—but she reminds herself she had also driven through a blinding rainstorm. There were many times it looked like she would not make it home. A sudden torrent materialized as she took one of the corners on the Junction road, and her car began to stall. Somehow it did not cut out completely, or else she would have been swept into the banking or, worse, down into the river. At another spot, the water was starting to come in through the floorboards. She navigated around several landslides. The largest one she managed to just squeeze by would definitely have closed the road. It reminded her of the time a storm was chasing her; she had raced it across Portland, escaping into St. Thomas, and finally back to Kingston, and as she drove, the storm got worse and worse, the roads behind her impassible moments after she had driven through them.

When she checks, her phone is clogged with voice mails screaming, "Where the hell are you?" "Why you not here at the Gold Birthday Bash?" Of all her betrayals, this will probably be one she won't be allowed to live down. Flora plans to go over to Lilac as soon as she finishes work. She will eat leftovers, rub Lilac's exhausted feet, and guffaw at Lilac's retelling of everything she had missed: the Captains of Industry with their ever-younger trophy females, or their ever-scalpeled wives; the Euro-trash and Diplomatic Corps always quick to hit the food and drink, sweating in their tight clothes as they dance with wild abandon inhabiting their very own tropical paradise; the bored younger generation keeping to themselves, sending text messages and conducting their own party; the eager dealmakers trading secrets over their rums, whiskeys, and beers; and the wannabees preening and exhibiting themselves, hoping to feature in the society section of the paper.

Just as Flora approaches the receptionist to tell her she will no longer wait, Crown and Battle come bustling into the room, apologizing. They escort her into a private office reserved for their most exclusive clients. Obviously, they think the Sea Fun World suit is going to garner them a great deal of money! She has no money to give them, and so if they aren't performing pro-bono, they will have to take the case on spec. Where is Mason when she needs him? Why had he left the firm to become a judge? And why had he been so indiscrete to have to flee to foreign?

The two men beam at her. "Everyone was surprised not to see you Saturday night!" That was Crown. "Yes, my dear, you were greatly missed." That was Battle. Flora does not ask who missed her but instead gets to the point. "Gentlemen, the morning is almost over, so let us get to the case at hand. Where do we stand?"

"Well," they say in unison, then Battle coughs and continues, "As you know, Madge is suing you for defamation. She is charging you with defaming her person and her business, and in so doing causing her loss of livelihood both current and future."

Now Crown's turn, Flora looks back and forth between the two as if at a tennis match. "She is also suing you for terroristic threatening and for emotional damage."

Now Battle, "Apparently she has put on a bit of weight."

Flora presses hard on Lilac's favorite sore spot, deep under the ball of her foot. "Ow, ow ow!" Lilac winces and cries out, which a normal person would take to mean stop, but Flora knows to press harder until Lilac cries, "Yes, yes, yes," which means time to back off and rub her foot generally. Flora applies more peppermint cream and rubs up and down the spine of Lilac's right foot.

"So the twerps kept me waiting for over an hour and then tried to talk me into mediation. I'm the one being sued, what's there to mediate? Madge just needs to drop the rass lawsuit."

"Maybe them smell you no have no money, so mediation it is."

"Ahah, but guess what?"

"What?"

"I have evidence. Evi-fucking-dence. When me describe the exact nature of the ev-i-dence, they change their croaking little tune. Madge can sue me from now till kingdom come. Her ass is grass."

Lilac switches feet. Her left foot is smaller than her right and always less crunchy or tight. Flora finds the favorite sore point on that foot but has to press much harder before Lilac begins her serenade of ows.

"Who, pray tell, painted your nails?" Flora points to Lilac's toenails, painted a garish neon yellow.

"I did."

"Punky pick the color?"

"Lef me."

"Punky did pick the color, didn't she?!"

"Bad pickney, lef me."

Convulsed with laughter, Flora shifts both feet onto her lap and begins to rub Lilac's swollen ankles and long slender calves. "So," she says between giggles, "tell me your favorite Golden moment."

"What mek you tink seh me did have time fi notice anything? I had an army of workers to oversee."

"Yes Miss Retirement, you are now an army general. Cho man, me know seh noting escape you, not one damn ting."

Lilac relents, "Okay, how about the time five of you ex's were all together."

"You too lie!"

"The judge chatting up a storm with Golden, while the politician nod him head in agreement. A little ways off the two scientists comparing their latest mobile gadget."

Flora falls off her chair onto the floor where she rolls back and forth holding her sides and gasping for air.

"But my favorite moment is when a certain aging Miss Jamaica sing in the style of Marilyn Monroe Happy Birthday to the feeble ag-ed Golden who can barely stand up without toppling over." Competing with Flora's howls, Lilac sings in a lisping, breathy, off-key voice, "Hap-py Bir-th-day Mis-ter Go-ld, Hap-py Bir-th-day to ye-w." And then she joins Flora on the floor rolling and screaming in laughter, they both singing, "Hap-py Bir-th-day Mis-ter Go-ld, Hap-py Bir-th-day to ye-w."

Chapter Twelve

The wind is generating a thick column of dirty froth as the sea dashes against the harbor wall, the spray leaping onto the road, as truck after overloaded, dust-spewing truck drives by. Flora looks in disbelief at Historic Falmouth and its transformation into a construction site. The wetlands to her left have been stripped bare, and there are two large machines in the distance scooping sand and dirt. Acres and acres of mangroves and other trees have been removed, and in their stead are pools of stagnant water with sticks poking out. She can't begin to imagine what is to take the place of the green that had been there her whole life. A shopping mall with in-bond stores owned by newly arrived Indians and Chinese carrying everything from diamonds to Prada to "Jamaica No Problem" t-shirts? Parking for tour buses? Some new attraction—how about a plantation theme park with costumed natives playing hard-working but happy slaves and visitors getting to play generous, good-natured masters? She looks at the ragged "Welcome to Historic Falmouth" sign with the list of historic sites that the tourist can visit and then past the sign at the massive development underway. Gone the little businesses along the street, gone the fishing beach. All dumped up, the land extended far out into the harbor by the contents of the insistent stream of trucks driving down from the quarry that had once been a hill at the mouth of the Martha Brae River. Rusting barges are everywhere. On one, welders work on large metal tubes. Untethered yellow containment buoys bounce on the surface of the choppy water, incapable of blocking any debris from sinking into the harbor.

The weather is too rough for the divers who are transplanting coral, as Flora watches their dive boats head into shore. An hour earlier, she had also been on a boat, documenting the cruise-ship pier construction, and had been impressed with the antlike hive of activity—massive metal pylons, an expanse of metal jutting out into the harbor, in the background the ruined old wharves, the stately courthouse, and then further down the shore, newly constructed concrete break waters, behind which totter decrepit Georgian buildings. She finds it hard to believe, but they say when the largest cruise ship in the world comes to dock, it will be the tallest edifice in Jamaica. Where will the 6,000 passengers go? What will they do? Lucky Madge, maybe she could have her dolphin handlers dressed in pirate and plantation costumes.

The midday sun is fierce; Flora cleans her dusty dark glasses while checking the time on her cell phone. She is waiting for Cliff, a friend of Jerome who is one of the divers removing the intact healthy coral before a large portion of the reef is dynamited and the harbor dredged to accommodate the mammoth ships. This is Nigel's transplantation scheme that he has been successfully peddling, yet Nigel was not hired by the European company in charge of the construction. Flora wonders if Cliff will show up. According to Jerome, Cliff has stories to tell. But will he have the courage to tell them? A few weeks earlier, Cliff had nearly drowned when a large piece of construction equipment hit him while he was surfacing. Apparently it is a very dangerous job. Why would you choose to destroy the reef if you were a diver? Could someone pay her enough to do that? Jerome has said he is going to join a dive team and videotape what they are doing. He has a camera so inconspicuous they won't notice what he is up to. Cliff is going to arrange for the inclusion of Jerome the imposter. Then what to do with the footage? She hasn't figured out that end of their conspiracy.

Flora waits another hour, but Cliff does not show. Fear? Forgetfulness? Something come up? Flora hopes he's okay, but she is annoyed. Hadn't she recently sworn off the north coast forever? And yet once again here she is forced to witness the destruction of Jamaica Land We Love. She waits for a convoy of trucks to pass, then pulls out onto the road. She'll take the old road along the coast for as long as she can but knows that within minutes, she'll be forced onto the new highway. She calls Jerome and asks him to meet her in Ochie. She'll buy them either late lunch or early dinner.

There are three cruise ships anchored when Flora makes it to Ocho Rios. Though stuck in traffic, she is glad to be in her car. If she were on foot, she would be constantly badgered by taxi drivers, hawkers, hustlers, self-proclaimed tour guides, who mistaking her for a tourist would be courting her with their very best American accents. Instead a skinny young man comes up to her car and puts his shaking hands through the passenger side of the window. "Please Mummy, help me. Nice Lady, I beg you. Please Mummy I beg you." She doesn't turn to examine him, but figures he is a crack head. The traffic is not moving. She feels a rising panic; her skin is crawling, and she wants to scratch it raw. "Please, Nice Lady, help me. I beg you." She reaches into her purse and gives him a hundred dollar bill, then closes her windows and locks her doors.

Flora dips her fragrant garlic naan into the mung bean dahl. It drips over her fingers as she transfers it to her mouth, and she closes her eyes and chews, concluding that maybe, just maybe, this is better than sex. She opens her eyes and looks across at Jerome, who is smiling at her, and decides she wants him to come home with her. She doesn't want to finish the drive alone, but what to do with his jeep? He can speed ahead and she can follow, frantically trying to keep up. That will make the drive definitely less dreary. They can chat on the phone every so often and pretend they are in a rally race.

"So what did Cliff say?"

"Him never show up! I waited an hour. Him never call."

"Hm. That not like him. Let me try reach him." Jerome calls but gets voice mail. "Hey Cliffy. Wagwan? How come you post the Prof? Call me back."

Flora combines mild but tangy aloo gobi with spicy ladies' fingers and agrees they go very well together.

"Would you take that job if them pay you enough?"

"No fucking way, could never pay me enough. Is rass nasty work in every way. Most time you cyan even see because all the silt—visibility is zero."

The restaurant is empty. Flora is grateful the cruise-ship throngs have no interest in her favorite restaurant. They go screaming down zip lines; what's to see as you zip? Flora has never tried. They go to Dunn's River Falls for entertainment, but food? Probably at this very moment eating happyhappyjoyjoy Flipper burgers while sipping on very sweet rum drinks.

"So Jerome, how you know Madge and Nigel?" Flora tries to sound neutral, but she can feel the tension in her voice and realizes she is looking at the plant just left of Jerome while asking the question.

"Nigel is the person teach me to dive. He was my mentor. We travel all over together. First I intern at the Marine Conservation Park, and then he hire me, and then we start doing projects together."

"Oh no Jerome, must be really disappointing how everything turn out then."

"No kidding. I did idolize him. Want to be him. Now me want fi kill him."

"My yout, don't say that! Though in truth is Madge me want to kill. Between the damn lawsuit and I think she's still in love with you!"

"Madge?" his voice spitting, his eyes red with rage. "She's in love with herself. She and Nigel deserve each other. They can burn in hell for all I care." This is Flora's first taste of Jerome angry. She's not sure she can handle him angry.

"Okay let's change the subject. Come home with me, and you can tell me everything when you ready. We will plot their demise." Flora raises her sweating water glass, Jerome sheepishly follows, and they clink glasses together. "To Madge and Nigel's demise and our triumph of the underdog."

Flora ruffles his hair, then spoons more food onto their plates. She feeds him some aloo gobi and then kisses the remains off his lips. Food always tastes best off a loved one's lips.

They make it to Kingston in record time. Most of the way, Flora doesn't even look where she is driving, just keeps her eye on Jerome's bumper, slowing down, swerving, speeding up when he does. They are both exhausted, but it is not late, and they are too agitated to sleep. Flora puts on a CD of Maria Callas singing Puccini arias. They sit together on the couch holding hands.

Flora is single minded. "Okay, I know this is hard to talk about, but indulge me." Jerome groans. Callas soars, her voice straining at the highest notes. "So you were in love with Madge and Nigel, you were very young, and they played some major head games with your sweet innocent head. Yes?"

"I was never in love with Madge. But yes, them spice up them empty relationship with me. Me did want please Nigel. And, really don't know why, but at the time did find Madge very sexy, and he want me to fuck her and so I oblige. Whole heap. I was very obliging. Okay? Nuff said! Why you so curious about this shit?"

"Because I am a pervert. Trust me, if you were the least bit interested I could outdo any of your stories I am sure!"

"Well, I'm not. I don't want to hear about your sordid past."

"Okay, how about my sordid present?" Flora tickles Jerome till he stops frowning. Maria Callas as Cio-Cio San is singing "Un bel di, vedremo"—her voice filled with longing, she sings how she will steadfastly wait until one fine day she will see smoke from a ship far out on the horizon, and her feckless Yankee lover will finally return to her. Flora turns up the music so she can feel the heartbreak, but Jerome's phone starts ringing, so she turns the music back down, listening all the more intently.

> *Mi metto là sul ciglio del colle e aspetto, e aspetto gran tempo e non mi pesa, la lunga attesa.* (I go to the edge of the hill and wait, I wait a long time, and it is no burden, this long wait.)

"What? Who dis? Dem what?" Jerome gets up and walks toward the window.

> *E uscito dalla folla cittadina, un uomo, un picciol punto s'avvia per la collina. Chi sarà? Chi sarà?* (Appearing out of the crowd in town, a man, a small speck, comes up the hill. Who will it be? Who will it be?)

"Who find him? Where dem find him?"

> *E un po' per non morire al primo incontro; ed egli alquanto in pena chiamerà, chiamerà: "Piccina mogliettina, olezzo di verbena" i nomi che mi dava al suo venire.* (A little so as not to die upon first meeting; and he much in sorrow will call, he will call out: "Little one, baby wife, oh fresh scent of verbena." The names he used to call me when he was here.)

Flora is weeping for Butterfly when Jerome turns to her and says, "Cliff. Some motherfucker kill him. One bullet straight through him head."

❂

Flora and Jerome have their first fight. Jerome insists he is leaving immediately to go home, pick up his diving gear, head to Falmouth by dawn, and get straight into the water. He is going to document whatever is taking place, and he is going to find out who killed Cliff and why. Flora begs him not to risk his life in such a senseless heroic gesture. Jerome calls her a neurotic, spineless, dilettante and slams the door behind him. Flora curls into a ball as she hears Jerome's jeep screeching out the driveway. She curses the night as she imagines all the ways Jerome will die an untimely and painful death: surfacing from the murky depths as the arm of some dredging equipment slams into him, knocking him unconscious; armed with a spear gun, a murderer firing a barb into Jerome's heart, leaving him to bleed to death; an assassin with a very powerful gun from very close range blowing Jerome's pretty head off; a truck careening around a corner, nudging Jerome's jeep ever so slightly, sending it tumbling end over end, then smashing into the boulders at the bottom of the ravine.

Flora curses the night and curses Jamaica, and not for the first time plans her escape. She will accept the Endowed Chair at MIT, the one her dear friend Chang offers every year and every year she turns down. Or she will start a lucrative consulting firm in New York while being a professor at Columbia University. Or she will move to Alaska and do nothing. She has done enough. She has done more than her share. Dilettante? Is that what you call someone who has devoted her life to championing what others have been too chicken shit to stand up for and be counted? She will leave this cursed land and never return. In the meantime . . . limbo, limbo, lim-bo—unlike Cio-Cio San, she can't pretend she isn't weary from this endless waiting.

Chapter Thirteen

Flora is sitting doodling on the legal pad she has been given as part of her official attendance package. She assiduously notes the frequency of certain words. So far, under "stakeholder" she has 12, "mitigation measures" 8, "sustainable" 33, "public-private partnership" 6, "community" 21, "renewable energy" 45. She is at the Prime Minister's Renewable Energy Taskforce Day-Long Focus Workshop (she is feeling quite unfocused), so there is no mystery to the phrase "renewable energy" topping the play list. She can't imagine anything else winning out at the end of the day except maybe "Jamaica," "God," or "hope." But the day stretches languidly out, and, who knows, some new jargon might suddenly be introduced and prove her completely wrong. Such is the thrill of life, just when you think you know it all, you don't. She wonders who among her esteemed colleagues might want to wager some bets. She looks around the room, but everyone seems to have their heads down, no doubt busy texting, web surfing, and checking their emails.

After a bubbly presentation by a large man flown in by the American Embassy to talk about "Alternate Energy," where he upped her "hope" count to 14 and where he spoke about "my dear friend" the Minister of Energy who he had apparently only met the day before but knew they were sworn brothers, the "dear friend" launches into an even more optimistic presentation on the ambitious options the government is considering—wind farms, wave energy, waste to energy, ethanol from every known plant, solar water heaters, solar golf carts, moon beams—did he really say moon beams or had she nodded off? Flora wonders what he does to get his head so shiny. She does not endorse the male obsession for shaving their heads at the slightest sign of balding or graying. When the Minister gets to the nuclear energy option, she finds *her* dear friend Milton Brown staring at him in disgust. Flora smirks at Milton who is shaking his head. He passes her a note that reads, *Can you believe what this jackass is saying?! We can't keep sewage out of Kingston Harbour but we are going to safely run a nuclear plant?* In reply, Flora has a coughing fit that conveniently removes her from the room for half an hour, by which time the workshop is paused for a beverage and snack break.

As Flora sips some fever grass tea that the government is promoting as part of its "Eat Jamaican" campaign, nibbles on a biscuit, and eats some imported fruit, she admits that Jerome is partially correct; yes, she is neurotic, everyone knows that, but dilettante? Until this moment, she would have strongly defended herself against such a charge, but really isn't she at this waste of time charade instead of planting a tree, or growing food, or inventing the cure for plastic, or finding Cliff's murderer? Clearly she is a dilettante. But spineless? No, no, no! Flora puts down her tea, flexes her painful left shoulder, and touches her spine. No, she has a spine. And so she walks out of the building and gets into her car, and instead of going to the office, she heads home. This neurotic dilettante has an article to finish on the failure of the bauxite industry to meet its restoration responsibilities, and she will not be further distracted until it is done.

CHAPTER THIRTEEN

Flora is rereading the *National Minerals Policy: Sustainable Development of the Minerals Industry* (6th Draft). It is a wholesome document filled with Vision, Objectives, Goals, Strategies, and lots of statements that begin, "The Government Will." She wonders who "The Government" is and in what way it "will" do anything? And who would know if "it" will or won't, has or hasn't done what "it" said "it" would do? For example, "Objective 7: To regulate the industry to ensure effective management of the environment . . ." has as Strategy 1: "The Government will: 1. Include social, environmental and economic considerations in the decision making process within the industry." Clearly, economic considerations always win out, case in point: one of the last remaining intact coastal bluffs on the north coast is about to be destroyed for limestone mining. Who cares if it has endemic species, rare Taino artifacts, unusual geological features, and just plain beauty? It is private property, and the owner can do whatever he pleases. The owner was rumored to be a well-known criminal. But aren't most large landowners, whether from past days of plantation slavery to current days of dons, drug lords, Ponzi schemers, and politicians on the take?

Flora can't stop yawning. She goes to the kitchen and sticks her head in the freezer to try and stay awake. She checks her phone for the umpteenth time, but not a word from Jerome. She longs for chips but doesn't have any, as she has stuck to her no plastic doctrine. Instead, she munches on a piece of near-frozen sugar cane. She calls Lilac but gets voice mail in the form of Punky chirping, "Sorry we did miss you call, (giggle) call again." Flora returns to her desk and starts adding to the middle section of her paper.

The policy clearly states that mineral operations must have "Life of Mine Plans" that "shall incorporate a mining plan, waste management plan, land rehabilitation plan and closure plan. Closure plans must clearly outline the possible impacts of closures on host communities and the natural environment." So one needs to have a plan but no requirement that one implement it, since Jamaica is littered with unrehabilitated lands and toxic waste from mining, so that in the middle of a desperate drought, potable water was sprayed onto a bauxite red sludge lake to keep it from drying up and the noxious dust blowing everywhere. Flora cites Case A in Manchester and includes photos of deeply scarred land and gaping pits, then cites Case B in St. Ann and attaches photos of deserted communities, homes in ruins with cracked walls and broken window panes, and barren scrub land that had once been productive farms. To illustrate this fact, she also attaches charts showing the epidemic of out migration and corresponding decline in local agricultural output, then she cites Case C in Clarendon and refers to her Appendix III, and then flings the National Minerals Policy across the room. Why the hell won't Jerome or Lilac phone her?

Flora is pacing, doing rounds on the tiled circumference of her kitchen and dining area. Lilac has finally answered her phone.

"So why you never leave me a message?"

"So why you never answer you phone?"

"Me did have things doing."

"Yeah like what?"

"Big people business. So what's wrong?"

Flora bursts into tears and proceeds to tell Lilac all about Jerome and Cliff, and Jerome risking his life to find out who killed Cliff, and why, and her fears, and . . . she is met with silence.

"Flora, you sure you ready fi dis?"

"Ready for what?"

"This is no joking matter. You sure you want to be mix up in all of dis?"

"I am not mixed up in anything. It's Jerome I'm worried about."

More silence, then a long sigh.

"Jerome is not a likle bwoy. He not like all the uptown spoilt boy pickney you used to. The one who need Mummy to hold him willy so him can pee straight. The one who think them is big man but need Mummy and Daddy rescue them at every turn. Jerome raise up by some serious people, and he know how to tek care of himself. Not the first time him deal wid dangerous business."

CHAPTER THIRTEEN

Flora stops her pacing and leans against the refrigerator for balance; she feels a bout of vertigo descending. "But wait, how come you know so rassclaat much about Jerome?"

More silence. Flora flashes on the scars on Jerome's body and remembers his story of dodging bullets under the sea. Maybe Lilac is right, but why does Lilac know something so fundamental about Jerome, and she, Flora, his lover, know nothing? Another long sigh.

"Awright, I should have told you, but me know Jerome from him a baby."

It is Flora's turn to say nothing.

"You don't remember, but I was friends with the Small girls. When you was spending time in Porty with you high-class white friend dem, I was with Liz, Ingrid, and Cathy in Mobay. You were in foreign when it happen, but I was in the car behind Liz when she die. Was a freak accident. Road get slick, Ingrid drive her mini too fast, car skid and flip over. Liz's neck snap, and just like that Jerome lose him mother."

"Bloodclaat Lilac, what else me don't know bout you?"

"Oh, a few things."

"But you know everything about me!"

"Well more or less, Florita, more or less."

At that, Flora hurls her phone down onto the granite tiles. As she watches her phone spill out its innards, she thinks, *Fabulous. I'm such a fucking idiot, now no one can reach me!*

It is three in the morning. Flora's eyes are swollen and red. Her hair is standing straight up from repeatedly pulling at it. She is wearing a threadbare Jamaica No Problem t-shirt and plaid pajama bottoms that are ripped in the crotch. She has just emailed her paper to an editor at MIT Press for inclusion in an anthology that includes several Nobel laureates. Lucky editor, because Flora's writing never needs editing. She writes with uncanny control and precision, rewriting until every sentence is exact and the whole seamless. Her writing is in contrast to her life. She remembers a colleague's astonishment upon meeting her after years of reading her work. She was in one of her stupid muddles, was it divorce from Husband Number Two? She had to laugh and forgive the colleague, "I'm nothing like my writing, I know!" The colleague tried to be chivalrous, but Flora let him off the hook. "No really, I'm a sort of idiot savant. No other explanation!"

Flora is rubbing her eyes and relishing her accomplishment—she's actually kept her promise to herself, gotten her work done, and proven she has a backbone—when she hears banging on her front door. If she had a gun, she would have gotten it. Instead, she watches with open mouth trying to scream, but no sound coming out, as the key turns in the lock, and Jerome walks into her house, followed by Lilac, and who is that behind Lilac? Ingrid?

"Flora, we been trying to reach you all night!" Did they say that in chorus?

Flora does her best to smooth her hair down and then points at the kitchen floor at her shattered phone.

"Oh sorry sweetie, never mean to upset you so bad."

Flora has vowed never to talk to Lilac again so doesn't respond to her but does notice that her friend looks like she's aged since the last time she saw her, only five days ago. She observes that Jerome has some sort of bandage on his shoulder but does not look closely; she does not want her fears about Jerome to be true. And there is Ingrid, stunning as ever, smiling at her with her famous green eyes that Jerome sort of shares, but his are brown with green tinges. Flora is sure she has completely lost her mind. They assemble in the living room and gawk at her, as if awaiting her command. She runs her hands through her hair and scratches her scalp. Then she looks at Jerome and pointing her chin at him says, "Okay, Jerome, you start. What the fuck is going on here?"

CHAPTER THIRTEEN

At the time of morning when the whistling of tree frogs turns to the chirping of birds, Flora chases the threesome out of her house, gets two ice packs out of her freezer, and lays on her couch with the larger pack on her head and the smaller on her face. Her brain is hurting. It is whirring round and round unable to stop trying to make sense. The part she especially can't figure out is exactly how the stolen sand fits in with the rest of it. She gets the relationship between the players, she gets why and how the sand was stolen, but what do those actions have to do with this other property that apparently Cliff lost his life over? Searching for certain details puts her brain into repeat mode, and there it remains stuck. Mason. If they chased him off the island, he must have the missing clues that she isn't seeing. She should go find him. God knows she could use the break.

The icepacks are losing their cool, but she doesn't want to get up. She adds a cushion over her face. The night has turned to day, but she needs darkness. She runs down the facts as she thinks she knows them: The large luxury resort-to-be that had been stalled at the beginning of construction, where once had been tall trees, now a wasteland of naked land, razed mangroves, dumped wetlands crisscrossed by half-built roads going nowhere, unfinished buildings, and random strewn construction materials, is also conveniently a transshipment point for drugs and guns, with boats and seaplanes arriving at night from the sea, small planes from the land—in Jamaica nothing that out of the ordinary.

Is this simply a matter of opportunism, maybe a way to make money when it seems to have run out? Or has drug trafficking, gun running, and money laundering always been part of the enterprise? And somehow sand stealing as well. The trucks that stole the sand came and went from the property, and sand that could not be immediately delivered was stored there. But why is she obsessing on sand stealing when that is not what Cliff got killed over, or is it also part of the picture? Or was he only killed after stumbling across the loading and unloading of boats and planes? Or is that just a coincidence, and was he killed for documenting the ridiculously ineffective transplanting of the coral and sea grasses, the blowing up of the reefs, the dredging and dumping of the harbor? Or was he just in the wrong place at the wrong time? If so, whom did they think they were killing? And who exactly is *they*? Most importantly, what is she to do with this—all that Jerome has told her—the footage he has given her? Why her? She doesn't relish the thought of gunmen barging into her home and killing her. Why is *she* saddled with this burden? She has way too many questions. There is a long list of people she needs to talk with and get some answers, but first, she must purchase a new phone. Though she has not slept in two nights, she might as well go to work; her staff needs to see their intrepid leader every now and again, and no doubt there is a pile of checks waiting for her signature.

Chapter Fourteen

"Oh Flora is you, didn't recognize your number. You calling from you office?"

"Mmhm, my cell not working so well."

"So to what do I deserve the pleasure of your voice?"

"Malcolm, me cyan hear nothing bout sand theft, story just disappear from off the face of the earth, what happen?"

"Well, seems like case never get reassign."

Flora remembers Lilac saying, "The trial not going go through den!"

"So the trial not going through? What, them settling out of court?"

"I don't really know, you know, but maybe, looking something like that."

Hush money, slush money. Flora wants to know where the money is coming from and where it is going, but she knows there is no way Malcolm will tell her.

"So tell me this, you know the hotel with the over water Polynesian-style rooms that stop build just after it start?"

Malcolm makes a noncommittal sound.

"Don't is your friend Baxter sell them that big piece of prime coastline?"

Malcolm makes another noncommittal sound.

"Your truck driver must have told you that is from there them did drive the trucks?"

"Flora I . . ."

"And don't your friend Baxter own a trucking and hauling business?"

"Flora what . . ."

"And don't him own a small plane charter company?"

"Flora, my dear, sorry, but I'm not following you. You know I would love to chat, but I have to run, have a damn meeting I am very late for."

"And don't him get contract to take divers out on him boats to blast the reef for the harbor dredging?"

"Flora, let's talk again soon, and you can explain what all of this is about, but I really have to go."

Flora shakes with rage. She can't believe she took money from these people.

Environment First is going to have to move. She can't continue to have her office under Malcolm's roof. It's bad enough taking money from Green washing oil corporations and PR-hungry local good-old-boy private-sector companies, but . . . what is the but? Surely murder has always been part of the picture; she just hasn't chosen to look closely at that corner of the frame before.

Flora is sitting in Hope Gardens. Hope, such a strange name for a slave plantation, but maybe it was the owner who had high hopes. John Tharp, who owned over 3,000 enslaved Africans and 10,000 acres, named his plantation Good Hope. He became the richest man in Jamaica, so surely his wishes were granted. But all over Jamaica are places with the name Hope—New Hope, Old Hope, Hope Bay, Hopewell, Good Hope. We are a hopeful people. Flora watches the children running around screaming, vying with each other to stone mangoes off the tree, climbing on top of each other to get to a mango-filled branch. An adult, who looks like maybe she works there, comes over to tell them to stop, but as soon as she walks away, the children resume right where they left off. Flora notices the paucity of adults. There must be five different school groups, but it seems like there is about one adult to every fifty children, a reflection of Jamaica's desperate demography perhaps.

She remembers her young days at Hope, the once home of her grandfather and father, and so she rather feels like it should be hers as well. She remembers being in a frilly white dress with pink roses, eating sticky cotton candy and getting hopelessly lost in the maze. Over the years the maze wore out, got mangy, and if you got lost you could just burrow through or climb out, but as a small child the maze was towering, imposing, and she was completely overwhelmed. Who knows, maybe that's where her fear of enclosed spaces began.

Flora traces her hand over the faux wood concrete bench and notices that there is a plaque for Michael Manley. She is sitting on a bench named for a deceased prime minister, under a very large tree that maybe her grandfather planted, or brought the seed to Jamaica from some other British Colony—British Honduras, British Guiana, British Ceylon, British Gold Coast Crown Colony. But as she removes the ants crawling over her, she studies the massive roots that snake in every direction for yards and yards and figures no, not planted by her grandfather, this tree has been there since slavery.

"Flora can you believe those jackasses were going to subdivide this place and turn it into a housing scheme?" Milton, his eyes wide, his springy white hair standing up in every direction, is gesturing widely.

"Ah Milton," Flora pats the bench. They are finally going to have lunch together. As he starts to sit, she cautions him, "Careful, don't sit on Michael!" Milton and Michael had been close friends.

"We have no open green spaces in Kingston, and they wanted to take this, pave it over, and put houses!" He is shaking his head in dismay.

"The only remaining spaces are all colonial, have you ever noticed?"

"Yes, there is Kings House, which, by the way, there were also plans to subdivide!"

"There is Up Park Camp, which I hear is also slated for development."

"Flora, we are absolutely mad!"

Flora looks with deep affection at her ancestral home, the colonial bandstand now a sort of gazebo, the wilting tropical flowers neatly planted like an English garden, the tall majestic trees with garbage strewn about their roots. "I think this should be mine. If I ruled the world, Hope Gardens would be mine."

"I knew your grandfather you know? Remarkable little fellow. Grew the sweetest strawberries. I once did a long interview with him—wonder where that is."

Flora stands up; her stomach is grumbling, and she is truly tired. She looks toward the little pond, with the island shaped like Jamaica, where once had been swans but now is choked with some invasive water lily. She points toward the island and says, "I hear the Chinese government has given money for a Chinese garden. What do you suppose that would be? Bamboo?"

Milton stands with difficulty, laughing and coughing at the same time. "Maybe they will also give us a panda bear to go with it!" They link arms and walk toward the restaurant, behind them the squeals of children chasing each other.

Flora orders a cup of soup and the combo plate. Vegan food is not really his thing, so Milton just orders a large bowl of soup and a guava juice. Flora knows he would prefer a beer. She orders a June plum-passion-fruit juice blend. She tries not to stare at Milton, who is looking unwell and very old. Flora is sure she isn't looking her best either.

"So you coming with me to the limestone mining hearing?"

Milton nods vigorously. "Wouldn't miss it for the world!"

Their soups arrive, and a grateful silence descends. A friend had complained that the soup at the restaurant is always "thyme soup," but Flora quite likes the salty thyme-infused pumpkin soup as she bites into a substantial dumpling. Milton is munching on a slab of yellow yam. Happiness. Flora does not want to break this spell by talking about unhappy realities. Who cares if Falmouth is ruined, if Cockpit Country is mined, if the Blue Mountains are deforested, if every river is polluted, if every beach is choked with plastic, she is in Hope Gardens, and the sun is playing on a majestic bank of clouds, so clean, so bright, so unreachable.

Flora shifts gears, and curses, as they round a hairpin turn and before them is revealed part of the new Mount Rosser by-pass road. There is a huge gash in the side of the mountain, and then, as they go around the next bend, there might as well be mountaintop mining, because the top of the mountain has been removed—West Virginia anyone? But where is the coal? It's just a road. The red of the bauxite soil is already staining everything. "Fuckers!" Flora screams as they drive under the overpass. "This used to be pastoral. This used to be picturesque. There used to be cows grazing!" Not that she's big on cows grazing, but maybe cows are better than bauxite extraction, less damaging than unnecessary, grandiose highways cutting across the interior of her island, especially a highway that was started in the middle, that connects to no other roads, and on which construction has had to be stopped, because the government ignored the warnings that they were building through geologically unstable terrain, and anyway the money has run out as it always does.

"Did I ever tell you about the time I drove around the island just after Independence?" Milton is sitting beside Flora, who can't believe she is driving to the cursed north coast yet again, this time for a useless meeting about mining a very healthy limestone forest. She has heard Milton's post-independence island sojourn many times so is happy when Derek perks up from the back in time to ask, "Prof, what happen to the sand theft case?"

"God Derek, please don't get her started on that, she'll crash the bloody car. You know, I used to go to that beach as a child. My father used to take me. They had these huge rays the size of a car."

"Mr. Brown, them never frighten you?"

"No, they were wonderful. The water was clear as glass. Not like now, it's so nasty, can't see a damn thing. I got sick the last time I swam there. God knows what is in that water."

"We could stop, eh Prof, and get a sample for testing? But I bet I could tell you off the top of my head a few tings in there, eh?"

"Well, back to the stealing of the sand, I have my theories. You know what I think? I think they are hiding something."

Flora blows her horn at a truck threatening to cross her path and snorts, "Well Milton, you are a genius! Of course they are hiding something!"

"No, I don't mean the sand, I mean it's a cover for something else."

"Exactly, and I can tell you what—drug and gun-running. Not very original I know."

"I did a little asking around about your friend who got killed, and sorry to say that's what my sources tell me. The bastards killed him because he not only stumbled across their activities, but apparently had put two and two together, you know, who and what and all that."

Derek whistles from the back. "Yes, very dangerous being a math wiz in Jamaica, knowing how to add up two and two."

Derek is going briskly through one of his classic PowerPoint presentations. Crisp, high-resolution images with concise, necessary facts about what there is in Porto Bueno Bluff that has greater value than digging it up to export to Florida, so they can further overdevelop and Jamaica can further devolve. Derek's images are not only pretty pictures of endemic birds, orchids, trees, (none of the endangered snakes, those make Jamaicans squirm), but also mining activities with oversized vehicles, dust flying, and the usual aftermath of gouges and gaping holes.

But almost no one in the room is paying any attention. The technocrats have already made up their minds, and as the technocrat in charge has pleaded with Flora on a number of occasions, when he thought she was getting overexcited and expecting too much of him and his governmental environment agency, "Cho Flora don't tek everything so serious, dis not my life, is only a job." The room is half empty. There won't be many jobs from the proposed limestone mining, and most are going to Chinese nationals, so unlike a public meeting for a new hotel or bauxite development, it is not packed with employees and the hopeful unemployed who have been bused in to give their support.

The Chamber of Commerce person chairing the meeting thanks Derek for his presentation and then launches into a speech about the need for balance—which she pronounces "ba-lan-ce"—that we must al-way-s ba-lan-ce be-tween eco-logi-cal con-cern-s and eco-no-mic con-cern-s. Then the same it's-only-a job man gets up and says that every care will be taken so that no damage will be seen from the highway. There will be a protective beauty strip. You won't be able to notice anything. He guarantees there will be no negative effects on tourism. Brand Jamaica will still be beautiful. There is a smattering of applause.

As Flora is wondering what is the best way to kill herself—drowning? Sleeping pills? Driving off the side of a ravine?—Milton pounds on the table with his fist, and shouts, "Madame Chairperson, have any of you listened to one word this young scientist from the university has just said? We have driven all the way from Kingston to participate in this disgusting charade, this pretense at process, this fraudulent poppy show. It is an insult, a damn insult." Madame Chair is banging her gavel, "Or-der! Order!" But Milton is on a roll. "And it's a damn disgrace that our government permits the digging up of our resources to send off to the richest country in the world. Let them dig up their own backyard. Haven't we learned anything? Are we still slaves or are we a sovereign independent nation?" Flora thinks she can answer that question, but instead Mr. It's-only-a-job says in that calm, flat, reasonable tone of the well-fed bureaucrat, "Milton, Milton, I don't know what you think we can do. But this is private property. We can't tell people what they can and cannot do on their property. They own it. They can do what they want to do with it." But Milton will have none of that. "Mr. French, you bloody well know that is not true. [Bang. "Or-der!" Bang. "Or-der!"] If there is bauxite under my house, or gold, or plutonium, or some mineral the government has decided is necessary for their foreign exchange, you better believe I don't own my property, you better believe it belongs to the Crown. That is British Common Law. That is what we have inherited in this God-forsaken place."

Milton has run out of steam, which Flora witnesses with sadness. Not so long ago, he would have been able to hold them captive for at least another half an hour. Instead, ba-lan-ce has been restored to the universe. "Thank you, Mr. Brown, for your input. We are grateful for all you have contribute over these many year. But I hope you will trust that the right decision are being made by our talented and dedicated technical team. Jamaica must develop. We cannot stand in the way of development. We must have balance. We must be prudent." Extraordinary impartiality demonstrated by the Chair, but there is no purpose pointing out conflicts of interest. No matter how many times she complains, no one ever sees a problem with having public hearings run by persons with obvious interest in the success of the development under question. Flora decides the best way to kill herself is to be a suicide bomber at a meeting like this, though she would prefer it to be really packed and every member of the government in attendance.

Chapter Fifteen

Flora wakes with a start, her heart racing. The room is very dark. She has no idea where she is, and searches for familiar objects but can't find any. A fan whirs overhead, and another fan is whirring from the foot of the bed. Flora tries to control her alarm. A pool of sweat has collected between her breasts. She gropes around till she finds the t-shirt she had been wearing when she went to bed and dries herself with it. Let's see: I got on a plane, I flew to Miami, then I flew to Washington, DC, and it's hot as hell. Ah yes, she is in an apartment that Mason and Kevin are borrowing from a diplomat friend.

She turns on her side and feels shift the Ethiopian food she had eaten not too many hours before. Flora recalls more details: she took the Metro from National Airport (she refuses to call it Ronald Reagan) to Dupont Circle and then walked three blocks to 17th and S, and voila, her boys greeted her with abundant hugs, supplied her with a very long drink, and gave her the tour of what seemed to be an art gallery of global exotica but is apparently someone's home. After innocuous chitchat (no, they hadn't broached "The Subject"), they walked up to Adams Morgan to have Ethiopian food at the last hold-out of such restaurants. Once there had been seven to choose from, now South

Asian seemed to be in vogue, or was it Mediterranean? She had counted restaurants by category but can't remember the count or typology. Kevin is leaving for Jamaica in the morning, so she'll have Mason to herself for two days before she also heads home; that comforting thought calms her enough to go back to sleep.

Flora and Mason are sitting in the shade near the rose garden at the Smithsonian. Flora has gone from flower to flower sniffing to see which roses have any scent and reporting back in ecstasy the few that do. She inhales the scent of a yellow-burnt-orange rose that transports her back to her grandfather's rose garden. "Mase, Mase, smell this one. Divine!" They had taken the Metro to Union Station, gone down to the Food Court to buy cold drinks and spicy samosas for their outing, and then trudged up to the Capitol, sitting at various fountains to cool off. They then went to the East Wing, the Hirshhorn, and the Museum of African Art, where they just exited. Tomorrow will be brunch with friends and in the evening a concert of chamber music at the Kennedy Center performed by the Tokyo Quartet. A superb weekend in the Capitol of the Free World—how lucky is she!

Flora lays her head on Mason's shoulder and strokes his arm. He has gained weight, a bit more fleshy around the cheeks when he smiles, his shirt straining over his stomach. The gray around his temples spreading, he is so tall, so handsome, so dignified. "But Mase, you need some sun bad bad. I'll fly back in a few weeks, and we go to the beach."

Mason laughs, "Beach? Are you crazy in this heat! And all dem people a bleach but you want me to be my authentic black self?"

"I just don't want you all ashy! Better be careful—Kevin thinks he is married to a black man!"

"Yes but mi hear seh you cyan be black and batty man!"

"Judge! Behave yourself! I'll come back, we'll rent a cottage in Rehoboth, and just like nice white people we will go to the beach!"

"Anything you say, my favorite browning!"

There is finally a discernable wind blowing. The sun will not set till late, but it has dipped toward the horizon, and the soup called DC air in summer is becoming easier to breathe.

"So tell me, what you do with your days?"

"Am writing my memoirs."

"Cho man, stop you foolishness! Seriously are you bored?"

"No really, I am writing my memoirs. I even have a publisher and a respectable advance."

"Hot shit! But Mase you cyan come home. Dem will kill you fi true. You naming names?"

"Well . . ."

"Dem will sue your rass, den kill you!"

"There will be a large team of lawyers looking over my every word."

They have to laugh at this, given that Mason, the lawyer, had combed through every Environment First contract, statement, document, press release, you name it, to make sure Flora wouldn't get sued.

"So am I in your memoirs?"

"Depends how much you pay me to keep you out!"

"Not one red cent you getting! They won't sell your book in Jamaica, you know that, right?"

"Well, maybe not, but it will get read there anyway, and the laws here are less hysterical about libel. We'll see." Mason strokes Flora's hair and rubs the nape of her neck. "Whatever happen with you and Madge? She still suing you?"

Flora makes up her face, "That bitch? My idiot lawyers (no offense!) let her idiot lawyers know that I had some damning evidence, and we have not heard a peep. But I bet you when me least expect it, watch her, she will spring something. These people just wait you out."

Mason nods in agreement and then yawns and stretches. "Let's walk. I'm getting peckish. How about falafels?"

"Yum!"

It's a long walk back up to Dupont Circle, but there is no rush. If need be, they can stop along the way at some gelateria, café, or bar, or sit and rest by yet another of the scores of fountains that litter Washington, DC.

۞

Mason is on the phone with Kevin. Flora can hear him chortling—they've been together ten years and still act like it's new love! She shifts her swollen ankles. She has her legs elevated above her heart as instructed by Dr. Supreme Court. Today is the furthest she has walked in memory. When they got home from their delicious and well-deserved meal of falafels—impeccably crispy on the outside, green and soft on the inside, dripping with tahini sauce, layered onto fresh and tangy tabouli, and eaten with a pile of thick Greek fries, all washed down with a pitcher of fresh lemonade—she had soaked her feet in a tub filled with Epsom salts and aromatherapy oils while Mason serenaded her with his latest opera discoveries that include remastered 1916 recordings of Caruso. This is the life. She absolutely could get used to it. No need to return to Jamaica. Jamaica is a very, very distant place.

"Okay Kevvy, miss you. I will, she's sitting right here. She is very well behaved and such good company. Love you too, night night." Mason comes over and kisses Flora on the top of her head. "That is from Kevin." Then he kisses Flora on the lips, "That is from me!"

"How is our boy?"

"Oh, he's been gone less than a day and already up to mischief! Here, give me those feet." Flora gratefully transfers her feet from the awkward position above her head to Mason's lap. He touches her ankles and she winces. They are still swollen; maybe a bucket of ice should be next. Mason rubs her feet, and she starts to fade in and out of consciousness.

"Oh shit, did I fall asleep?"

"Yep, snoring and all."

"You too lie!"

"I am a judge. I cannot tell a lie!"

"Okay, then tell me this, did Malcolm dem steal their own sand? And if so what the fuck for?"

'"Well I don't know about Malcolm. I don't think he's personally involved, but some of his associates definitely are."

"But why?"

"I know, even in Jamaica where we excel at cutting down the tree to get to the fruit, seems crazy to destroy your own property that you're supposed to be developing, but I hear the financing fell through for their crack-head schemes."

"Yes, the silver lining of the global market meltdown!"

"I also heard about some serious gambling debts both of the usual sort and of the risky financial investment sort."

"Ahah. Not to mention it get very cash intensive to live the high life dem boys like to live."

"Yes, my dear, over leveraged, bad investments, those pyramid schemes we know all too well, that sort of thing."

"But I thought the big boys got their money out before it all went belly up for the rest of us. I heard they flew over and threatened you-know-who till he coughed up the money."

"Yes, I heard that too, but not sure they got all their money back."

"Rahtid! But tell me this, how Baxter fit into the picture?"

"Now you talking! Mr. Under-the-radar. Well him and him partner Kid Capone, the number one Mobay Don, control that whole coast from into Hanover, through St. James, Trelawney, and parts of St. Ann. Capone control the politicians, and if someting a gwan you can bet your bottom dollar Baxter getting some of that money."

"But how him connect up with the international money?"

"Not hard. You have this mafia and that mafia, and this cartel and that cartel, and all sorts of unsavory characters who have way too much money that needs to be laundered or who need money quick. Tourism is a good ploy, and Baxter has an all-access pass and all the toys." Malcolm makes the sound of money cascading, "Kching! Kching! Bingo! You just won the jackpot! It's a very frothy mix of organized crime and unorganized, or should we say disorganized, crime!"

"And strange bedfellows."

"Oh yes, literally!"

"Jesus fucking krist! So who threaten you?"

"Hmm. Is more like who didn't threaten me! Let's just say I had it on the highest authority that was best for me to leave post haste."

"This does not make me happy, you cyan come home!"

"Oh, of course I can. Case is over. Who remembers any of it? We're on to our next crisis and then the one after that. I'll be home over the Christmas holidays. We're having a family reunion. My parents' fiftieth wedding anniversary is New Year's Day."

"How romantic getting married on the first day of the year!"

"Yes, very romantic, or then again maybe had to do with the less romantic fact of my mother's pregnancy and my grandfather's shotgun!"

"Such dangerous beginnings! I just want you to be safe. I couldn't stand anything happening to you. Please promise me you'll be safe!"

"I promise, but look who is talking! You seem to be getting into some high water yourself, and I'm not sure you even know how deep you in!"

"True, true. Unfortunately very true. Speaking of which, I brought you a pile of DVDs with a whole heap of scary footage on them. They are for safe-keeping, so keep them safe! Though you can include as much as you want in your memoirs long as you dedicate the book to me."

"I am planning a whole chapter on you!"

"Is that all I'm worth?"

"Well, give me some more gossip, and maybe I can stretch you out for longer than a chapter. What's happening with you and that very cute boy?"

"You mean Jerome?"

"Why, you have more than one cute boy at the moment?"

"God no. I barely have energy for one. Old age is a terrible thing, though you don't seem to be suffering."

"Yes, well, if you can't manage, you can lend him to me."

"I'll tell Kevin."

"Oh he'll be there too, honey!"

"Mason stop it! By the way, tell me you are not in a certain dead ambassador's collection of illicit videos. Please!"

"Actually, Florita darling, I have some DVDs of my own I need for you to keep."

"I cannot believe this! You don't really expect me to risk going through customs with pictures of you sucking some boy's cock—or is it the other way around?"

"You make it sound so sordid, so crude! I am an officer and a gentleman! I would never put you in such an awkward position—now Jerome on the other hand."

"Mason!"

"No seriously, there is at a bank a safe box in your name. I'll give you those details in writing. But you will hopefully never have to reveal who is on those tapes!"

"But why me, Mase?"

"Because you, Florita, are the person I most trust with my life."

Chapter Sixteen

She has spent an entire weekend missing no one, never wondering what was happening to anyone or worrying about anyplace under threat. Unfortunately, her flight, though the first of the morning, is delayed, and Flora's bubble is bursting, her idyllic time with Mason fast fading. Sitting in limbo, neither there nor here, the nagging feelings of incompletion and restlessness return. She doesn't want to buy a book, and anyway wouldn't be able to concentrate enough to read it, so instead gives Verizon her credit card number and checks her email.

First up, she replies to Derek.

Subject: re: Oh Happy Day!
Darling Dr. Derek. Congratulations. Those dimwits have finally made you a Ph.D.!!! I will throw you a Wild Party in celebration. Just send me the guest list, food and liquor requirements and I'm on it! Oh and of course pick the date you want. And we are definitely not inviting anyone on your committee!!!!

LOVE YOU XXOOXX

Subject: Paper Accepted

Dear Prof. Smith,

Thank you for your paper on the failure of Bauxite Lands Rehabilitation in Jamaica. As always, it is of the highest quality and has been accepted by our Peer-Review Panel with NO changes. Your paper will be a welcome and important addition to the anthology, and MIT Press is extremely grateful for your taking the time to send us something original to include. As you are no doubt aware, you are in very eminent company. Please again accept our kudos on your excellent work.

We are all anxious to see you again and are hoping you will be back with us very soon. Prof. Chang will be in touch shortly with an invitation for the book launch and conference, and a task force of international scientists addressing Climate Change Policy for Small Island States that we are hoping you will join.

Warmly,
Charles
Charles Peabody, Ph.D.
Senior Science Editor
MIT Press
www.mitpress.edu

The mention of Chang makes her smile. She had planned to call him from DC then remembered he wouldn't be in Boston this time of year and was probably out of reach, on some mountaintop—Kilimanjaro was it? She looks forward to catching up—she has some ideas she needs to run by him.

Despite her swearing off talking to Lilac, she does open an email from her:

> Subject: Forgive me nuh?
> You get a new phone yet? You still mad at me? You know me never mean to upset you so! You know I love you more than anyone on this planet (except of course Punky!). CALL ME!
>
> Subject: INVITATION TO BAUXITE REHABILITATION TREE PLANTING
> CEREMONY
> Dear Ms. Florra Smith:
> The Bauxite Board and Shanlugongqu Corp. cordially request your presence at the Ground Breaking Ceremony for the Rehabilitation of lands successfully mined and recently closed. A shuttle will be provided for all attendees. Please see attachment for all information pertaining to the ceremony. We look forward to your presence, or that of your representative, at this event.
>
> Shereen James (Miss)
> Communications Manager
> Shanlugongqu Corp. Jamaica Division

Flora's contentment is now completely drained away. Shanlugongqu? Who the . . .? Oh yes, now she remembers, the Chinese have bought out the government's portion of the failing bauxite enterprise previously owned by the Russian Oligarch. Why oh why would they think she would want to attend their sham tree-planting ceremony and let them use Environment First to validate their empty claims to corporate environmental responsibility? And since when have the Chinese cared about such appearances? The Bauxite Board and the Ministry of Mining must be behind the event, probably to do with some international money they are begging or some convention they have recently signed. Luckily, the immediate boarding of Flora's plane is announced, in the usual incomprehensible way that announcements are made in airports, so she has no time to fire off an email telling Miss James, the Bauxite Board, and Shanlugongqu Corp. exactly where they can shove their invitation.

❂

Though signs forbid cellular phone use in the customs area, everyone (except Flora) is on their mobile. The Visitors line is moving right along, thank you very much, but the Jamaica Nationals and Caricom Citizens line slowly inches forward, with over a hundred people in front of her. Wonderful! What was she thinking arriving in the middle of the day, and why can't Jamaican Nationals have a line of our own? Why do we have to share with Caricom Nationals? At least three flights seem to have just landed. Someone says one is a charter—where are Jamaicans chartering home from?

It takes exactly an hour for Flora to get her passport stamped. She heads to the Nothing to Declare line with her backpack and computer bag, and asks the passport officer how she's doing. The officer replies, "Could be better, but am alive so can't complain, must give thanks and praise to God for another day." Indeed. Jamaicans are always counting blessings, thankful for small mercies. Flora is convinced that the more you have, the more you whine. She, who has just had the most luxurious and privileged weekend, has been whining (to herself, of course, but she is prepared to whine to anyone who will listen) about how long it has taken to get out of the airport.

She tells the polite JUTA lady at the door, no she doesn't need a taxi. How times have changed, so decorous and regimented, no one rushing at you and bodily trying to put you into his vehicle. We are getting way too civilized. As Flora searches for her car keys, she hears a familiar little voice squeaking, "Aunty! Aunty!" and feels a small child lunge into her and then clasp firmly onto her legs. She lifts Punky into her arms, smothers her with kisses, and hugs her tight. It doesn't take Flora long to find Punky's grandmother, leaning innocently against a column, watching them with delight.

There is no point, really. No point asking Lilac who she is there to meet. No point questioning Lilac as to how she knew what flight she was on. No point holding on to her not-speaking-to-Lilac policy. Lilac is an irresistible force of nature. Instead, Flora shifts Punky onto her hip and stands shaking her head at her friend until their mutual smiles turn into laughter. Lilac comes over, picks up Flora's computer bag, and tickles Punky, who squirms in Flora's arms. "Punky you so smart, how you find Aunty so quick."

"Mi did see her soon she come out."

"Yep can't miss Flora." Lilac kisses Flora. "No one else in the world look like our Florita. Don't?" Flora has no idea why, but she is blushing. "So how was the trip? How's Mason?"

Flora stands on her toes to give Lilac a kiss in return. "Trip was fabulosity, will tell you all shortly. You coming to my place or I going to yours?"

"Punky you want to go to Nana's or Aunty's house?"

"Aunty Flora, we go Aunty's."

"Okay. Then come with me, and we will be at Aunty's in two twos."

Punky climbs down, and Lilac exchanges Flora's computer bag for Punky. "Oh by the way, have something for you, it's your same number." Lilac hands Flora the exact replica of her last phone. "I didn't think you'd want an upgrade, but if you do, no problem. Just let me know what phone you want, and I will get it."

The three are sprawled on Flora's living room floor. Flora is programming her new phone. Lilac colors with Punky in a coloring book featuring fruits and vegetables. They work on a purple eggplant, while Lilac supplies phone numbers and suggests people who should not be forgotten. Flora can't remember half of those who had been in her phone and is glad for the excuse to "lose" certain people.

"You have Karen Phillips?"

"You mad? Why would I want her number? She is a complete whackodoodledoo." Flora reaches for another in Lilac's array of patties. So far she has eaten a lentil, a pumpkin, and is about to eat a callaloo patty. Welcome home!

"Punky, your grandmother makes the most delicious patties. Speaking of which, how much would you charge to cater Derek's Ph.D. party?"

"Wow, you mean him finally finish?"

"Hey! Not his fault!"

"You know me wouldn't charge. We can buy the ingredients together."

"No way. I'm not going to let you pay for one striking thing."

Lilac rolls her eyes. Punky displays her eggplant proudly, "Aunty look!"

Flora scoots Lilac out of the way so she and Punky can color a pumpkin. "Orange, Punky. Find me the orange crayon, and we're on our way." Punky exuberantly covers the entire page in orange. Flora tries to add highlights to the pumpkin, some green at its stem, an outline, so the pumpkin has a shape. Lilac is leaning against the couch watching the action, her long legs crossed at the ankles. Flora looks up at Lilac and mouths, "We have to talk." Lilac looks over to Punky, then back to Flora, and nods. Flora feels a cresting wave of pity for Lilac for all that she has exacted of her friend these many years. Nonetheless she steels herself, presses forward. "Tell me something," Flora can feel Lilac flinch. Flora glances at Punky, who is deeply occupied, then turns her gaze to Lilac. "Did you and Ingrid ever . . .?" Lilac can't help smiling at Flora's tenaciousness but shakes her head no. Flora gives her an are-you-sure look, to which Lilac answers, "Not Ingrid, Liz." Flora is dumbfounded, "Liz? Liz Small? You mean Jerome's mom?" Lilac nods.

Punky has no more space to fill with her orange crayon; the room is very quiet; the two adults are staring at each other, not saying a word. Punky turns a few pages, "Aunty what next? What next?" Lilac rolls over to Punky, kisses her on the nose, and takes the coloring book. “My turn baby girl, let’s pick a fruit this time, how about we color the watermelon?”

Flora goes into the kitchen and pours water into glasses. The glasses are full, but she stands clutching the water bottle in her hand. She counts to a hundred and tries not to hyperventilate. There is no way they can have this conversation with a three-year-old in the room. Liz? When? Flora puts the glasses onto a bamboo tray she inherited from her parents. It is decorated with scenes of river rafting on the Rio Grande, something they had done on their honeymoon. She sets the tray down on the floor and reaches for the black crayon. “I’m coloring the seeds. Punky, what you and Nana going to color?” Punky searches for the right shade of pink and then starts filling in the watermelon flesh. Her body is all that separates Lilac and Flora, and all that they have not said, and cannot yet say.

Chapter Seventeen

Flora stands in Ingrid's living room, fighting a feeling that she has been there before. Of course she's been there, it's the Small family home, and she would have attended birthday parties and other gatherings when she was in school. She vaguely remembers being part of a group of girls crowded under a big tamarind tree, turning a bucket, filled with salted ice, out of which came the most delicious coconut ice cream. Or is the familiarity just the old-style house when so few still exist? Apart from two consulates, Swallowtail is the last original house and property in the area. Everything else has been turned into townhouses with names like The Grande Oakes, Cumberland Meadows Estate, Ackee Glade Manors, Mango Walk Mews; what once had been mango trees is nothing but concrete, twenty homes crammed where one had been. Flora walks over to the big picture window that shockingly has no burglar bars marring the view. The tamarind tree is indeed still there. She flushes as she locates where she and Jerome had been parked that first night. What a sensible fellow to not bring her into his childhood bedroom that she would have known as his mother's before he was born!

Flora steps outside into the fading evening light. A cool breeze brings a scent of jasmine and a longing for the sea and the clouds turning coral. Oh, to be on the point with Jerome looking out at the horizon. As she walks toward the tamarind tree, three large dogs bound over wagging their tails. The chocolate lab wags its entire rear end. The black lab jumps on her and licks her face.

"Sheeba down! God that dog. Sheeba! Down this very minute!" Flora is amazed that Sheeba actually obeys. "Flora, my dear, I'm so sorry. Forgive my dogs' bad manners. You okay?"

"Yeah man, I'm fine. They never bother me. I like dogs."

"Good. Most people are petrified. They are great big menaces, but sweet menaces, isn't that so, my darlings?" Ingrid introduces Sheeba, Bugsby, and Rex to Flora. The dogs crowd around Ingrid, and then go back over to Flora for full body sniffs and petting. Flora tries to remember the last time she was alone with Ingrid. Was it Negril Beach when she was like sixteen, her last summer before going to college? She discovers that Sheeba has the softest ears, reassuring to touch, over and over. Her head down, all Flora can see is Ingrid's ripped jeans and bare feet. She forces herself to look up.

Ingrid is smiling. "Sheeba likes you."

"Oh, I think Sheeba would like anyone!" Flora feels like she's been sent to the headmistress's office—when will the interrogation begin? What is her punishment? Instead, Ingrid walks over and strokes Flora's hair, and then massages her neck and shoulders, her touch first tender and then strong. Flora feels years of disappointment rising into her throat and fears she is going to dissolve into helpless sobs.

She feels Ingrid's breath close to her ear, "You know Jerome is very fond of you?"

"Is he?" The tears are starting. "I am very fond of him." The tears are flowing. "Ingrid, I'm really sorry . . . do you mind?" She means, "I am a bad person, aren't I?" A wave of pain spreads from her chest across her body. "Do you mind me being with Jerome?"

"Flora, my love, mind? How could I mind? You are the best thing to happen to Jerome in years." Flora slowly realizes there is no punishment. How could she have forgotten? Limbo is a place without torment, only salt tears and sighs. Holding tightly onto Ingrid, Flora cries the tears of one who has finally received benediction.

⁂

They are sitting in the long back porch. It is quiet except for the sound of roosting birds and tree frogs. Bats dart about. The porch is filled with plants. There are blooming orchids hanging. The smell of jasmine is very strong. Ingrid takes a flower and lets it linger by Flora's nose, puts it in Flora's hair, and then sticks one behind her own ear. They are sitting at a narrow table painted in bright colors like the bookcase at Jerome's. Flora points to the table and says, "You make this?" Ingrid nods. She brings them soup: a cold soup made from cucumbers, tomatoes, and avocado, garnished with cilantro. Second course is penne pasta with olives, basil, broccoli, and red peppers. Ingrid boasts that everything comes from her gardens except the pasta and olives. A while after the meal, they have cocoa tea: Jamaican chocolate, nutmeg, cinnamon leaves, and sugar, into which they dip jackass corn—hard coconut biscuits.

The only light comes from a large yellow and red candle that is hollowing out as it burns. Ingrid has draped a light blanket over them.

"Don't you miss Espie? Don't you get lonely in this big house by yourself?"

"Sure I do. That's why I like when Jerome comes to town, but he doesn't like to come to town. Of course, now he has motivation to come a bit more often." Ingrid tickles Flora for emphasis. Flora buries herself deeper into Ingrid's lap. "Actually, I get to see Espie soon. I'm heading to Rome week after next."

"That's great."

"Yeah. You should come. We're going to Venice for the Biennale—Espie has a few pieces in the show—these days she's doing these huge installations. You'd love them!"

"Cool! I want to see. Show me pictures. But, Ingrid, she going to keep living half the year in Italy?"

Ingrid kisses her teeth. "Espie become so Jamaican, she treat her boy pickney like babies. I mean really! Trevor can look after himself goddamn it."

"But he's her baby."

"Since when is a twenty-three-year-old a baby?"

"I mean he's the last one."

"Oh please! Anyway, once it get too cold she suddenly remember she have grandchildren over here to look after!"

Flora laughs. Unlike her closest friends who started making babies very young—Lilac had her first child at nineteen—Flora has missed out on this having children thing. She had the chance, but it was never convenient, she'd always gotten pregnant by the wrong men. And she had been convinced she would have made the worst mother. One abortion too many, and she'd finally gotten the doctor to tie her tubes. She'd been begging for years but had always been denied, told she was too young not to procreate.

"Jerome's dad is joining us, then we go spend a little time with him in Geneva, then we'll be home."

"Oh, so Jerome is going as well." Flora realizes she hasn't seen or talked to Jerome in over a week and has no idea how he is. "Good for Jerome to get away for a while. I'm really worried about him."

"Well, you should come too. We're all worried about you."

"Seriously wish I could. Ingrid, I need a *new life,* but I don't know how to go about it."

"What you mean?"

"My life. I'm stuck. I don't know why I'm doing what I'm doing anymore. I don't even know what I'm doing."

"Ah, midlife crisis!"

"Nah, not that cliché. I just want a . . . different . . . life."

"It's easy. Just blindly step off the precipice. Don't look before you jump. Travel aimlessly. Go hang with Jerome in the bush. Just stop being so responsible!"

"Me responsible? Shit!"

"You're the most responsible person I know. I think it's high time you stopped trying to save the world."

Chapter Eighteen

Flora is sitting on the bench looking up at the roof of *Eco Yard* wondering how to dismantle it. She has just had a board meeting, where she unfortunately burst into tears upon presenting the projected fourth quarter figures, which show that come January they will not be able to meet payroll. At their successful fundraiser, most of the generous donors gave only to the endowment, the income from which has plummeted by half due to the government's nifty debt exchange. No one wants to give money for administration or programs, and this time she has no fundraising magic tricks. She is no one's hero at the moment and hasn't been featured in the newspaper in months. Her last letter to the editor wasn't even published!

Flora relives the shame of her tears. What the fuck is wrong with her? Clearly she's depressed. She looks back at the roof and curses Malcolm. The board cannot understand her desire to move. They have never understood her longing to have Environment First independent, unbeholden, with a home of its own. They think Malcolm has become oh so generous and don't see the conflict in taking money from that which they are supposed to be fighting against. She has spent years trying to find Environment First a property to own, but money has always been the bitch.

Flora winces as she relives the board's quickness to suggest that yes, well, maybe she's been doing this too long, maybe she should go back to academia, maybe someone younger, more energetic, less jaded, more idealistic (who, Punky?) should be found to replace her. Oh no, not that she would ever really be replaceable, Sandy had chirped. Flora needs a whole new dictionary, a whole other language to curse in, because she has worked her way through every curse word she knows. Her deadbeat board members have opinions on everything but are incapable of actually doing what they are supposed to do—raise money—that's right, not have opinions, just raise goddamn money. Well, she'll show their sorry asses. More energetic? Did they really think she was feeble and aged? Had they taken a look at themselves lately? She is the one who founded Environment First, and they absolutely have no right to take it away from her.

Ah, but why care? Flora longs to sleep, to lie down and feel the warmth of the sun and the cool of the shade, and to fade into oblivion. She can't remember the last time she's had a good night's sleep. To sleep all the way through a night, how does one accomplish that? What was it that Ingrid said? Step off the precipice without looking? Travel aimlessly? How ridiculous! Easy for Ingrid to say because evidently she is independently wealthy—how else can she be so glib in advocating casual freedoms? Flora has columns of numbers to face, which—start at the top, start at the bottom—just never reconcile.

The bench is way too uncomfortable for attempting oblivion. She has two choices: call the board's bluff and say, "You know what? You are soooooo right, thank you for pointing out what a wretch of a person I am. I quit!"—or—she can get back on the horse and gallop across the field jumping over high hurdles—that is, once again be the focus of attention by the media. But how? Cliff's murder? No one will touch that. Environmental destruction? Big yawn. Hmm, there must be something. How about contaminated food? People get worked up over that.

Flora sits at her desk carefully rereading the newspapers. Maybe there is something she has missed. She knows she's been distracted, hasn't been vigilant. There's a lot of infighting in the party in power, that and the murder count (is it up? is it down?) seem to be taking up most of the ink. But she does notice a small story about a fellow Caribbean island banning plastic bags. Ahah, that's a no-brainer; Jamaica is awash in everything plastic, including bags. She can generate a media blitz on plastic.

Flora turns on the radio to the final hour of Mark My Word—the Mark McKensie show, the tag for which is "If it matters to you, it matters to Mark."

"But Mr. McKensie, you know is only in Jamaica dis kind o' ting can happen."

The irate caller gets Mark's famous guffaw, "Is that so, caller. You don't think this kind of thing happens anywhere else in the world?"

"Nah, sah, is only in Jamaica we have such bad mind, tiefing politicians."

Another guffaw, "Well, I don't know about that."

"Let me tell you, Mr. McKensie, you know how much money di government borrow fi build di new finance centre and you see one block of concrete lay?"

"Well, no caller, I have to give you that."

"Where the money gone to?"

"Good question caller, very good question!'

"And rememba all di sand dem tief? Was big big news but now long long time you cyan hear one ting! Anyone get prosecute, Mr. McKensie? Anyone get charge wid dat crime?"

"Caller, you know you really on to something. I fear we seem to have the attention span of toddlers. We seem to be incapable of bringing anything to closure, or anyone to justice. Quite a while ago, I took a tour of where the sand was stolen, and let me tell you, if they can't find one person to prosecute then might as well we all pack up our bags and call it a day. Anyway, thanks for calling and do call again. We have to take a break and pay our bills. I'm

Mark McKensie, and you are listening to Mark My Word. We'll be back shortly."

Flora is walking Mark McKensie along a section of Palisadoes beach that is covered in plastic as far as the eye can see: bags of every type, plastic bottles and containers of all sizes, some opaque, some transparent, plastics in bright and neutral colors, some broken into tiny bits, others completely intact, some growing barnacles. Hair, car, and food products predominate. She notes that the once towering dunes have been flattened for a "protection and rehabilitation" project that will substitute the natural protection for an artificial one, a wall of rocks trucked in from some other place of devastation. Flora contemplates slitting her wrists then wading into the waves, but instead she has to pay attention to Mark, so he will do a show on the topic, Plastic Pollution. She had stood there and watched as a bulldozer tore into the native plants. She had thought of the lone man in front of the tanks in Tiananmen Square, but she could not bring herself to lie down in front of the bulldozer. It's certainly not the first time she wished she had such fortitude, nor can she forgive her cowardice, but the show must go on—she has to show up to witness the next bulldozer.

"Flora, where does all this crap come from?"

"Some is dumped at sea, but most is from land, thrown into streams, gutters, and gullies, and eventually finds its way here. We'll take a uptown tour, but first we'll look at the mangroves so you can see the vast biodiversity of plastics. Well, what is left of the mangroves, since they are being destroyed to rehabilitate them."

McKensie guffaws, "Isn't this all supposed to be some protected area? Didn't we sign an international agreement saying we will protect it? Why isn't it being protected?"

"It is being protected, don't you see? We humans are protecting nature from herself with engineering feats and a four-lane highway going nowhere."

McKensie snickers, "Oh yes, I see the logic."

"Well, and to make matters worse, these dunes, where we are standing right now, were designated, by a special commission set up to study them, as absolutely never to be destroyed, but instead to be strengthened with more native flora."

They laugh at her unintended pun. Flora was always asked at school, each wit thinking they had invented the witticism, "Where is Fauna?" If Lilac was around, Flora would point to her, and the nickname had stuck for a while, but she likes to claim she was named after devastating hurricane Flora, not plant life! Her mother, to the contrary, insisted that she was neither named after a hurricane nor flowers, but a great aunt. Flora scoffs at such timid beginnings.

Mark puts his arm around Flora as they walk toward her car. "But Flora, my dear, I hear you are suing the government yet again. Don't you fear for your life sometimes?"

"Truthfully? Yes, sometimes. But trust me, what I increasingly fear for is my sanity."

They stand by a break in the mangroves. The calm harbor water sparkles. Three pelicans fly into view, dive, settle, and then take off again. Mark kicks at the plastic garbage that blocks their way. The mangrove roots are clogged. The stench is unbearable. Fish float belly up. A weathered canoe comes into view and heads toward them. Flora waves at the elder man punting the canoe, and his face lights up, "Good Morning, Miss Flora." She holds the canoe while he steps barefoot into the mud and garbage. She takes his hand, "Maas Sam, long time, mi well glad fi see you." Flora introduces Mark, then she and Mark get into the canoe, avoiding as best they can any contact with the filthy water of Kingston Harbour.

Mark puts a handkerchief over his nose, "What's with the dead fish?"

Flora shrugs, "Could be anything. We've had three oil spills in two weeks. Could be some chemical leaking. Maas Sam, how long you see the dead fish dem?"

"Not long, tink seh yesterday morning mi did first notice dem." He points at fish jumping out of the water, gasping for air. "Dem fish soon dead."

Flora knows that enterprising Jamaicans will have been gathering up the dead fish by the bucket load and selling them. The last fish kill the newspaper referred to as a "gift from the sea." She's seen fishermen reeling in fish from right beside the raw sewage outflow. Is it foolish to warn poor people that the fish they are eating is contaminated in god knows how many ways? But if you live on a garbage dump, what's to be finicky about food contamination? She had told some children collecting dead fish not to eat them and then felt stupid. Food is food; get it how you can. Who is she to lecture on safety from the comforts of her privileged life? But don't poor people have the same right she does to eat clean food? Oh shut up, she's sick of these everlasting arguments that can't be resolved no matter how many times they churn in her mind.

She forces her attention to Mark, who is engaging their boatsman, "How long you been a fisherman, Maas Sam?"

"Oh, since mi a likle bwoy. Use to fish fus wid me grandada, den mi fadda and uncle dem. Is Port Royal we come from."

"Aho, so you know this harbor very well!"

"Yes sir, Mr. Mark, like di back o' mi hand." He poles them into a quiet section where they are surrounded by mangroves. "Plenty bird av nest hereso."

"You ever see crocodiles?"

"Oh yes, and dolphin too. Mostly early morning and again evening time you see di dolphin dem. But not like before. Everyting scarce now, Mr. Mark."

"Everything but plastic!" The three gaze out at the array of plastics caught up in the mangroves and watch as the baby birds nest in plastic bags. Their contemplation is interrupted by the sound of a plane landing. They watch as scores of birds take flight, startled by the noise.

"Alright Flora, I've seen enough."

"But McKensie, I have so much more to show you."

"No need, trust me I know what gullies and river banks and garbage dumps look like. We will devote an entire show to the problem of plastics, recycling, solid waste, sewage, everything. On the drive back we can talk about who else you think I should have on the show with you."

"Maas Sam, you listen to Mr. McKensie show?"

"Every day. Never miss it!"

"Then you know him is a busy man, so please tek us back to shore. Another day you and me go all bout, go to the cays, all bout."

"Yes Miss Flora, long time you don't come stay by us."

"Mi know, mi know. But that soon change. Promise."

Chapter Nineteen

The sun has just begun to rise over the mountains, but has not yet spread her goodwill into downtown Kingston. Through the dim light, Flora follows in Lilac's wake as they trek deep into Coronation Market. Behind them, skillfully maneuvering in tight spaces and narrow turns is Mousy, Lilac's cartman, who proudly informs Flora that he has been Miss Samuels' cartman since he was a boy. Flora observes that Miss Samuels might as well be the queen on visitation the way she is adored at the market. Only the best for Miss Lilac; vendors have her goods selected and put aside—no waiting for her royal highness—others go into their secret stashes when they see her coming. She knows them all by name, asks after various family members and associates, knows all their ailments and concerns, and has an eagle eye for the slightest imperfection, at which point she feigns deep disappointment and heartbreak to which the offending vendor begs forgiveness by plying her with more brawta, a little something extra for Miss Samuels. Flora shakes her head at each performance. "Bwoy Lilac you no easy!" But Lilac does not break out of character and pays Flora no mind.

"Bammy? Bammy? Bammy?" "Sorry, darling, not buying any bammy today." "Chocolate. Who want chocolate, pimento, nutmeg, cinnamon leaf?" "Early buyer. God bless the cheerful early buyer." "Everyting a sell out! Me wan go home watch me woman." "Lime. Mi 'av lime big as mi 'ead." "Garlic. Who want garlic?" "Me 'ave basin, two 'undred give you basin." "Blouse sell off, three bills blouse done it." "Toothpaste, shoelace, belt." Anything you want, it is there. Gospel music blasts from a stall, and nearby vendors dance and sing along: "The Holy Ghost power is moving just like a magnet." Flora is tempted to join in, the contagion is so great. "It's moving here, moving there, moving everywhere, Holy Ghost power moving just like a magnet."

Flora tries to remember what obscure item she needs that might be in the market, but they are there to shop for Derek's party. He informed her he wants ital food, strictly natural, only. She's decided the long Ph.D. process has done him in, and she can't blame him if after finally becoming Dr. Derek, he turns his back on the world and retreats to the mountains as a Rasta. But in honor of his Trinidadian roots, Flora and Lilac are insisting on roti. So they will make roti, ital patties, sip—a huge pot of simmering ital soup with everything possible in it—plus roast yam, roast breadfruit, fried plantain, and natural juices.

Lilac seems to have bought a week's worth of ingredients. Flora wonders how Mousy manages to push his cart. Maybe he should make two trips. There are baskets piled with yams, cocos, dasheens, sweet potatoes, "Irish" potatoes, plantains, corn, pumpkins, dried coconuts, an entire stem of green bananas, breadfruits, ackee, callaloo, bok choi, okras, carrots, onions; there are scotch bonnets in every color, the most fragrant "St. Andrew" thyme, oregano, marjoram, ginger; there are red peas, black-eyed peas, and peanuts. For the fruit juices, there are June plums, pineapples, limes, passion fruits, guavas. No wonder Lilac is queen of the market!

Mousy carefully loads all the items into Lilac's van, at which point it dawns on Flora that there is no Mousy to carefully unload said items on the other end, so she and Lilac will have to become Mousy. She hopes one of Lilac's workers will be around, but this time of morning? Maybe the security guard can help! Mousy goes out into the street and commands traffic to stop then directs Lilac as she expertly gets out of their very tight space. They wave thanks and are on their way.

"Well, Lilac Samuels, me never think me could admire you more than me already do, but mek a tell you: you the tops. You the cat's meow. You bigger than Bob Marley. You sweeter than condense milk. You the cherry on top the sundae."

Lilac shakes with laughter, "The cherry on the sundae? Where you get that from?"

"Oh, probably some bwoy on the street! Why, you prefer to be the icing on the cake?"

Flora can't remember the last time she threw a party. She worries about the neighbors; is she really going to have things roasting in her backyard and cooking on a coal pot? What if guests bring drums to beat or instruments to play and smoke weed? She hadn't bargained on any of this! She and Lilac are strolling through her yard looking where to set up the food, where to put up the tent, where the sound system should go. Should she invite the neighbors so they can't complain, won't call the police?

Flora is grateful they had the help of Big Mac, the security guard, as they carted the loads of produce into Lilac's professional pantry, but she still carried her share and feels like she deserves a nap. When they were done unloading and putting away all the produce, she had stood in the kitchen gaping at all the gleaming equipment that could be whipped into action to feed hundreds of people. She is astonished that she knows someone who owns such equipment and knows how to use it. But luckily they only need to feed about seventy and mainly using the most primitive cooking methods possible.

Flora slides onto the hammock strung under her mango tree. "Lawd, Lilac, me need a break." She pats beside her for Lilac, but instead Lilac says she soon come and goes into the house. Flora stretches out on the hammock holding onto the pole so it won't swing. She doesn't want to add motion sickness to her existing complaints. Her phone falls out of her pocket and, like a Pavlovian bell, prompts her to hit autodial:

"Jerome my darling, you mus be cussing my rass how mi dash you weh."

"Prof? Rahtid! Is my favorite Professor dis?"

"Boogie forgive me for being out of touch. I've been in a dreadful state, didn't want to inflict it on you. You alright? How's your shoulder?"

"Where you calling from?"

"Under my mango tree."

"Sweet me to hear your voice, you see. "

"Can you come spend some time before you take off for Bella Italia? Mi long fi see you."

"Well could be arranged. When you thinking of?"

"When you leaving exactly?"

"Middle of next week."

"Alright, come for Derek's party, and then I'll have a surprise for you. Am going to take off work so just you and me can spend some time together, okay?"

"Sounds good."

"You never answer me about your shoulder."

"Oh, still sore, but coming along."

"Well, is you right side and you left handed so you not totally useless!"

"Eh eh. You feisty and out of order!"

"You better believe it. Oh, oh, Lilac is heading this way. We planning Derek's party, so I will call you back in a bit with details. Okay, my darlingest one?"

"Will be waiting with bated breath. Latas."

Flora jumps out of the hammock to help Lilac, who is carrying a very heavy tray. They sit down at the wrought iron table after Flora brushes off the leaves. The smells wafting up to her are of coconut milk, vanilla, nutmeg, and cinnamon leaf—Lilac has made them cornmeal porridge. Flora bends down to inhale and swoons. There is mint tea for a countervailing aroma and a bowl of fresh fruit to clean the palate. Flora no longer feels the need for a nap.

"Lilac, this proves you are the cherry on top the sundae! Mmmm. My fave. Can't tell you the last time I had cornmeal porridge."

"Probably the last time I made it."

Flora cuts her eye at Lilac, spoons several servings of porridge into her mouth, then starts humming "Heaven—I'm in heaven."

"I just spoke to your boy Jerome."

"My boy?"

"Well, as you have led me to understand, you've known him way longer than me. From babyhood apparently."

"That is most correct. You going see him before them head off a Italy?"

"Yep."

"Well, well, bad pickney, that mus improve your mood."

"That obvious, huh?"

"Mm hmm."

Flora fills up her bowl with more porridge. She has always eaten twice as fast as Lilac. "So why you wait so long to tell me about you and Jerome?"

"Well, at first me never want to interfere, you know, wanted you to have you likle fun, and I didn't know was going to get serious; after all, you did swear seh you not going see him again. And you must admit, Florita, with you and man, me never know which way it going!"

"Will have to give you that, though of course you know better than to believe me when I say such things! You ever notice the only times you and me fall out is over man? How long me stop speak to you when you marry the pickney dem eedyat father? And remember you refuse come to my fairy tale society wedding to the one who will remain nameless?"

"But we don't fall out over Jerome! We fall out because me keep secrets from you."

Flora pushes her empty bowl aside. "Okay, then tell me about you and Liz. I mean don't you think it a bit kinky, yes even for me, to be having a love affair with my best friend's lover's son? I mean it's like me fucking your son, Lilac."

"Oh please! Spare me the melodrama. You might recall that I happen to have a son, and far as me know you two never . . ."

"Oh my God. Perish the thought. Yes, me and my godson Omar have never had not one incestuous thought! Pity him stuck in foreign, but we are Facebook friends. I have photos of his twins on my laptop!"

Lilac giggles at that. "How come you and me not Facebook friends?"

"I didn't even know you were on Facebook!"

"I'm not!"

"Okay, back to the painful topic."

"Me and Liz. Well, can't quite exactly explain it. As you know was good friends with all three sisters, somehow me and Liz just end up together and cyan stay apart, even when she with Fontaine and me was with you know who."

"So you start off as like a teenage crush kind of thing?"

"E'heh."

"But then it come serious, and you cyan stop even when you both married with children?"

Lilac covers her face in her hands.

Flora moves her chair over to Lilac and hugs her. "Sweetpea, I'm so sorry, me never know you did suffer so. Why you never ever tell me?" Lilac shakes her head and shrugs. "And then the car crash. You saw it, how absolutely awful! Did you hate Ingrid? How could you forgive Ingrid? Poor Ingrid—how could she forgive herself?"

"Hate Ingrid? You mussi mad. Was accident, and anyway was Ingrid who did arrange things so me and Liz could still see each other. When Liz dead can't do nothing about that. You have to take care of the living. And Ingrid, talk bout hard luck—she lose her sister, she lose her son. And Fontaine family fight against her raising Jerome. Poor baby, him was all over the place between this set of grandparent, that set of grandparent. But you have to give it to Jerome daddy—stand up to him family when him turn ambassador and have to leave Jamaica. When Jerome say he not going, and is Ingrid him want to live with, Fontaine tell his parents like it or lump it, but a so it going to go."

Flora leans against Lilac, and serves them each a bowl of fruit salad. Her motto has always been "When in doubt . . . eat!" Smiling mischievously, Flora says, "Okay, I have a confession for you."

"Bumbo!"

"Well, since you know everything about me, this probably won't be news to you but . . ."

"Go on."

"Negril . . . I was sixteen . . ."

"Go on, nuh!"

"I was alone with a certain Ingrid Small, the most seductive female on the planet."

"No!"

"Yes!"

Chapter Twenty

Flora is happy, a sensation so rare of late that she isn't sure to trust it. But she gives in to this feeling of joy and well-being, whether it will last or not. While she watches the bustle of her backyard transforming into a festive ground, her stomach does butterfly flips, her heart is light and warm, and it's not just the sight of Jerome in surfer shorts and skinny tank top that stirs her emotions. She is doing something that will bring people together and give them enjoyment. She, Flora Smith, that "awful woman," is doing something that does not involve lecturing, nagging, begging, haranguing, being the messenger of doom, suing anyone.

Shelly directs staff, as they unload containers of food that then go into warming dishes with flames under them. Devon, though skeptical that such a thing is possible, is setting up the alcohol-free bar. Lilac is chatting with Livity and Lion, the two Rastas who are watching over the bubbling sip and manning the roasting food. Jerome brought the two with him. They are children of Ras Knowledge's brother, so cousins of a sort. Punky sits on Livity's knee chewing a piece of corn that was spooned out of the sip just for her. Ingrid, Miss Ital herself, is stringing handmade lanterns. She has already decorated the tables with greenery and placed floral bouquets at strategic points. Jerome is testing the sound system.

When he'd volunteered to DJ, Flora protested, because how would they be able to dance, not to mention slip away every so often, if he was in charge of the music and MCing? But he reassured her that these are the days of iTunes mixes already programmed into his laptop, and so of course they'll be able to dance and slip away. But, he cautions, he has to be careful, he will wear the sling for his shoulder to remind himself that his injury is not completely healed. Flora rolls her eyes and points out that he isn't wearing it now, so when is he planning to put it on? He explains that sling and condom will go on at the same time. In response, she punches him in the arm, just a little reminder of his injury.

Flora walks by the food, admiring the set-up for customized rotis. All utensils, serving and eating ware, are reusable or compostable, absolutely no plastic, no styrofoam. When she goes on Mark My Word, she'll be able to elaborate proudly on how one can have a perfectly stylish party and create no garbage. Maybe she should start a blog with these sorts of tips. It could be called Green Jamaica Runnings and would include the most up-to-the-minute in Green Chic and Conscious Consumption! Is this where three degrees of higher learning have landed her? Brave new world—she should rush over to tell Ingrid she's had a breakthrough, and that she is on the verge of jumping off the precipice!

While she greets guests and gets them mingling, Flora enjoys the blend of world music Jerome is playing, mainly Brazilian and African music. Finally, Derek shows up with an entourage of about twenty. To signal the Party Boy's arrival, Jerome plays the Mighty Sparrow's classic "Dan is de Man," and Flora watches with delight as Derek shrieks, yells, jumps up and down, and bursts into tears as three sisters, two brothers, his mother, two aunts, and an uncle accost him. He had no idea! The party is now officially started.

Jerome hands Derek the microphone. He introduces each member of his family and then gestures to Flora to come join them.

"Prof you ketch me! What a sweet surprise. I can't thank you enough for organizing this thing. Thanks to you and everyone who helped out. I see Miss Lilac handling the food, so bwoy, I intend to eat good good tonight. Prof, come say a few words. Everyone, this is my favorite professor."

"Well, Derek you better be careful talking about favorite professors, because you don't graduate yet, and I see we have here a number of faculty members, including the head of your department and the dean of your school, upon whom your graduating depends!"

Everyone laughs, and Derek hugs Flora.

"But really we're here to celebrate our darling Dr. Derek, a person of outstanding brilliance, generosity, and goodness. I know your family anxious for you to get your ass home to Trinidad, but we all been so lucky to have you here these many years, and I for one hope you lingah likle while longer! We must thank Lilac Samuels and her family and associates for the delicious food tonight. I am about to go pile whole heap of food into my calabash, and I encourage all of you to do the same. And then face boy DJ Jerome is going to spin some serious music, and we will dance the night away. I am so very very happy that we can all be together tonight. So everyone congratulate Dr. Derek—clap him!"

Flora watches Jerome sleeping. He is lying on his left side facing away from her, his right arm still in its sling. It looks so uncomfortable, and she wants to take it off but doesn't want to disturb him. In accordance with the law, they had locked the music off at two, well, more like two thirty, but within the acceptable range. They had stayed outside till about four, cleaning up and chatting with Derek and his family and various stragglers. She and Jerome fell asleep about six, and she's managed to sleep all of four hours! The plan is to pretty much stay in bed till they head over to Ingrid's in the late afternoon, but she is already restless.

Flora, who usually thrashes through any night, tries to lie as still as possible. She watches Jerome's back as it gently lifts and falls with each breath and thinks, *"I am still happy. Can this be possible?"* She controls her desire to laugh out loud, as she remembers her favorite moments: Dancing lasciviously with Milton and Jerome to Arrow's "Hot Hot Hot" then Dragon Lee's "Tiny Winey." Milton, his shirt soaked through, had to take a seat afterward and guzzle coconut water, while Jerome and Flora kept dancing. The entire party converging, spontaneously hugging each other, dancing and singing along ("Everybody come and celebrate . . . and everybody say, oo,a,a,oo,a,a, I love my country, oo,a,a,oo,a,a, I feeling irie") as Jerome played David Rudder's "High Mas" three times in a row. Derek's sisters putting on a special dance exhibition to the latest Soca-Chutney Bhangra-inspired tune, and then being joined by their mother and aunts when Jerome played two favorite Bollywood hits sung by Asha Bhosle. Derek, his brothers, and uncle joined in and did the male roles, and got everyone line dancing disco style. This led Jerome to start a disco set. Lilac, Derek, and Flora doing the bump to "Ring My Bell" and the hustle to "Got to be Real." And Flora silently crying, watching Ingrid, Lilac, and Jerome dancing to Sylvester's live version of Patti LaBelle's song, "You Are My Friend." Flora tears up again as she recalls the words, because yes, she has been looking in all the wrong places, all the love and understanding she's ever needed has been there all along.

Chapter Twenty-One

As Flora watches the unloading of Jerome's jeep, and then the loading of gear into the two canoes, she is overcome with doubt. It had seemed like such a great idea, but that was before Jerome got hurt. Maybe taking off to some isolated cay for swimming, diving, and playing Lost-on-a-Desert-Isle is not such a good idea, especially since he has to get on a plane in just a few days. What if something happens, and they really are stranded? Flora can imagine the extreme irritation this would cause. It would turn into one of those Flora-Creates-Chaos stories that friends love to tell. She has no desire to add to the already extensive body of narratives of the You-Will-Never-Believe-What-Flora-Did type. Jerome seems not in the least bit worried. He claims that this is just what the doctor ordered—must be a bush doctor or Dr. Derek—but Flora makes no objections.

Maas Sam is supervising his grand- and great grandsons in correctly loading the boats. He barks at Junior, his youngest helper, when he carelessly flings a bag into the hold. Jerome takes Junior aside and explains the system of storing things according to weight, size, and need to access. This wins Junior's immediate devotion. He follows Jerome around, imitating everything Jerome does, and tries to impress Jerome with some moves learned from the last Chinese marshal arts movie he watched. His sound effects are especially theatrical. Flora, Maas Sam, and his daughter, Janice, watch the puppy-like adoration and laugh. Janice is Junior's grandmother, and a very successful businesswoman, buying and selling seafood, as well as owning and running the renowned Janice's Cook Shop, that brings all sorts of people to Port Royal to eat fresh fish. She is featured in travel guides to Jamaica, standing in front of her restaurant, beaming at the camera while holding a platter of fish smothered in onions, peppers, and pickles, and golden crisp bammies. Janice is a big, strong woman and knows the sea as well as any fisherman.

The two canoes are loaded, and they are just waiting for some extra ice that Junior's father Eddie has gone to get. Flora walks over to where Jerome and Junior lean against *Yellow Bird*, the newer of the two boats. The east horizon is getting lighter, maybe approaching dawn. Junior points at Flora and says to Jerome, "Is you modda dat?" Jerome smiles and says no. "Is you aunty den?" Jerome laughs and says no, is him friend. Junior frowns, unable to comprehend the relationship between his new best friend and the person his great grandfather calls Miss Flora. Jerome looks at Flora and then says to Junior, "You think we look alike?" Junior shrugs. He has lost interest in the topic.

Flora is glad for the darkness. There is no getting around the fact that she is twenty years older than Jerome. If they stay together and are out in public, he will have to get used to these embarrassing moments, but she is sure she never will. She glances at Jerome and wonders if they look alike. Not really. She supposes, to many Jamaicans, brown people are an indistinguishable group, but Jerome is a much deeper brown than her currently pallid self. Maybe their noses are sort of alike, and they both have full lips, but their faces aren't shaped the same way—hers is much rounder, his cheek bones much sharper. And of course their eyes—he has the Ingrid cat eyes; she has her mother's dark brown eyes—their eyes are nothing alike. Eddie arrives with the ice, and Flora is grateful that the bustle has resumed.

Maas Sam stands holding on to the bowline; in the faint light, he guides his grandson Shaba as he pilots them through the channel. Flora is sitting in the middle of the canoe—she'll join Maas Sam when he sits down. Shaba has his son, Jayjay, beside him in the stern. Flora looks out at the other boat. Eddie is captaining, Jerome at bow, in the middle Junior has his head in Janice's lap. The early morning sea is calm. All is quiet except for the sound of their engines and their boats slicing across the water. Flora watches Jerome pointing straight ahead. She relaxes. He is in his element. She has made a good choice. Eddie guns the engine, and they speed away. But Maas Sam's boat *Lady Luck* continues her relaxed pace. He is in no hurry. They will get there when they get there. They enter the open sea, and Maas Sam sits down. Flora moves up beside him and watches him peering over the edge into the dark water. She wonders what he's looking at. It's been so very long since she has done this. She used to love these outings. She could definitely learn to love them again.

The relationship between Flora's and Maas Sam's families goes back to before either were born. From what her father told her, Flora's grandfather was fascinated by Port Royal. In addition to being a naturalist, he was an amateur archeologist and used to spend a lot of time poking around hoping to find something rare. He was on the board of the Institute of Jamaica and chair of the Port Royal Historical Society and so had free rein. He used to take Flora's father, from an early age, with him on his Port Royal outings. According to what Maas Sam heard told, the first Professor Smith loved a rum and was well known in the Port Royal rum bars. Whenever Flora hears stories about her grandfather in Port Royal, she wonders if he didn't like the easy ladies as well. Did he harbor wicked pirate fantasies in his quiet little Englishman head? She used to wonder if there weren't some relatives she is unaware of, some "outside" progeny, but she has never come across any.

"Miss Flora, mi ever tell you bout you grandmother?"

"You knew my grandmother?"

"No mi neva know her, but mi fadda did tell me bout the time she come out with you grandfadda on him boat. She cover from head to toe. She have on veil. She have hat with a veil. Him did tink seh she was white witch of Rosehall!"

They chuckle at such a silly apparition. But Flora always hurts for her father when she thinks how he must have felt, at aged seven, his mother gone. It was one of many things they never talked about. They too had gone out on the boat together—she a child and her father a grown man. Maas Sam was in his prime then, good-looking, jaunty, confident.

"Your modda now, she never too love your fadda tek you out to sea."

"My mother was terrified of the water. Poor thing. Was torture, she stand watching as we disappear out of sight. She sure one day we not going return."

"My modda did tell me some time Miss May stay crying inside the house, and don't rest till you come back. One day a big wind come up and we reach back late. When we reach, lawks, she was all a tremble. You remember?"

Flora remembers her mother smothering her, holding her so tightly. Her mother was shaking and crying. And her father sternly said, "May, stop this, you will frighten the child. Do not frighten the child!" Did anyone care that the mother had been so afraid? Did anyone try and comfort her? No. Maas Sam had pontificated, "Miss May, don't frighten. You must have faith in the Lord. Father God look over us and protect us. As I walk through the valley of darkness, I feareth not. Don't worry youself missus, mi will never let harm come to you likle girl."

CHAPTER TWENTY-ONE

The eastern sky is ablaze. Blood red eats at the blackness, changing it to blue. *Lucky Lady* travels directly east, and as the sun rises, first as a red ball and then pulsing fingers of golden light, Flora sees the cay, the tall coconut trees signaling land. Maas Sam's family has planted the trees over many years, steadily replacing ones blown down by storms. Maas Sam stands up and directs the boat's course around the coral heads, over the reef, and into the little lagoon, until they arrive alongside the canary-colored boat that looks like it has been sitting there for quite some time. As Jerome, Junior, and Eddie stroll over to greet them, Jayjay displays his string of fish that he caught dragging a line off the side of the boat. Shaba proudly pats his son's head and sends him off to Janice, while the rest unload. Jerome continues to hold Flora after helping her off the boat. Junior, watching this display of affection, scowls then, pouting, goes to stand by his father. Maas Sam sharply orders Junior to do something useful and throws a bag for him to carry, while grumbling, "Dese today bwoy pickney, dem too sof, too spoil, too useless!"

When they reach Janice, Flora is tickled to see the shy Jayjay now animated telling his grandmother his fish tales and how the big one that she is now scaling almost got away. Junior sulks under a coconut tree and throws stones at crabs. Janice has piled fried bammy, festival and Johnnycakes on two large plates, she has callaloo and cabbage seasoned with country pepper in a big black pan, and fish soup left over from her restaurant heating in a dutchy over an open fire. She is going to fry the fish that Jayjay has brought her. Flora's mouth waters as she looks at the big bottle of homemade pickles. She doesn't eat fish anymore, but she intends to cover everything in the tangy mix of vinegar, spices, hot peppers, and pickled vegetables. She must remember to get some from Janice to take home to Lilac. Those two women should have a serious cook-off.

Flora watches Jerome go over to rescue Junior. He tells Junior that they have the very important task of picking coconuts. Junior demurs and feigns disinterest but then can't resist showing off and races to find a tree, crowing when he is first to the top of his tree. He starts flinging down coconuts and gets screamed at by Eddie to stop acting the fool. Maas Sam kisses his teeth and declares that the boy needs a proper beating to set him straight. Janice retorts that she is told it's his great grandfather that the boy favors. Maas Sam stalks off in a huff. Janice raises her eyebrows at Flora and points her lips at her father's back, "But cooya—you see what I mean Flora? Same said bad pickney!" Speaking of bad pickney, what the hell is Jerome doing climbing a coconut tree with an injured shoulder?

After eating, provisions, gear, tackle, and ice are fussed over, and then the two boats take off again. Janice has to physically pick up Junior and place him into *Yellow Bird* because he will not get in the boat. He screams that he wants to stay and play with Jerome, he does not want to go fishing, he hates fishing! Everyone ignores his tantrum. As Flora and Jerome wave at the departing boats, Flora pokes Jerome and laughs, "Lawd Jerome, you find you match, that pickney desperately in love with you, worse than Madge even!" Jerome gives Flora a watch-yourself look and then, wincing, goes to soak his sore shoulder in the lagoon. Flora grins at Jerome floating on his back looking like a contented seal. The island of Jamaica is behind him muted in the distance, her mountains peaked with clouds piled one on top of the other.

Flora finds the shadiest spot and attaches her usually-under-the-mango-tree hammock to two almond trees. Then she gathers things she might need. A few coconuts for water, just one more Johnnycake, one more bammy for snacking. She strips naked, partially covering herself with a Bob Marley "One Love" sarong she'd bought in the Philippines when she'd attended a United Nations sponsored conference on coral reefs (was it the UN's Decade of the Coral Reef?), then she covers her face with a towel to block the glare, and, whistling "I'm in Heaven," settles down for a nap.

CHAPTER TWENTY-ONE

Water dripping on her belly wakes Flora. She removes the towel from her face and sees Jerome smiling at her. He licks her belly button and then works his way up to her breasts. Flora fingers his thick, tightly curled hair then lifts his face so that they can kiss. He is very salty. Flora strokes Jerome's shoulder.

"Hi, my love. How is your shoulder?"

"Not bad."

"Ingrid will kill me if I get you worse injured before your trip."

"Nah man, the only injuries Ingrid would blame you for is if me throw out mi back or if me get a really bad case of pussy burn." Jerome strokes his mouth as he says that and Flora splutters with laughter.

"Ingrid should know a thing or two about that!"

"No kidding!"

"Well, I have no complaints with her as your role model."

"Me neither."

"Boogie, tell me this, you happy we're here?"

"Never been happier!"

"Is that so?"

"Mm hmm."

"Show me how happy then."

"Intend to."

◌

When the others return from sea, Flora and Jerome are bobbing in the lagoon after having gone on a long swim/snorkel around the cay. Jerome managed quite well doing a one-armed stroke but mainly propelled himself underwater using his fins. As *Yellow Bird* draws alongside them, Junior does a backward summersault into the water inches from Jerome, who grabs him and holds him under. Then the two go into a protracted splash attack, and Flora heads to the beach. She waves at Jayjay, who with Shaba's tutelage is steering *Lucky Lady* into shore. He is full of concentration and focus. Flora decides that Jayjay will be the expert boatman and master fisherman. Junior can be the tour guide, the hustler. He can wear bling and talk with a twang to tourists who he will escort out on his boat. Jayjay will be the repository of Maas Sam's great knowledge. Junior will anticipate every new fad.

"Flora, is Jerome cook all this?" Flora can tell, from the spreading smile on Janice's face, that she is overjoyed to see that while they were away, a big pot of rice and peas has been cooking, and the black pan is full of steamed vegetables, and that in the embers sweet potato, yam, and plantain slices have slowly roasted in foil. "All mi have fi do is throw some lobster and crab in a pot, and dinner will be ready!"

"Well, I helped!"

Janice rolls her eyes.

"I did! I cut everything up."

"Mek I tell you, you ketch one fine young gentleman. You better watch youself or me will tief him!"

"Miss Janice, you see that cutlass over there? Don't mek me have to use it pon you!"

Janice straightens up and, hands akimbo, towers over Flora. "Me never hear you too good first time, repeat what you did say again for me nuh?"

When Maas Sam, Eddie, Shaba, and Jayjay come upon the two women, they are mystified as to why the two are clinging to each other, laughing so hard that they can barely stand up. Maas Sam clucks, "Eh eh, is what sick you two?" But he can't help smiling. Flora can feel his nostalgia, she knows that seeing her and Janice together takes Maas Sam back to a time when his life stretched ahead of him, and the end of the line seemed as far away as the horizon.

The night is solidly dark. There is a sliver of a moon already getting ready to set. A steady breeze brings the smell of the sea and the soothing rustle of leaves. The only other sounds are the waves against the reef and the occasional cry of a bird. Flora looks at the multitude of stars and anticipates watching them march across the sky—the Big Dipper as night falls, Scorpio lasting through the middle night, and Orion arriving in the late night and still there at sunrise; this trio shift their positions as the year unfolds. The sky always comforts her, assuring her a position in the universe, and that if lost she can be found.

Jerome has made them a windbreak out of fallen coconut fronds and has put down layers of bedding so that they won't get damp as the night progresses. Flora nestles into him, and he pulls the sleeping bag closer around them. She inhales his scent and slowly caresses him. There is so much she wants to say but chooses restraint. She will not do her usual, blurting out whatever is on her mind. She will prove to herself that, better late than never, she's finally learned something about conducting relationships. She will not ruin their evening by bringing up their age difference; still, she needs reassuring.

"Jerome sweetie, tell me something, when you come back from Italy, you want us to start spending more time together? I mean, I'd like to spend more time with you."

"Yeah, I'd like that as well."

"I mean, you can continue to see whoever you want. I'm not possessive. But I just wondering if you want us to be . . . you know."

"Flora, I want to be with you—okay?"

"I'm sorry, I'm being silly."

"You're not being silly."

"Well, I feel ridiculous. You know what though, I been thinking really hard, and I'm starting to see my new life. The thing is, I want you to know me in other ways. I mean, I'm not a complete ditz!"

"Prof, how you can say that! What mek you say that?"

"I dunno, sometimes I think I must look pretty fool fool to you. I mean you did call me a dilettante!"

"Oh please! You are not serious! Or you really don't have any idea what I think of you, do you?"

"No, I don't actually!"

"Okay, let me tell you."

"Please do."

"Is long time now, but I still remember the first time I heard you on the radio. Me did think, watch youself, you going fall in love with this one."

"You heard me on the radio?"

"Plenty times. You always so funny and smart, and I think bwoy, I want to get to know this woman, would like travel all around Jamaica with her."

"No!"

"Is because of you me start document all the shit me was seeing. I did remember you complaining about scientists studying everything to death and not doing anything to stop the carnage. That was your word—*carnage*. You said, 'I don't know how these people can sleep at night.'"

"I said that?"

"Uh huh. Remember seeing you on the news one time. Was a public meeting, think it was limestone mining, some new cement something, and the minister was telling one pack of lies, and you stood up and said, "Honorable Minister, not to be disrespectful, but I would suggest that you consider a career in writing after you leave politics because what you just said is total fiction."

"Oh god, I do remember that one. Oh my god!"

"Of course me take you serious. I would do anything for you, to help you. You do so much. You deserve so much."

Flora is stunned. She wills herself not to cry. She shifts so that she can put her head on Jerome's shoulder—first checking to make sure it's his left shoulder. And then she covers his face in kisses and says, "Jerome, no one has ever said anything like this to me, never. I can't even begin to tell you how much what you just said means to me."

She can feel him smiling, and then after a long pause he says, "And by the way, I know what bothering you . . . me know seh you think people going laugh after you, but stop worry about the age thing. None of that matter to me, so just don't stress about it. I'm you biggest fan. True, true. I love you. Eventually you going get used to that."

Chapter Twenty-Two

Flora, who has just emailed her hot-off-the-press, highly original prospectus to Chang at MIT, is in her office whistling loudly. Her staff, one by one, find excuses to come in and check on her. Flora smiles at each and answers their bogus questions with patience and good humor. She knows they will gather and whisper as to what might be going on with her. She calls a staff meeting, and they crowd back into her office. Still smiling and whistling, Flora asks her staff if any of them would like to take over the running of Environment First? Would anyone like to move up in the ranks to become Executive Director? Does anyone have that sort of ambition? She gets no verbal response. They fiddle and shift about and avoid eye contact with her. They look at their hands, at paperwork, at objects on the wall.

"You mean all of you are fine with what you're doing? None of you have thought, *Well, if I ruled the world, I would do things differently*?"

There are a few giggles. But surely ruling the world and running Environment First is not the same thing. No one seems to want to take over Flora's empire.

"Okay. So none of you want my job. So I ask you, do you know anyone who might like to have my job?"

There are more giggles and vigorous shaking of heads.

"What would you think about me resigning and the board finding someone to take my place?"

There is now frightened silence. Where is this strange game going? Keisha bravely pipes up, "Prof, we don't think anyone is qualified to take over, and we don't want anyone else but you. Personally, I will quit if someone else is hired."

Flora opens and then closes her mouth. That is not at all the answer she expected, and this is not at all going the way she imagined. She sighs. "Keisha, I really appreciate that sentiment, but I just want you to know that the board has suggested I resign, and so I am considering it. Thought I'd get a sense of where my staff would stand on the issue."

They all start talking at the same time, "Resign?!" "Nah man Prof!" "Mussi mad!" "Cyan work!" Keisha again speaks for the group, "Prof, as the staff rep, I will go and talk to the board. I will make it absolutely clear that if you are removed, we are all quitting."

Flora wants to say, "Yes, but what if I really, really want to leave? Sure, it was the board's suggestion, but now it's what I desperately want to do." But she realizes she has upset her loyal, hardworking staff, and she just doesn't have it in her to break their hearts. But soon she will have to. She will make a proposal to her board that they find her replacement. She will train that person, and there will be an orderly transition, but this is all going to be much harder than she can manage, so she will have to find some other way to tell her staff that she will not be with them forever.

Flora opens her arms and says, "Okay, group hug!" The confused group huddles. "I love you guys. You really are the best. I'm sorry I'm such a mess, but hey, you can't say I don't try my damn hardest to save Jamaica!"

CHAPTER TWENTY-TWO

The parrots hop from branch to branch, making a racket. The late afternoon light makes the hills glow. In such moments, Flora realizes how much she worships the island she lives on. She does not have to get on a plane or a cruise ship to be bathed in the miracle that is tropical light getting ready to kiss the land goodnight.

She has been wandering through Hope Gardens daydreaming, imagining her grandfather also walking through the gardens, holding his young son's hand, explaining this plant, and that tree, and the mystery of a disappeared mother. She is divining, connecting to her DNA through random footsteps, walking here, then there, remembering her first steps under the riotous canopy of bougainvillea—a plant brought from the other side of the world and now so commonplace. Where is her mother in this picture? She doesn't associate her mother with Hope Gardens at all. She associates her mother with her medical practice on Hope Road, where Flora would go after school to do her homework and impatiently wait to go home.

Flora has a burning desire, a set of goals, a finely conceived plan. She stands under the parrot tree and looks at two buildings in varying stages of decay—one seemingly still functional, the other close to ruin. She wonders what were their original uses, and does she really want to inherit the karma that goes with occupying a slave plantation building? But what isn't? The very university she taught at is on land that was once two plantations. There is no getting away from the tentacles of history. What to do? You can ignore, you can acknowledge, you can transform. There must be better choices. But maybe there aren't.

Flora gets out her phone and searches her contacts.

"Milton, how you do?"

"Not so good."

"Sorry to hear that." But Flora is on a mission, "Tell me something, when you were fighting the Hope Gardens development, did you by any chance research the buildings on the property?"

"Actually yes, I know quite a bit about them."

"I knew you would. You are such a frigging genius!"

"What you want to know?"

"I'm interested in some of the buildings and was wondering what they have been used for."

"Well, I need to talk with you anyway. It's too late now for me to come, the gate is going to close soon, but why don't we meet tomorrow?"

⚬

Flora is shocked when she sees Milton. His skin looks gray, his face puffy, his spirit lagging. She knows he hasn't been looking well for quite a while, but she had such a great time with him at Derek's party, she had fooled herself into thinking otherwise. She is sitting at their usual spot on the Michael Manley bench, but Milton remains standing, so she gets up.

"Milton my love, what's wrong?"

He doesn't meet her gaze, but instead looks irritably around him. "Will tell you in a minute. Show me what you talking about."

"Okay, it's this way."

They walk across the pocked road, onto the field, with lines of what in England would be rose bushes but here is just a nondescript collection of whatever tropical plants some Englishman like her grandfather once thought were pretty, so we now think are pretty. She points them toward the parrot tree, but they have to stop as Milton is convulsed with coughing. He is bent over, shakily holding onto Flora. She rubs his back while he catches his breath. Then they proceed; she knows better than to suggest otherwise.

They stand in front of the almost functioning structure. It is made of bricks, but has a modern addition made from cheap wood. It has a few broken windows and parts of the roof peeling away. The day before, Flora had walked up the steps and peeked inside. It looked like government offices, now abandoned.

"Ah, this was the great house. It's not very grand, so I don't know if there was a grander home at an earlier stage, or whether the owners weren't ostentatious. Anyway, this is where they lived."

CHAPTER TWENTY-TWO

Flora can't quite picture it. She knows that what is left of the aqueduct is close by, but she can't envision this place as a sugar plantation. In her mind, it is always botanical gardens, an open space that people enjoy. Whatever it is or was, its heyday is over. It is like all Jamaican public institutions, perpetually on the verge of ruination, yet still clinging to life. She walks them over to the adjoining lot, on which stands another brick building but totally covered in bush. To get a closer look, they will have to climb through a fence and fight their way across someone's pumpkin patch. Given Milton's condition, they will stay where they are, peering over. Flora already knows from a previous visit what it looks like inside: a precarious wooden floor with missing, sagging, and broken boards; garbage and broken glass strewn about; rows of tall archways that look like doors. Why so many doors, or are they windows?

"Now this no one seems to know for sure. Some say church, some say slave hospital, I think it might have been some sort of storage."

Flora likes the fact that, unlike the master's home, it is a place of competing stories, a place without known, direct lineage. A bastard or an orphan, really, and waiting for her to adopt it.

"Flora, what's your interest?"

"This, Milton, is the International Institute for Environmental Sciences and Advocacy's Kingston office!"

He looks at her with incomprehension, to which she simply laughs and guides them over to a bench under the parrot tree. She can no longer read the name on the bench and wonders to whose departed soul it is dedicated. She would like a bench of her own. Maybe Milton and she can share a bench and be forever joined in mortality. But what if he is destined for somewhere other than Limbo? She helps him sit.

"Sweetheart, thanks so much for your help. Now, tell me what is going on with you."

"Flora, I'm sorry, but I have very bad news."

She holds his hand. It is cold and hard. His hands are usually warm and soft.

"I've been diagnosed with lung cancer. The prognosis is very bad, and I've decided to not do anything heroic. Just going to put my things in order best I can."

"Shit! Milton my love, I'm so sorry." Flora puts her arm around his shoulder and squeezes him into her—never a big man, he seems smaller than ever. She wants to cry, "Milton you can't leave me, please not now!" but instead she says, "I will do anything for you. You know that right? Please let me know what I can do."

"Well, my daughter is moving back. For ages she's been wanting to leave Canada and come home, so she quit her job and is coming this week. She will move in with me and take care of everything, and when I'm gone, she will get the house, so that works out."

Flora thinks of her many hours at Milton's home, sitting on the upstairs patio, watching the assortment of his beloved birds flitting around, looking out at Kingston below, arguing loudly into the dead of night. All their plans together that now will never be actualized—she feels such a burst of terrified adrenalin that she can hardly stay still.

"What you can do, Flora, is help me sort through my papers. I want to get them in order. I want to give you all my information on the different battles, you know . . . the sewage in the harbor, beach access problems, air pollution with the cement factory—you know that was my first battle back in the fifties?"

"Remember all our bauxite work together? Man, we had some grand old times. Some crazy crazy times. I can't imagine having to do any of this without you. That is the hard truth, my friend."

Milton chuckles and then has another coughing fit but doesn't wait for full recovery to continue, "Remember the time we snuck into the bauxite lands up by Discovery Bay and then pretended we were lost tourists who had wandered off course?"

Flora laughs herself into her own coughing fit. It was one of their more entertaining moments. With two people hardly more recognizable in Jamaica, who would believe they were tourists?

"Oh god, Milton. I love you cyan done. You have always been my hero. You blazed the trail, and I have simply followed in your footsteps."

"Ah Flora. Not so it go. You have been my inspiration on many, many occasions. I would have given up a long time ago without you."

Flora covers her face. She can scarcely hang on, but she must. The adrenaline surges again, and she bolts upright. "Okay, when do we start? When do I come over and we get cracking on your papers?"

"Give me till next week. Have some tidying up to do."

Flora helps Milton to his feet, and they silently stand together holding hands, staring off into their separate memories. Flora is remembering the times she and Milton have danced together, all their love of life tightly packed into such tiny moments. She has no idea what he is remembering.

Chapter Twenty-Three

Flora is in the studio, with heavy headphones she's just put on, into which blares a commercial for the latest 5-G wireless service. She fears the catchy jingle will lodge in her brain. She obsessively adjusts the large microphone hanging in front of her to just the right position and swivels in her chair, which she knows is an absolute no-no, but she can't stop. Her stomach is in knots and her mouth dry. *Wow*, she thinks, *I am out of practice!* McKensie gives Flora a quick pat on the shoulders as he walks behind her. He settles into his chair, smiles, and gives her a thumbs-up, then puts on his headphones and waves at his producer and technician, who are through a glass window in an adjoining room. Flora hears the bubbly theme song to Mark My Word, then the deep, syrupy radio voice of McKensie.

"Greetings, listeners, and welcome to Mark My Word. I am your host, Mark McKensie. Today, we have a very exciting line-up. I have in studio with me the gorgeous, passionate, always impressive, always provocative Professor Flora Smith, CEO and Executive Director of the environmental NGO, Environment First. We are also going to have joining us a number of informative and knowledgeable guests, and as always we look forward to taking your calls and hearing what you the listener have to say about what is going on in your community. Today, I am very proud to say we are dedicating the entire Mark My Word show to our precious Jamaican environment. So sit tight and get ready for a very engaging three hours. I promise you will not be disappointed! Stay tuned—we will be right back." A quick break for another set of commercials and that annoying jingle again!

"So, Professor Flora Smith, a warm welcome to you. "

"Thanks Mark, very happy to be on your show. It's been a while."

"Yes, unfortunately way too long, but we intend to make up for that today. Professor, please tell our listening audience a bit about yourself. I mean I am looking at your CV, and I can't even pronounce half of what is written in it."

Flora hates this part of any show, and giggles to prove that she's just a regular gal.

"I mean you are extremely well educated—you have not one, not two, but three degrees, it says here, in Geography, Biochemistry, and Mineralogy. Folks, we are talking a doctorate from MIT. Did you know that we have a Jamaican with a Ph.D. from the Massachusetts Institute of Technology, one of the most high-ranking, most influential scientific institutions in the world? Listen here, Jamaica, I tell you we must be proud of our achievements. We are such a small country, but we manage to achieve so much. I know we celebrate our musicians and our athletes, but we must also celebrate our scientists and our scholars as well. We must value education and knowledge. But tell me, Flora, what is mineralogy?"

Flora is very anxious to get to her topic—polluting plastics—but she knows she must first demonstrate her scientific and street credibility, and she needs to prove that she too is Jamaican and belongs. So as quickly as possible, though without sounding rushed, using simple language, throwing in self-effacing humorous anecdotes and Jamaicanisms, she gets through the getting-to-know-you portion.

She explains her educational background, references her mother the lady doctor, her grandfather and father the plant experts. She explains mineralogy by joking with Mark, reminiscing about their helicopter trip to view the sand mining and her hopping in and out of the helicopter before security could stop her from taking samples. These very same samples were then used successfully in court to identify the sand that had been stolen: science at work for the common good. And yes, pity the case has mysteriously vanished, and justice has not yet been served.

Continuing on the mineralogy track, she talks a bit about her research on bauxite mining, emphasizing its negative effects on the soul of Jamaica—stalwart rural Jamaicans and their very necessary way of life. Then she tells how she started her NGO to try and solve solid waste problems, to improve the lives of Jamaicans living in and around garbage dumps, to stop sewage continuing to pollute Kingston Harbour, which, listeners, just happens to be one of the natural wonders of the world.

And finally Flora tells a very moving story about how the very same day she was in despair and going to give up, a dusty, tired, thirsty young man walked in off the street and into her office and told her she was his last chance. He had done everything possible, tried to meet with the owner of the violating company, wrote letters to every government agency, met with every relevant political representative and private sector organization, went to every media outlet, and nothing, no one would listen, and no one would care.

He took her to his community and showed her how it had been turned into a toxic waste dump by an industrial company owned by a powerful Jamaican with political connections. She was outraged and pledged her organizational support. So Environment First and his community, working closely in partnership, successfully sued the company and the government. And now that community no longer lives with poisonous chemicals fouling their water. No more hazardous waste oozing everywhere, making their children sickly; giving the old people headaches; having to close the school doors and send the children home when the odors and noxious vapors get too strong; even sometimes not being able to hold church, stopping good law-abiding citizens from being able to worship together.

CHAPTER TWENTY-THREE

"This," Flora declares, "is why I get out of bed every morning, and in the face of impossible odds, keep doing what I do." If there had been a sound track, the stringed instruments would have come to a final crescendo right there. But, what Flora has left out from this triumphant narrative is the awful and inconvenient truth: she long ago used up her mental and emotional reserves and is absolutely sick of trying to save human beings from themselves and from destroying the planet.

Flora is grateful for the long break of news, sports, weather, the one o'clock winning numbers, and of course lots of commercials, every one vying to own their quota of seconds on the highest rated news talk show. During the break, Mark takes Flora out onto the balcony to escape the blasting air-conditioning in the studio. One of the station's orderlies brings them glasses of water; as they refresh themselves, they gossip about various rumors of the usual sex, money, and power sort, and commiserate over Milton. Then it's time to return to their seats and don their earphones.

"Welcome back to Mark My Word. I am your host, Mark McKensie, and today I am a very lucky man, because in studio with me for the entire show is the very lovely, very knowledgeable Professor Flora Smith. We are talking about what we need to do to take better care of our precious Jamaican environment. Flora, the other day you took me for a long walk along Palisadoes Beach, and I just couldn't believe the plastic garbage everywhere. We seem to be drowning in plastic."

"Mark, you're so right. As far as the eye could see was plastic of every conceivable type, and what I think many of your listeners don't know is that this plastic, which by the way is made out of many scarce resources like petroleum and water, anyway, this plastic will be around not only long after we are all dead and gone, but will still be here after ten lifetimes have come and gone. So we need to change our manufacturing and consuming habits, because like you just said, we are drowning in plastic. And you know, it's not that hard to do, because just the other night I threw a party for over seventy people, and we didn't use one plastic thing, and we created no garbage."

"That sounds good Flora! Now, on the phone with us, we have an old-timer who can tell us about how it used to be and about the changes he has seen. Samuel Wiltshire from Port Royal is a fisherman from many generations of fishermen. He kindly took us on his boat to show us the awful plague that is plastic pollution. Maas Sam, the other day you told me that you know the harbor like the back of your hand."

"Well, Mr. McKensie, that is so. I learn from my grandfadda and fadda and uncle dem, and I learn my grandsons and great grandsons and try pass on the knowledge me did receive. Myself now, I never have no son, but me have one daughter who can drive boat and handle fish pot and any kind of fishing just as good as any man. And since woman more sensible dan man, I always happy to have her along with me."

"Ha ha! Maas Sam says woman more sensible than man. I am sure Flora would agree with you. What you say to that, Professor?"

"I say Maas Sam is a man of proven wisdom."

"Ha ha. Well, I can't let pass the fact that Maas Sam's daughter is the famous Janice Wiltshire, who owns Janice's Cook House. Maas Sam, please tell your daughter that any excuse I can come up with I head to Port Royal for her food. Whenever friends or family come from foreign, we go straight from the airport and pay Miss Janice a visit."

"I am sure she is listening, so she must be very please to know that, Mr. Mark."

"Okay, so back to the topic at hand. Tell me how things have changed since you started out."

"Awright. Well when me was a likle bwoy, the water inside the harbor clear clear clear. Could see all the way to the bottom. When the ship dem use to come in, we dive down to get di penny the white people dem throw down fi we. Mek me tell you could see dat penny all the way down. People used to swim cross the harbor.

Dem even keep race. In them time, shark plenty, but nobody worry bout dem because the shark dem have plenty fi eat, and not concern wid us human. Fish dem plenty plenty, Mr. Mark. Nowadays most of them fish gone. Never ever see them again, and now everything is scarce. We have fi go further and further fi find fish. Tek you all two tree day, and you still don't ketch what you use to ketch in one hour. The reef dem cover wid nasty green moss and it killing off the coral.

"Now me know seh fisherman get blame fi why no more fish, and me the first to say dem who have bad practice, like dem who use dynamite, dem who poison di water fi ketch fish, dem who use compressor and dem who dive nighttime, dem who ketch di breeda, and don't trow back the baby, dem should get punish, tek weh dem license, tek weh dem boat, fine dem, put dem inna prison and some a dem me say just drown dem right dere and den and done wid it. But, Mr. Mark, is not we di fisherman cut down all di mangrove, and dig up di seagrass, and dredge and dump up and destroy all the fish nursery dem. Is not we pour filth and garbage inna di sea. Is not we build big hotel and housing development right pon top di shoreline and mash it up. Is not we bring whole heap a plastic bokle and plastic bag inna dis ya country. No sah. Is not fi we. And so I can tell you Massa God fish soon soon done, and if we go on like dis, when my great grandson Jayjay, him is as smart as a whip, when him time come fi have fi him owna boat, nothing lef fi him, and den what him fi do? What him fi do? Tief? Is that what we want, Mr. McKensie? I ask you, do we want to breed more tief?"

Mark McKensie actually sighs loudly. "Maas Sam, Flora is correct; you are a wise man indeed. You are a Samuel, but you certainly have the wisdom of a Solomon. Thank you very much for taking the time to share your insights with us."

"You are very welcome. Miss Flora family and my own family go back far to her grandfadda and my fadda, so any time I can help out Miss Flora she only need to ask."

Flora is so proud of Maas Sam that she is vibrating with emotion and afraid to speak. And bless his soul, he has basically told the large listening audience that she is a genuine Jamaican. Her father might be a white man, but she has deep Jamaican roots and is down with the common folk!

❂

They are well into the second hour of the show, and it's all been fine, but Flora is still afraid something is going to go terribly wrong. She and Mark sit very quietly through the next string of commercials. Flora is amused that even someone as upbeat as McKensie has gotten quickly beaten down by the horrible realities of his show's topic. Welcome to her world!

"So Professor Smith, you and I were in Maas Sam's boat, and he took us to see the baby birds nesting in plastic scandal bags, and everywhere I looked I just couldn't believe all the rubbish. What are we to do about this?"

Flora knows the only answer that would matter to Jamaicans: all she needs to say is that plastics mirror female hormones and "turn man into woman," and that would be the end of plastics in Jamaica. But she is on her professorial bandwagon, so she controls her popularist urges and proceeds with a different logic. "Well, Bermuda just banned plastic bags. Italy, the largest user of plastic bags in Europe, is banning them. Countries in Africa, Asia, all over the world, are banning plastic bags, and we need to do the same in Jamaica. That's the first step."

"How about recycling? Wouldn't that help with our plastic bottle problem?"

"Well, we don't have genuine recycling in Jamaica. Basically, a few people take their plastic bottles to a place like Environment First, and they get picked up and stored, and then when there are enough, they are shipped off to China. Now that's a huge waste of energy. And what happens when it gets to China or wherever else it ends up? Out of sight out of mind, those are our solutions. Instead, none of this should be allowed in the first place. An importer should not be allowed to bring anything into this country that they cannot properly account for its correct disposal. Real recycling would require that the plastic would be reused, or made into something useful, not just dumped somewhere else. Other countries in the Caribbean are turning plastic waste into things like construction materials. That is not the perfect solution, but it is better than just shipping them off to pollute someone else's country. The other thing that needs to happen is there needs to be a return fee like we still have for some glass-bottled drinks. If there was a value to the plastic bottles, you better believe that people would not be throwing them in the rivers, gullies, gutters, and in the streets, for it all to wash into the sea, and end up on our beaches. If there is a value, people will be making a living collecting those very same bottles. The thing, McKensie, is, I might be a scientist, but this is not rocket science. This is just common sense!"

Another top of the hour newsbreak, and they are into the third hour. Flora had told Mark she wanted to keep the environmental topics all public health issues, the things Jamaicans might care about: garbage, sewage, burning rubbish, air pollution. She told him to stay away from things Jamaicans don't like: wild animals, too many trees, untidiness, the disgrace of dinginess and disorder. But he insisted he wants to include biodiversity, and so has Dave Roper, a government biologist, speak on conserving Jamaican biological diversity, including talk of endemic and endangered species: crocodiles, sea turtles, snakes, bats, birds, butterflies, snails, lizards, all sorts of creatures Jamaicans couldn't care less about, or are hostile toward. There is talk of conserving habitat, of the dangers of deforestation, soil erosion, loss of habitation. Flora is glad for the break from having to talk, but knows this tack is only going to lead to backlash, and so she isn't in the least surprised by the listener who calls the second the biodiversity enthusiast stops speaking.

"Mr. McKensie, I always listen you show and appreciate all you trying to do, but dese people you have on, what dem call demself? En-vi-someting-mental-or-the-other? Cho, dem is just rich white people who don't want black people to have what dem have. Dem just a fight gainst black people progress. Dem seh don't cut down the tree. So how dem big house get build? Dem seh don't pollute di air, but what dem big fancy Prado use fi drive? Dem seh keep all di bush because crocodile and lizard and snake muss live, but how we human suppose fi live? Is only because is primitive dem want fi keep us. Dem want to keep us like inna di time of di Arawak dem, when people a walk round naked and chew pon leaf and chase afta food wid bow and arrow and spear. But it cyan work so. If you read you Bible you know dat God put man to have dominion over all things on this earth. Everything is fi we use, so must use it. Dig out di mountain, mine di bauxite, cut di tree dem, mine di river fi rock and sand. Whatever it take we mus have development, mus have job, we don't need all dem tree tree round di place just nasty up di place, we need more road, we need more car, we need more house, we need whole heap more job, we need modernize, we need develop. Dats what we need ina Jamaica. We don't want no more fi live in board house wid no light, no running water, wid bullfrog and peeniewally and whole heap o ignorance! Eedyat ting dat! Mr. McKensie, pure foolishness dese people a chat."

During the commercial break, Mark and Flora roar with laughter, and run around the studio giving each other high fives. They need to release the tensions that have been building over the almost three hours. They had been shaking their heads, and covering their faces in dismay, through the last caller's rant, but after the fact it seems virtuoso, a masterful analysis really.

"Welcome back listeners. If you've stuck it out with us, you, I am sure, have been as riveted as I have been to this very important discussion we've been having on what to do about taking better care of our precious Jamaican environment. Those of you who have not wandered off are about to be rewarded, because on the line we now have the original, I'm telling you Father God broke the mold after he made this gentleman, our most beloved of journalists, our elder statesman, the don himself, Mr. Milt-the-Lion Brown! Milton, it's great to have you on the program."

"Well, thank you Mark, it's great to be on with you, and with my most dear friend, Flora, but I don't know about that intro, don't you think it a bit over the top? I mean elder statesman, the don himself? Rubbish!"

"Ha ha. You know Milton I miss hearing you on the radio. I love reading your Sunday column "Wake Up and Smell the Coffee," but I really wish you still had your radio show. Wait, wait, let me take that back. If you were still on the radio, no one would be listening to me at all!"

"Mark, you are a real old jinal! You're right though, I do miss being on radio and talking with the callers and all that, speaking of which, I must say a word or two to your last caller, and I certainly hope he's still listening."

"Oh yes, go right ahead, I was going to ask you to comment."

"Well, I certainly understand where he is coming from, but let me say this: I am proud to call myself an environmentalist (yes, caller that is the word), and I am certainly not rich (being blacklisted by a certain Jamaican government saw to that!). And I'm definitely not white. It's radio, so you can't see me, but trust me, I'm as black as the ace of spades. Furthermore, I come from a line of Native Baptist ministers. If the caller knows any history at all, and I doubt he does, but let's give him the benefit of the doubt, he will know that the Native Baptists fought for the emancipation of the slaves and set up free villages and so on. My father was in Marcus Garvey's inner circle. So no one can accuse my family of ever doing the bidding of white people.

"What the caller doesn't realize is that he is a victim of mental slavery. Without knowing it, he has caught the disease of the very people he claims to loathe. He has bought into all that Judeo-Christian poppycock about humans having dominion over the earth. That is just people making up stories to justify their greed and stupidity. The fact of the matter is we don't own this earth, we borrow it from our children and grandchildren, and we have the duty to return it to the library of life in at least better shape than we found it. The caller talks about board house and ignorance. Well I grew up in a one-room board house with no running water, and no electricity, and we had so many peeniewallies the trees were alight with them. And what this ignoramous does not understand is that he is actually dependent on bullfrogs and peeniewallies, and birds and bats, and that if they are healthy, he will be healthy, and if they are extinct, he will be extinct.

"Unfortunately, we have these wrongheaded attitudes toward nature in Jamaica. I have fought against these attitudes most of my life, and, Mark, since you have labeled me a senior statesman, your listeners know I am not a young man. I have fought for the Jamaican people to have access to our beaches, which more and more we are completely excluded from. I have fought for Jamaican people to have clean water to drink, clean air to breathe, decent wages, a good education, nutritious locally grown food to eat, to be treated with dignity and justice. But I have also fought for this place, this island we call Jamaica, that existed before there were human beings, that existed before there were sailing ships, and murdered Tainos, and enslaved Africans, before there was private property and before there was empire. And I say to you here and now, to my final breath, no matter how frustrating, how hopeless, how discouraging, I will continue to fight, along with co-patriots like Flora Smith, the bravest woman I know. Mark my word, Mark McKensie, I will continue to fight for Jamaica till my final breath, and I encourage all your listeners to do the same."

Chapter Twenty-Four

Flora has done it yet again. Her media strategy worked, and she has once more succeeded in getting the spotlight focused on herself, Environment First, and her environmental topic of the day. The newspaper headlines and editorials scream: "Plastic Plague!" "Jamaica Drowning in Plastic!" "Ban Plastic Bags!" "Jamaica's Plastic Invasion!" There are dramatic photos of beaches and mangroves choked in plastic, baby birds nesting among plastic bags, offending gullies, gutters, and streams strewn with garbage. The newspaper websites run shocking slideshows and video clips that Flora supplied. The various articles and editorials misquote her to varying degrees, but the message is loud and clear: Professor Flora Smith, world-renowned Jamaican scientist, environmental lobbyist, CEO and Executive Director of Environment First, urgently raises the alarm that Jamaica has a monumental problem with solid waste pollution from plastic products that need to be reduced, regulated, recycled, and banned!

So yes, she has whipped up a hysterical focus on Plastic Pollution; she is on the front page of every newspaper, requested on the major talk shows. One editorial even questions why she hasn't been bestowed with such an honor already and suggests she should be immediately granted the Order of Jamaica for her efforts to save Jamaica's environment from the ravages of ignorance and greed. The phones at Environment First have been swamped with congratulations, questions as to how the person calling can help, questions about where and how to recycle, people offering their own innovative, entrepreneurial solutions that they want Environment First to partner in or give a stamp of approval. And her two original goals have been met: the Board is once again slavering at her feet, and the money is flowing back into Environment First's anemic coffers. Their second fundraiser, which is in three and a half weeks, will no doubt be successful, and she will have once again dodged the NGO-funding-collapse bullet.

On one level, Flora is satisfied that she has done what she set out to do. It is the pleasure an artist might feel in a painting well executed, an athlete might take in a race well run. It is the pride of good workmanship. But she has no delusions that she has accomplished anything substantial. Rather, she is sure this topic will be like all the others, a one-hit-wonder, and this cycle of crisis–attention–no attention–next crisis will just repeat itself over and over, world without end, and she has moved beyond her ability to endure yet another cycle.

What does bring her genuine joy, though, is a surprise at the end of her day. As Flora is gathering her things to leave, Crown and Battle march into her office with a dozen red roses in a crystal vase and announce, in their usual tag-team style, that Madge has withdrawn her defamation case. They report to Flora that when they showed Madge's lawyers a little taste of the evidence their client holds, within minutes of the adjournment of their meeting, they got a call from Madge's principal attorney saying he had received instructions to cease all legal proceedings against Flora Smith and Environment First, and such actuality expressed in written form would be arriving the following morning.

CHAPTER TWENTY-FOUR

Battle puts three long-stemmed glasses on Flora's desk, Crown pops a bottle of bubbly, and they toast to the end of this nuisance suit. Battle tells Flora the added good news that they have been assured by Madge's attorney they will neither fight costs nor any punitive damages. Crown fills their glasses again, and they toast to Madge having to spend a shitload of money. Crown then tells Flora that in recognition of her unselfish dedication and unrelenting efforts on behalf of the citizens of Jamaica, Crown, Battle and Harding intend to charge Environment First absolutely nothing. And Battle adds that they will also donate to Environment First their portion of any awarded monies. At this point, Flora feels the weight of her world come crashing down on her. She collapses into her chair, covers her face in her hands, and sobs.

Flora has made it home. Her every bone, every muscle, her entire being aches. Though she always manages to talk herself out of the indulgence, tonight she fills her bathtub to the top with hot water and adds a sprinkling of bath salts and a tiny bit of coconut oil. She places her laptop by the tub, selects Beethoven's Ninth Symphony, puts the volume on maximum, sinks into the water, and lies utterly still. She wants to think of absolutely nothing. When it starts to get tepid, she drains out some of the water and adds more hot water and a bit more coconut oil. She hums along with the music when the refrain comes around. She is just starting to feel like she might make it through the night when her phone rings. Why oh why did she bring it into the bathroom! Oh yeah, because she has been waiting for this call.

"Mase darling!"

"Florita! Sorry to take so long getting back to you. Was stuck in meetings in New York, and then on the train coming back, was sitting in the quiet car, so no yakking on the cell phone!"

"Were you meeting with your agent?"

"Yes, agent and editor and a few lawyers!"

"Hee hee. Tell me this, you really calling your memoirs *Boom Bye Bye*?"

"So far publisher loves title and lawyers have okayed it, so yes! Speaking of lawyers, congrats on your defeat of the Madge. My boys Crown and Battle texted me and then I got your voice message. Am thrilled for you!"

"Well, my dear, what a relief! I tell you that thing's been hanging over my head for way too long. But you know who really we owe the victory to?"

"Who?"

"Jerome. His footage was the damning evidence."

"True."

"I mean all the reports and what not we got through the Access to Information Act didn't bother them one bit. Even when records showed how many dolphins they themselves had cited as dying in their very own care!"

"Picture worth a thousand words! Guess harder to explain your dead dolphin floating belly up when it's on video. But check this out, rumor has it Madge moving back to Caymans."

"Rass how dat one pass me? But why?"

"Guess Nigel will take over the Jamaica attractions. She's selling the Florida and Mexico franchises. I hear some new regulations coming in will make things in Florida a bit more complicated. The ones in Mexico selling for a pile of money to one of those Spanish hotel chains. If you throw in the money them just make on the public offering, Madge can retire to the Caymans and spend her days counting her tax-free billions. Smart move."

"Yes, but you know the real reason she moving back home to Caymans, don't?"

"No. Why?"

"Jerome! She cyan face the disgrace, not just losing a law case to me but having to see me and Jerome together."

"Meow Florita! You too wicked! You do it so well, but me don't think being bitchy suit you my dear."

As if to underscore Mason's point, "The Ode to Joy" begins with the very deep baritone lecturing: *O Freunde, nicht diese Töne! Sondern lasst uns angenehmere anstimmen und freudenvollere!* (*Oh friends, not these tones! Let us raise our voices in more pleasing and joyful sounds!*) Time to stop the negativity, the sniping and griping because: *Alle Menschen werden Brüder, wo dein sanfter Flügel weilt.* (*All men become brothers where your gentle wing rests.*) We are all brothers and sisters: this was the "We Are The World" anthem almost two centuries before Michael Jackson was born. And no wonder Europe decided to claim Beethoven's setting of Schiller's rapture as their very own anthem, because they were the world, that is, they had consumed the world, so might as well be singing about *Alle Menschen werden Brüder*. Flora leans over and puts the music on pause.

"Flora, where the hell are you?"

"In the bathtub. And hold on a second, I have to add some more hot water. . . . Okay, I'm back. Main thing is am really relieved Jerome is in Italy. Am very afraid for him. Am sure Nigel and Madge can figure out where our footage comes from."

"Yeah, but there isn't anything they can do about it."

"Hope you're right."

"Oh but sorry, just remembered the real reason wanted to call you! I read your proposal on the train. Professor Smith, you are brilliant, absofuckinglutely brilliant."

Flora glows with Mason's praise. "So Judge you like?"

"Like? Like is nowhere superlative enough! What is MIT saying?"

"According to Chang, they are over the moon. President, trustees, everyone vying to support. There apparently is already a South Asian billionaire who wants to adapt my model to India, though the scale is so different I don't really see how. Chang says all the major foundations—Gates, Soros, Ford, Clinton, Macarthur, Rockefeller—all want to give money. It's the model of development they have all been waiting to support. Or some such shit.

Chang is coming down next week for five days for site visits, and he and I will talk about the nitty-gritty details, set up a timeline, and all that. He says he even has Shanghai and Taipei money that's ready to go. So we even have a two-China solution!"

"Wonderful, Florita! Congrats, I'm damn proud of you!"

"So will you be on my board, be my special advisor, be on the faculty?"

"But mus! I can't believe you are even considering me! I'd be honored. Have you told your EF board yet?

"Nope, will do after our fundraiser."

"The International Institute of Environmental Sciences and Advocacy. You go girl. Jamaica to the world!"

Flora drains out the water then showers to get the oily residue off her body. She sings along with the chorus while she washes out the bathtub.

Freude trinken alle Wesen	*All creatures drink joy*
An den Brüsten der Natur;	*At nature's breasts;*
Alle Guten, alle Bösen,	*All good, all evil*
Folgen ihrer Rosenspur.	*Follow her rose-petalled path.*
Küsse gab sie uns und Reben,	*Kisses she gave us and vines*
Einen Freund, geprüft im Tod;	*A friend, proven onto death;*
Wollust ward dem Wurm gegeben,	*Pleasure was given to the worm,*
Und der Cherub steht vor Gott!	*And the Cherub stands before God.*

Flora once attended a performance of the Ninth in Vienna that had a chorale of almost a thousand singers. Perhaps heaven would be like that—all that celestial singing. Now that she's stepped off the precipice, can she leave Limbo? But she isn't quite sure whether she's still falling, or whether she's landed, or whether the precipice was really just a few inches high, and not a leap at all, more like an ordinary step, but in a direction previously unknown to her, neither up nor down, not north, south, east, or west.

Chapter Twenty-Five

Flora is on Milton's second-floor patio, trying to feed him various concoctions Lilac has sent along. There is a beetroot drink that is supposed to be good for the blood. And what is wrong with Milton's blood? It's his lungs, Lilac, his lungs! One goddamn cigarette too many. Thousands too many. Lilac has made a dessert (oh yes, she knows Milton likes the sweet life) of tapioca pearls in warm coconut milk, with stewed guavas and bananas. If Milton isn't up for it, Flora will volunteer to finish what he can't.

"Milton darling, until this moment me never realize seh Lilac one Obeah Woman! Now everything about her make sense!"

"Don't let my daughter see me eating any of this. She has me on a very bland diet!"

"What the hell for? Must eat tasty nutritious food!"

"Well, she says sugar is bad. And especially since I'm an addict!"

"Lawd have mercy, she been in Canada way too long. Anyway, the only sugar in any of this is natural yummy good for you fructose. I never knew you were diabetic?"

"I'm not!"

Flora watches Milton with as much satisfaction as if she had prepared the food he is relishing. Flora rubs his head. For the first time that she can recall, his hair has been cut and tamed (no doubt the daughter again.) "I going tell Lilac to send food for you everyday. You looking better already!"

They stand in Milton's study where Flora surveys the wall-to-ceiling stacks of papers, books, and god-knows-what. What was the "tidying" Milton said he was going to do? Where could they possibly begin? But Milton apparently knows what everything is and has a "system." He walks Flora around the piles, and explains that they are sorted by subject matter, except when they are sorted by event, except when they are sorted by date. He says he has managed to transfer all his photos into digital format, and that his daughter has been scanning all his articles written before the digital age, so his articles and other writings will be accessible.

"Way to go! Your daughter sounds like she has the strength of ten people!"

"I guess. She's been sort of pent up, you know, languishing in Canada, and now that she's finally escaped, she has all this energy unleashed!"

"Okay, so do you want me to just box all the piles and store them until the Milton Brown Library and Archive has been built?" Flora is thinking, *Please don't tell me we have to go through each pile, because we will be here till kingdom come!*

"Well, we don't have to go through every piece of paper (Flora tries to suppress her glee), but it will save you time later if we have some sort of system. Best you have a good idea what is here and have a preliminary database."

"As painful as it is for me to admit, you are very correct. I tell you what, I'll bring Keisha with me next time. She's obsessed with setting up systems. And will also bring Dr. Derek because he is Dr. Data and also has muscles for carrying boxes!"

"Great plan. Now we can just go back and sit on the patio and have a bit more of that delectable dessert your Obeah Woman made!"

Flora has just put away some leftovers and is saying goodbye to Milton, when his daughter arrives laden with boxes of supplies of the frightening bedridden sort: plastic bed liners, adult diapers, skin lotions, alcohol swabs. Flora can almost smell Milton's last days ahead. It makes her want to vomit. The daughter studied to be a nurse but never finished her Canada boards and instead worked for twenty-five years in administration at a Toronto hospital. As if in testament to this fact, following in her wake are three men carrying parts to a hospital bed that is to be assembled. Flora waves, says they have to catch up, will have a nice long chat next time, and quickly escapes.

Back at Environment First, Flora and Keisha are outside on the bench having a quick meeting. The O'Tahiti apple tree is dropping its blossoms leaving a purple carpet at their feet. Flora will miss that tree. She looks around, thinking about what she will miss and what she won't. After Keisha came back fuming from her meeting with the board—they had quibbled and denied suggesting Flora resign, had only been suggesting maybe she needed a break, maybe she needed to reconsider her approach, maybe she. . . . Flora had taken Keisha into her confidence, told her about her plans for the International Institute for Environmental Sciences and Advocacy, and asked if she'd like to jump ship. Keisha had thrown her arms around Flora and embarrassed them both. Flora has been identifying everyone she would like to take along into her new empire. She has chosen Keisha as her office manager for Kingston Headquarters, the Hope Garden Headquarters to be exact, that old shell of a building at Hope for which she has elaborate eco-architectural dreams.

Flora remains outside. One small step for . . .? One large step for . . .? She fingers her Institute's prospectus, and considers, yes, this is probably her best work to date. And after so many years of worrying about a multitude of social and environmental problems, grappling and struggling for solutions, it came to her whole—the big picture, all the little pieces and how they fit together. She was walking around the cay thinking about being on a tiny coral atoll, while looking at Jamaica in the distance, and she went back to her hammock under the almond trees, their leaves turned to brilliant shades of yellow, orange, and red—our island autumn—and she thought about the seasons she loves in Jamaica, the changing of the almond leaves, the floral eruption of the Pouii, the mango blossoms painting the hillsides red, the Lignum Vitae covered in yellow butterflies, each fruit, all year, rolling out during its time. She lay down in the hammock, closed her eyes, and boom, it all came to her. She had jotted down a few notes, a few talking points, and when they got home that night, she had gone straight to her computer and by six in the morning had her first draft written. It was so simple, and so obvious; why hadn't anyone tried it before?

The elegant concept behind the International Institute of Environmental Sciences and Advocacy is, instead of the typical academic separation of scientific knowledge from activism, the ethical principle behind the pursuit of scientific knowledge would be environmental advocacy and just social solutions. The approach would bring together law, media, technology, scientific and academic research, indigenous and local knowledge, and environmental and social activism and weave them together in application to urgent, persistent, entrenched problems.

Flora would like a well-funded division to go twenty-four/seven countering the lies, cover-ups, and deception with evi-fucking-dence. But she is also aware that people like to ignore the truths that stare them in their face, so the evidence would have to be combined with state-of-the-art media campaigns that wash people's brains. If Jamaicans can overnight become the largest per capita consumers of cranberry drinks, surely they can be equally convinced to love trees!

Flora will accept an Endowed Chair as MIT Professor of Environmental Sciences and Advocacy, but she isn't going to have to spend much time at MIT, which was what had always stopped her in the past. She and Chang will oversee the design of the new degree program, and she will be director of the Institute, which will start out with a number of study sites in Jamaica. But the Institute will not just be for academics, or for those pursuing a degree, or for those needing to escape winter for a few weeks to attend meetings, or do research, or "study abroad." There will be a variety of ways people from all walks of life can participate: environmental research; small-scale technological inventions and adaptations; training in media and legal advocacy; training in running NGOs, activism, and organizing societal change; training in conservation and agriculture; interventions to transform bankrupt development models, build community capacity, and improve standards of living without raping the Earth. Utopia and why not!

The challenge at this point is acquiring the parcels of land they have their eyes on. There is a large government holding fast-tracked for divestment that has a very attractive combination of surprisingly intact wetlands, shoreline, and marine ecosystems, and interior lands that have already been used for a variety of agricultural and housing development schemes. Since it already has multiple usages, they could build the main campus, conference and research center on the disturbed upland parcels, while stopping the planned destruction of the relatively undisturbed shoreline sections. With the money that has been pledged, plus with some debt swap deals, they expect to be able to convince the government of Jamaica that this is the way to go. Flora is also hoping they will be able to purchase the St. Mary lands near Jerome to keep them in conservation and small-scale Jamaica-focused agriculture. And they anticipate getting access to lots of coffee and timber deforested public land in the Blue Mountains to replant and restore.

But she's going to have to reconsider her timing for telling her board. It's a small island, already too many people know, and especially with Chang showing up next week, one of them is going to hear something, and someone will spill the beans. It's best she send the board the letter she drafted laying out her succession plan that they find a replacement she will train. And if they don't find someone?

Chapter Twenty-Six

Flora returns to Milton with reinforcements: Keisha and Derek. She is disturbed to see the hospital bed centrally placed in the living room but relieved to see that Milton is not in it. He is very breathy, however, and easily tired. Flora thinks about when he will no longer be able to go up and down the stairs and so won't be able to leave the house unless someone carries him out. Milton perks up at the sight of his crew and insists on showing Keisha and Derek around the yard. Derek and Flora help him down the steps, and then they walk very slowly from vantage point to vantage point: the view first Kingston, starting with Hope Gardens directly below, and then spreading out all the way past Kingston Harbour, to St. Catherine and Clarendon beyond.

After a suitable rest, the three manage to get Milton upstairs in one piece, but they have to stop every two steps or so for him to rest, and Flora is terrified that she is hastening Milton's death. The look the daughter gives them when they finally make it to the top only reinforces this fear.

"Daddy, you're not to overexert yourself. You really need to not be walking about."

"Nonsense child! When it's time for me to be bedridden I will take to my bed. Until then, I am going to have as normal a life as possible!"

"Suit yourself. There has never been any point arguing with you, and lord knows I'm not about to start now!" She stalks off. Milton looks at Flora and shakes his head. Flora can't help but laugh. These sorts of arguments between child and parent are all too familiar. But luckily, her parents did not die tragic deaths. Her father had died of a massive heart attack, so there was no lingering, and her mother had followed five years later. She was healthy and vibrant to almost the end, and Flora isn't really sure what her mother died of. May was in good health, but then like a lot of people after the Christmas holidays got a bad flu, which became pneumonia. She went into the hospital and never came back out.

Ms. Systems Manager and Dr. Data are fast at work. Flora's job is to assemble the archival boxes, Milton's to sit and direct traffic. Keisha and Derek have a cataloguing system for the contents of each box by subject, date, and content description/comments, and everything is cross-referenced. Derek prints out bar-coded labels for each box. There is also a color code and old-fashioned writ, large, something the eye can see, like: Hellshire Beach, or Kingston Harbour, or Cement Company, or Bauxite Mining. All of Milton's books are getting a label with his name on it plus a color code for subject. There are nonfiction books on many topics plus literature from every region. Milton is an autodidact and over-prepared for everything. He drowns you in facts you don't really want or need, but the moment will come when he has exactly the information you haven't been able to find anywhere.

Keisha and Derek check their cataloging with Milton, who okays it or suggests revisions. Flora packs; Keisha, who has the most legible writing, scribes something that will make sense later; and Derek adds color coding, tapes the cover shut, and carries the box over to similarly coded boxes. As more and more boxes are packed, and Milton's piles start to dwindle, Flora begins to feel a suffocating dread. They are transforming this room that is living and breathing Milton into a mausoleum. Shouldn't they wait for him to die before doing this? But then he wouldn't be around to tell them what to do. Flora looks at Milton, who is definitely flagging. Is he just tired, or is this as depressing to him as it is to her? Flora suggests a break. Derek and Keisha reassure her that they can manage, and if they come across something they can't figure out, they will ask. Flora takes Milton by the hand and leads him to the bed, which he gratefully gets into. She adjusts it to the angle that he requests then goes to get him some coconut water. When she returns, he has fallen asleep.

Chapter Twenty-Seven

Flora is picking up Chang at Norman Manley International Airport "where the local time is . . .," the "local" time sounding nothing like a Jamaican voice and exactly like the local time at Miami International Airport. She has just parked and gotten to the meeting area when there he is, walking through the exit doors. They embrace for a long time. It's been over a year since they last saw each other. They've been friends for almost twenty years. Though only eight years older than Flora, Chang was one of her professors at MIT. A math prodigy, he got his doctorate in physics at age twenty-four and at age thirty was part of a team to win the Nobel for proving the existence of some cosmic particle and solving an obscure centuries-old math problem. And then Chang had said, "So what?" and decided to apply himself to more mundane and practical problems. In addition to continuing as an esteemed professor and administrator at MIT, he has become Mr. Gadget, establishing a well-funded, international nonprofit organization called Small Steps, which works with brainiacs to create engineering solutions for our abused planet while improving the lives of the poorest—how to make dirty water clean, how to run your home on a solar-powered battery, that sort of thing.

Chang is dressed for the tropics, in red and black plaid Bermuda shorts, yellow and red hibiscus patterned aloha shirt, and sandals. He's from the Pacific Island of Taiwan. As soon as they get the Institute up and running in the Caribbean, next in line for their Institute expansion plans are small island states in the Pacific. Chang's outfit allows him to show off his magnificent physique. A cyclist, rock climber, and mountaineer, he has not a millimeter of fat on him.

"Ah Florita, I love the way the air feels in Jamaica, reminds me of home. I'm so happy to be out of Boston!" He takes deep breaths, and sucks in the heavy, humid air.

"Imagine that! And you were always trying to get me to move there!"

"Ha! But you are coming to the book launch and conference, yes?"

"Of course! We'll do our New England nostalgia road-trip, admire the autumn leaves, and I'll pour maple syrup on everything."

"Let's do that! We thought we'd announce the Institute at the launch; is that okay with you?"

"It's all good." Flora and Chang embrace again and head to the car park.

At the airport roundabout, Flora heads them in the direction of Port Royal. It's midafternoon and still very hot. Maybe they can go by the lighthouse on the way back.

First stop is Janice's, where Chang is to sample the lion fish, an invasive species that the government is trying to eliminate. Janice has a large tour group, and is in a frenzy, so they just say a quick hello. Maas Sam, with Jayjay in tow, takes them into the kitchen to get food and beers, and they go outside and sit under a young breadfruit tree. One of the primary foci of the Institute will be fishery conservation and restoration. Maas Sam, who is head of the fishermen's association for the south coast, will be one of the key players. Maas Sam is explaining to Chang the current fishery-conservation-zone laws, and Flora is translating when necessary.

"Di 'ting, Mr. Chin,"

CHAPTER TWENTY-SEVEN

"Chang, Maas Sam, him name Chang not Chin."

"Sorry, di 'ting, Mr. Chang, is the way the law stay now, de only ting you cyan do in de conservation area is fish. You can dump sewage, you can build hotel, you can dredge, you can do any and everyting but fish. That cyan work!"

"No kidding. Mr. Sam,"

"Chang, it's Mr. Wiltshire or Maas Sam, but not Mr. Sam,"

"Oh sorry, Maas Sam, that definitely will not work."

"Is dat we tell di politician dem, but dem won't listen!"

"You have that problem here too, huh? Well, we'll find a way to make them listen, and if they still won't, we just find a workaround. Communities been organizing ourselves long before politicians existed, so if they don't want to be part of the solution, we'll just do without them."

"Is dat me always tell Miss Flora, we need fi self-sufficient, don't need no meddlin politician dem."

Chang gives two thumbs up to Janice's spicy lion fish dish and sends Jayjay in for another round of beer. Flora declines, but Maas Sam accepts. They walk over to the fishing beach where Maas Sam and his associates keep their boats and fishing gear. The extended Wiltshire family is one of the few fisher folk who have adopted conservation methods, such as larger mesh size and not catching the popular reef-grazing parrot fish. Chang talks about some technological innovations that might be helpful and suggests proven traditional Hawaiian shoreline aquaculture as practices maybe they can try here? Flora is doubtful. You have to have fish to start with, so they'd have to find a coastal area that actually has some fish. Maas Sam mulls over where that might be. Flora sees Jayjay listening intently to what the adults are saying. She is curious about his educational foundations. How well can he read and write? What are his formal math skills? With Janice as his grandmother, wouldn't she have made sure he is learning properly? Flora will find a way to test him and see that, if he needs it, he gets remedial help. She'll teach him herself if necessary. She wants him to have the best of all worlds. He is a future she will invest in.

Next stop is the surfing beach; the waves are negligible, so there aren't any surfers in the water, but Chang is enjoying being by the sea.

"I didn't know Jamaicans surf."

"We do have one one, two two, have a few really exciting young surfers actually. You want to try surfing in Jamaica? I could bring you out here one morning, but I'd suggest you not swallow any of the water; there's a malfunctioning sewage plant up the way."

"Oh shit!"

"Literally!"

They can see Lime Cay and the ships in the channel waiting in line to get into the Port of Kingston. The two walk toward the lighthouse, ahead the sweep of the St. Thomas coastline and the mountains that are part of Flora's molecular structure. She always feels uneasy in places where there are no mountains, as if something as necessary as her arm or leg is missing. Just around the next corner, in the middle distance, is the iconic Palisadoes shipwreck, which Flora points out to Chang and reminds him that they walked to it his last visit. Since she was a child, she has watched the bulk of the ship battered by insistent waves, hulk breaking apart, the flaking metal rusted and pocked with cavities. Last time she checked, the wreck was someone's home. It has been stripped of anything valuable, but there it is, stuck in the sand these many decades.

"I'm really impressed with Maas Sam. Soon as I get back, I have meetings with funding agencies who want to give money for the fishery conservation program in specific, and I will stress how the only way to be successful is to have people like Maas Sam leading the way."

"Good. But you know I'm always very conflicted about the fishers."

"How so?"

"Well, I don't think we should be fishing at all. Humans have sucked all the fish out of the oceans, there is none left for the creatures that actually live there. We really need to stop."

"I agree with you. That's why I believe in aquaculture done properly, of course. Done the traditional way before there was GMO fish and before there was fossil fuel-based fish feed!"

"The thing, though, is the fishermen I know tend to feel more in control of their lives and enjoy their lives more than most Jamaicans. I guess some of the old-time subsistence farmers are a bit like that as well. Their lives are their own. That's why I'm conflicted, I don't like killing fish, but I like the lifestyle that goes with it. Now that's cognitive dissonance if ever there was!"

"Yeah, well, the thing is to create more and more ways that people can have that feeling about themselves, you know, they have a way of feeding themselves and others, so they have some agency and liberty. But at the same time build up the capacity of nature to replenish herself instead of sucking her dry."

Flora tries to keep them on the "good" beach in their little walk, but they still wade through large patches of plastic garbage. Chang doesn't say anything, but she knows he is thinking, *"What is wrong with you people—how can you allow this!"* And it fills her with a mixture of mortification and rage. What IS wrong with us that we think this is okay? That only places tourists see need to be attended to? If the head of our nation, the Queen of England, were visiting, everything in her path would be cleaned up, painted, given the veneer of care. When the King and Queen of Spain were visiting Spanish Town, the capitol when Spain owned Jamaica, plants were placed in strategic places along their journey, only to be removed once their highnesses had driven past. Streetlights that had been erected for Cricket World Cup, to light up the downtown streets that the middle and upper classes rather not venture onto, were taken down as soon as the matches were over. No, ordinary Jamaicans don't deserve foliage on their journey, don't deserve clean beaches, clean seawater, functioning garbage disposal, don't deserve to be able to walk safely where they live, because apparently they don't deserve to live.

Flora knows she is exuding despair because Chang gives her another hug before getting in the car and rubs her tense left shoulder as they drive. "Florita, there are simple solutions to solid waste problems that have worked in countries poorer than Jamaica. Don't worry, we will make them work here." They go back to the roundabout, this time heading toward Kingston. "Oh my god, what is that?" They are passing a concrete gateway painted with large Chinese characters. It is headquarters for the road "rehabilitation" project, the kill-the-mangroves-to-save-the-harbor project. Chang reads the Chinese characters and bursts out laughing.

As they drive along, Flora glances over at Chang and chuckles at his incredulous expression as he looks out at the strangely barren landscape of scraped sand denuded of plant life, new sections of road in various stages of construction, with a smattering of machines scattered about, piles of huge boulders, and a ceaseless wall of rocks. There is no one to be seen working on the entire strip; it's too late in the day, or maybe they are on strike.

"For god's sake, what do they think they are doing here?"

"Chang, what is wrong with you? You're an engineer. Can't you tell that they are protecting the harbor from a category five hurricane or tsunami?"

"You're joking, right?"

"Dead serious!"

"Are they using Chinese workers?"

"Well, it's a loan from the Chinese government that we're already paying the interest on. And as you saw from the headquarters, it's a Chinese company in charge, so there are Chinese supervisors who show up every now and then in air-conditioned SUVs and then disappear again. It's odd though, no Chinese workers. Unlike all other Chinese-funded development projects in Jamaica, this one doesn't come with Chinese workers. Though I hear that since the project is so behind schedule this will change, and Chinese workers are about to be brought in. But for now, apart from a few laborers and big machinery operators, seems to be mainly work for truck drivers. But the project has like five layers of private companies and government agencies, so rest assured, a lot of money has passed hands, and bottom line, that's all that really matters."

Chapter Twenty-Eight

After driving for two hours, Flora pulls over at the top of Spur Tree so Chang can have a look at the sweeping vista below, except it's very hazy, and it's hard to see much of anything. He's toned down his tropical outfit a tad, wearing the same shorts, but no aloha shirt. Instead he has a t-shirt that reads, "This Is Your Brain on Stupid" with a caricature of George W. Bush. Flora points downward in the direction of the bauxite plant that for over a year has been out of commission during the aluminum glut-induced global bauxite crash and then not restarted because, rumor has it, the company is holding out to have its own coal-burning power plant. It is eerie to see the enormous plant rendered useless, everything turned off, standing dark and still, and the neighboring communities slowly starving while it stays closed. Chang tells Flora, he can't make out any details, but he remembers it from their previous trip, when she gave him her painfully thorough bauxite destruction tour. He had felt like he was back in Taipei, or Delhi, Beijing, or Mexico City, the way his lungs had felt by the end of the tour. The caustic smell is something you ingest, the taste lingers, he had to chew a wad of gum to try and get the repulsive taste out of his mouth.

CHAPTER TWENTY-EIGHT

As Flora drives them down Spur Tree, she terrorizes Chang by overtaking a slow-moving convoy of trucks. The fact that she is overtaking around a corner makes it worse, but she knows better than to be stuck behind any brake-riding road hog going down the longest, steepest incline in Jamaica. She chuckles at her passenger, who has never accepted the insanity of Jamaican driving, though Flora finds Boston drivers way more frightening.

She wishes she could take them for a quick detour to Treasure Beach, but no time for meandering, they are on an absurdly tight schedule. She gets to enjoy the sea for two seconds as they pass along the Black River coastline, but then it's back to nothing but road and whatever happens to be on the side, usually bush, billboards, and bars. Flora notices that Chang has gotten a bit subdued.

"Sweetie, you okay? Has my driving completely freaked you out? You getting carsick? You need us to stop?"

"Well, I do need to pee."

"No problem. This is Jamaica and man stan up and piss where him like. You can pick a tree, a wall, or just use a tire of our vehicle. Let me know your preferred spot and I'll pull over."

They stop by a turn-off with a large banyan tree. While Chang pees, Flora munches on banana fritters she's just squeezed half a lime over and drinks some ginger beer. She's wondering how Milton is doing and glad that Lilac promised to visit him. When Chang returns, she shows him the various food choices, and as he rummages to find what he wants, Flora's phone rings.

"Ms. Silo! Natasha girl, belated congrats on winning the environmental writers' award. And thanks so much for doing that long piece on Plastic Pollution. Beg you pardon, meant to email and tell you thanks."

"Oh, you very welcome. It's the least me can do!"

"So what's up?"

"Well heard about your Institute and think it sounds awesome. Was wondering if I could get an exclusive?"

"Rahtid, word travel fast in a dis ya country. Who you hear bout it from?

"Sorry Prof, but I'd rather not say. You know us journalists and our sources."

Since Flora is Natasha's primary source, she wonders how protected she ever is! "Eh heh. Well, the truth my dear is that it not official yet. Am on a site visit with one of my colleagues from foreign right now. We have some details to iron out. Probably take another month or so. But rest assured, soon as it's official you get the feature okay?"

"Yeah man, no problem. One other thing . . ."

"Eh heh?"

"I need to talk to you about Cliff Edwards."

"Bumba, what you know about Cliff?"

"That's what I need to talk with you about."

"Okay. Well, Ms. Silo, clearly you and me need to get together. I am tied up this week, but soon as I'm clear, you can come over to my place, and we can have a very private conversation. How that sound?"

"Sounds great, thanks."

"Oh, by the way, have you been to see Milton?"

"No, not yet. How him doing?"

"Am on the road so haven't seen him today, but if I was you, I would get my ass over there right now, if not sooner."

Natasha kisses her teeth in consternation, "Lawd have mercy Flora, that not sounding good, at all, at all!

There is a large sign: Fountain Blue Estates. Flora turns into the road that the sign indicates, but as they drive up the incline into the interior of the development, it is clear that there are no houses. There is a recreation area with a basketball court but no hoops. There are solar street lamps that have no bulbs in them, cul-de-sacs, and roads that trail off into dirt tracks: a planned community that never got built. Why start with solar streetlights and basketball court before anyone lives there? These are just some aspects of a completely mismanaged government holding. Groves of mango trees planted as a cash crop, but the fruit never sold (at least not by the authorities!). Acres of sprawling haphazard agriculture, cattle grazing, trees planted for biofuels, none of it bringing in any significant income, and all of it to be divested.

They drive wherever a road takes them, reaching a dead end and turning around, going down some grassy track, ending up in someone's yard, and again turning around. There is a Great House cum Visitor Lodge that has kayaks and other water-sport toys strewn in the backyard, even though it is not near the shore. Flora wonders when last anyone stayed there. Clearly everything of the usual sort—tourism, cash crops, cattle, energy (there was even a plan for an oil refinery)—has been tried, but with no overarching plan, and none of it has worked. She knows that she can make the Institute succeed. You have to have the big picture and all the details; otherwise, all you have are uncoordinated, disparate, competing pieces, or a grandiose shell with nothing in it.

As they head back down to get to the shoreline side of the property, Chang is again animated, "I can see it Florita, I really can. We would need a proper surveying and assessment. But it's a substantial piece of property, already has a fair bit of infrastructure in place, though of course in disrepair, but with the right architects and designers this could be state of the art. I have absolutely no doubts, my girl, no doubts at all."

Flora had gotten the key to the gate, which regulates admission into the shoreline section of the property, by requesting permission to show a visiting scientist around. Swampy, fairly undamaged wetlands, with about 140 acres of mangrove forests, it is already the site of scientific study, mainly birds and crocodiles, so the authorities are used to scientists requesting permission. Ah, the privilege of access. Chang locks the gate behind them, and they drive through the bush, along a narrow, sandy track to its end.

As they walk on the finely grained white-sand beach (a rarity on the south coast), Flora points to the signature red mangrove islet close by the sheltering reef, where birds sit preening on the exposed rocks and stand very still or stalk in the lagoon. As they wade, she is stunned by the clarity of the water. She can see two crabs mating (or are they fighting?) in the sea grass. She can see the individual specks of sand on the sea floor. She can't remember seawater this clean, this translucent, since she was a child. It makes her think of what Maas Sam was saying about Kingston Harbour. Mother of God forgive us if it used to look like this!

Chang tells Flora he feels the urgency of saving this place from being pimped for tourism. He had seen all of it in photos, especially the spectacular ones taken at sunset—the islet backlit, the sky in pinks, reds, and oranges—but though some of the photos better capture the beauty of a particular bit of landscape—that tree leaning over the water and reflected back onto itself in perfect symmetry—nothing, neither still nor moving photography, can capture the essential value of the whole. They both earnestly wish: Let this stay as it is. Please, let something stay as it is, unimproved by men.

Looking westward, Flora points at a massive edifice in the distance, "God, Flora, if we can see it from here, must be huge."

"Well, big is always better. I hear they are ripping apart the surrounding area to build a golf course. Just what Jamaica needs, another golf course!"

Flora wonders where the water will come from to keep the golf course oh so green. Cockpit country aquifer? Piped in from Black River? Stolen from one of the springs nearby? She also wonders what Malcolm must make of this latest betrayal; *his* request for a golf course permit was turned down. But then again, his "seven-star" development is long stalled, first because of the global economic meltdown, then the tragicomedy with the sand theft and the consequent collapse of his business partnership.

Malcolm has been avoiding her since the time she called to grill him about Baxter. One occasion, she actually saw him on the street trying to hide behind a lamppost; another time, when she walked by him in a restaurant he pretended to be completely engrossed in his phone. But she did corner him at a Rotary event where, impossibly, they were both receiving national service awards—his service was job creation, hers was environmental education. When she resumed her line of questioning, he vehemently denied that his friend Baxter might have anything to do with Cliff's murder, or sand theft, or drug running, or any criminality whatsoever. And he turned from his usual amiable self into a thug, a side of him she had heard about but never experienced. He stood extremely close to her, looked her straight in the eye, and said in the measured tone of the ruling class Jamaican bully, "This . . . is . . . the . . . last . . . I . . . ever . . . want . . . to . . . hear . . . of . . . this. Do . . . you . . . understand . . . me?"

Chang interrupts her unpleasant recollections. "But Flora, if that resort is the vision the government has for Jamaica, why will they go along with us?"

"Forget vision, Chang, who gives a shit. It's about money and power. They need the money. The IMF has instructed them to divest, divest, divest. So if we get there with the money first, and they won't take it, gonna look a bit funky to their money masters, no?"

"Okay, I hear you. I'll go meet with the IMF soon as I have a promissory on the last of the money. I already have meetings with the State Department lined up."

"Attaboy Chang. My hero to the rescue!"

They walk in silence up the beach to a horseshoe-shaped bay into which restless pelicans circle and dive, circle and dive. Flora tries to put out of her mind the horror of the bay being dredged, walls and groynes erected, sand glued down to keep it in place, and fat, oiled tourists lolling about to the cheerful sound of sanitized Jamaican music and the roar of jet skis, while Jamaican servants hand them drinks, and braid their hair, and trade sex for the dream of visas.

They head into the swamp: towering brown and red mangroves through which the sky perfects blue. Tiny crabs and brightly colored red and yellow insects crawl on each other in the oozing mud and float on little colonies in the water. Birdcalls fill the air. The eyes of crocodiles appear and disappear. Flora and Chang follow the animals' wakes, as they glide stealthily across the pond into the safety of the mangroves. Why anyone would want to destroy this Flora cannot comprehend, but she holds no illusions, almost no one else in Jamaica thinks as she does, and unless they buy this property, it and everything on it is doomed.

Chapter Twenty-Nine

Flora is so exhausted from driving Chang all over the island that she has vowed to park her car indefinitely and is grateful to Lilac for taking him to the airport. He'll be back soon enough, so she doesn't feel too bad about her failure in hospitality. When he returns, he'll have some heavy hitters with him, several Nobel Laureates, a few billionaires known for their philanthropy who are always keen to be in the right place at the right time, and maybe the likes of Bill Clinton. Flora's head hurts at the thought of having to work with a multitude of handlers and PR firms to guarantee everything is up to each prima donna's standards, that they get proper access to all the right people, and that they are treated like royalty. Fontaine! That's whom she needs. She needs Jerome's dad to handle this diplomatic minefield.

Flora drags herself over to her laptop. As it's booting up, she thinks about the amount of ground they covered in five days: Port Royal, from Kingston to the western edge of St. Elizabeth; then deep into Cockpit Country, St. James and Trelawny; down the north coast to St. Mary, into Portland up the Rio Grande valley on some "roads" that so scared Flora she had the urge to close her eyes while she drove; into the Blue and John Crow Mountains; then home and Hope Gardens. They didn't have time to go by boat to the south coast fishing communities, from Hellshire all the way along the coast to Old Harbour, Portland Bight, Treasure Beach, Black River, and beyond. Who would guess that a small island could be so big!

Flora is thrilled to see an email from Jerome, who says he's very good. They had a great time in Venice and Rome and are now in a part of Italy he's never been to before on the southeastern coast. He really enjoyed being with his dad. And, since Fontaine is to retire within the year, he's trying to persuade his father to move home to Jamaica. He has attached photos. The happy family: Jerome, Fontaine, Ingrid, Espie, Trevor, Paolo, and a very attractive young woman, who looks Ethiopian, and seems to be Trevor's girlfriend. Flora thinks Jerome should stay in Europe for another month, hang out with his family and dad, and stay away from anyone with evil intent.

Flora emails Jerome that she's delighted he is having a lovely time, and she looks forward to traveling with him in Italia one of these days. She tells him she just saw Pearl and Aisha and their very cute kids (Flora, still not quite understanding the familial relations in that complex household, isn't sure whether to refer to them as his cousins, or his sisters, or? so doesn't) and to tell Espie that the guesthouse looks in tip-top shape and is fully booked. But most importantly, she needs to talk to his dad ASAP, needs to hire him immediately. Jerome should bring his dad back to Jamaica with him. Please ask Fontaine to Skype or call her. It is very urgent! Oh, and she loves and misses him.

When Lilac returns, Flora is in bed hiding with the covers drawn up over her head. Lilac pulls them off Flora's face, "Bad pickney, what happen, you okay?"

"Mi dead." Flora hides back under the bedclothes.

Lilac sits on the bed beside Flora. "Well me don't want chat wid no duppy!"

Flora reluctantly sits up. "Chang get off okay?"

"Mm hmm."

"So Sweetpea, where Punky? How come you without you side kick?"

"I just drop her off at her parents. Shelly taking some days off, poor thing, she really need a break, so she will have Punky to herself for a few days."

"Ah too sweet. Is Devon taking time off as well?"

"No way! He's in charge of the Janice branding deal, been showing her around our kitchens and factories. Tomorrow they checking out bottling and distribution. So no rest for him!"

Flora had given Lilac a bottle of Janice's pickles, and she immediately called up Janice and suggested they go into business together. "Wow, the Janice thing moving fast. I soon get my commission!"

❁

Driving up to Milton's, Flora tells Lilac how much she loves being a passenger, less stress, more interesting, you get to look around, check out the scenery. She is grateful not to be doing this alone. Lilac has told her of Milton's quickening decline; he has stopped eating and is being fed liquids, so Lilac has been making purees, consommé, shakes. It's time for baby food. Flora muses on the fact that dying sure ain't pretty, neither is being born for that matter, the beginning and the end emphatically lack dignity.

They sit in Milton's driveway while Lilac fields a call from Devon. So far everything seems to be going smoothly with Janice. When they get out of the car, Flora is startled that Lilac isn't carrying anything for Milton. They go upstairs and gather around his hospital bed. On the tray is medication of some sort, opiates? Milton seems to be asleep, but very restless, his arms make jerky movements, he kicks his legs, and then he is still for a while, then the jerking begins again. He wakes with a start and opens his eyes wide. His eyes are milky. Flora and Lilac stand on either side of him. Flora takes his hand and strokes it; the skin feels clammy, she kisses his forehead, again clammy; and speaks into his ear, "Milton, it's Flora." Milton turns his head in her direction and makes a sound that might be a laugh, might be a groan. His dentures are out, and his mouth is caved in. His skin, which seems to be glowing from some internal light, is clinging tightly to his cheekbones and temples. His structure is showing through. The room smells the way Flora imagined it the day the hospital bed arrived.

Milton lurches upright and says in a wheezing, but almost normal, tone of voice, "Flora, my darling. You bring you Obeah Woman with you?"

Lilac gently turns his head toward her, "I'm on this side, Milton."

"Ahah, good, I have my two angels to look over me." He lies back down, moans in pain, closes his eyes, and is gone again. Flora holds his left hand, Lilac his right. He has shrunk since Flora last saw him, not so many days before, and with his close haircut that makes his ears stick out, he is like a child with a terrible aging disease. Milton, my love, where have you gone? He returns to his cycle of twitching and stillness and twitching. And then he cries out, "No, Danny. No!" and looks about completely confused. His daughter comes rushing into the room. She takes a rag, dips it into a bowl of ice and some sort of alcohol (is it bay rum, or white rum, or something used in Canadian hospitals?), and tenderly wipes his face and his exposed chest.

"Daddy thinks his brother is here with him. For days now he's been having conversations with him."

Flora remembers Danny, Milton's older brother. They sounded exactly alike; if you weren't looking, you couldn't tell them apart. Danny lived in Tampa, Florida, and has been dead for over ten years. Flora bites down on her index finger. She watches as Milton's daughter gives him an injection, opiates indeed. As the daughter places the needle back on the tray, Lilac asks her how she's holding up. In reply, her face crinkles, she starts to cry, her shoulders shaking. As Flora and Lilac move quickly to comfort her, Flora thinks, "Danny, I beg you, come get your brother. Take him home. Please. It is time to take him home."

Chapter Thirty

At four in the afternoon, in assent with Flora's ban on driving, an Embassy car arrives at *Eco Yard* and delivers her to the US Embassy, and a photo op with Ambassador Ann Robertson, who is presenting a large check (literally large, though the sum could be bigger) to Environment First for the Embassy-sponsored "Yes We Can" Urban Solid Waste Project. Already scattered in several communities are barrels for garbage with "Yes We Can," and "A Gift from the People of the USA" stenciled on them. Most of the original barrels are still where they were placed, but a few have been captured for collecting water and cooking pan chicken. Flora, who has warned the Embassy to expect an accelerating attrition, is holding one end of the check, while Ambassador Robertson is holding the other. Embassy staff and various members of the press click away. "Over here, Ambassador Robertson, look this way please. Prof, smile nuh? That's better, you so pretty when you smile!"

After the photo op, Flora, the Ambassador, her Director of Protocol, and the Director of Public Relations go into a conference room to meet—about the Institute, not Yes We Can or anything else to do with Environment First. Ambassador Robertson is 110 percent behind the Institute. It is exactly the sort of bilateral, win-win, equal partnership that they are looking for. She and President Carter have been saying for decades that there must be a way for a powerful country like the United States to partner with smaller, less wealthy countries in more equitable and sustainable ways. And the Institute, which builds capacity rather than continuing extractive models of development, which does not take anything away from Jamaica or the people of Jamaica, on the contrary, treats the Jamaican partners with dignity and respect, is really the best example she has seen to date.

"You know, Flora, my favorite part of your Prospectus is your plan to have trust funds for all the communities that get involved. It's always bothered me that so much research gets done in communities, but people there just don't receive any tangible benefits."

Robertson, who began her career as an intern under Jimmy Carter, and was on the board of the Jimmy Carter Center, drops his name at least once a conversation. The other name she works into any conversation is her boss, Hilary Clinton. She worked on Clinton's presidential campaign, and Flora suspects she has her job thanks to Mrs. Clinton, as the Ambassador calls her. Flora is super okay with all that, because Robertson has already let the State Department know it needs to be green lights all the way for the Institute. And she has promised Flora that when Chang has his meetings with the State Department, she'll make sure the highest levels attend, and if not able to attend, they will be fully briefed. She will do it herself if necessary. Oh happy day! Flora cannot see how the Jamaican government will be able to stand up to this much pressure!

Ambassador Robertson excuses herself, as she has to get ready for an event at the Chinese Embassy. She and Flora embrace goodbye. Flora, rather overcome, gushingly thanks the Ambassador for her and her staff's invaluable support and impulsively kisses her hand. Flora has no idea where that gallant gesture came from and trusts Ann won't take it the wrong way! She returns to the protocol and public relations directors, and they go over the upcoming visit. The Ambassador has already given them the go-ahead to host a dinner in honor of the visiting team, and is it true the President of MIT and Presidents Carter and Clinton are coming? Flora says it's really in Chang's hands, and she'll make sure he updates them as soon as he knows who will be in the delegation. Flora tells them that Ambassador Fontaine will oversee protocol for the visit on the Jamaica side, and that information scores Flora major points with the Americans. They are beaming at her. "Flora, we just love working with you!" says the Director of Public Relations. "Yep, you're the best!" says the Director of Protocol. Good Lord, why has she been playing in the Little League all these years, when the Big League was available?

Flora declines the kind offer of an Embassy car ride home, and instead, upon retrieving her cell phone from security, calls her new chauffeur, who conveniently lives three minutes away, to come get her. Lilac almost loses control of the car when Flora tells her about kissing Ambassador Robertson's hand. If they weren't stuck in the inevitable line of traffic waiting to turn onto Monroe Road, she would have pulled over. Instead, Lilac is bent over the steering wheel howling with laughter. Flora, who thinks it's amusing but not that hilarious, is nonetheless pleased; she considers it her duty to keep Lilac entertained—why else would Lilac stick with her?

Once inside her Beverly Hills apartment, Lilac starts cracking up again. "Bad pickney, tell me again, you did not kiss the US Ambassador's hand?"

"I was overcome with gratitude . . . me get confused, tink seh me on a visitation to the Pope!"

They head into the kitchen. Lilac tells Flora she must be weak in the head and need some nutrition quick, quick. Lilac, who has been experimenting with Janice's sauce recipes, takes out of the oven a pan of crisp, thinly cut slices of jerk tofu. Flora probably needs some protein. Lilac gets a salad out of the fridge and serves Flora a plate of jerk tofu and salad. She makes Flora one of the shakes she'd been feeding Milton: protein powder, peanut butter, bananas, almond and oat milks, nutmeg, vanilla. This will fix any weaknesses in the head.

"You get any sleep last night?"

"Not a wink!"

"Figures!"

After eating, Flora goes to wash away the days' long string of absurdities. She stands in Lilac's stylishly hand-tiled shower comparing this apartment with the home in Mona, where Lilac and her mother lived, and in which Flora spent a lot of time. This apartment is quintessential Lilac. Even with the addition of Punky, it has hardly changed. It remains uncluttered, elegant, peaceful. Sure, Punky's room is awash in color, but it is also very tidy, everything in its place. Lilac's bedroom might as well belong to a Buddhist monk, one with impeccable taste. The few objects all have significance and all have beauty.

The Mona home on Palmetto Ave. was a typical Mona house: two small bedrooms (one converted into a study for Lilac); one slightly larger master bedroom; and maid's quarters in the back, which, since there was no maid, had been converted into an apartment that Flora rented a number of times—divorce number one, when she was writing her dissertation, when she was escaping from Husband Number Two. The Mona house was clean but not particularly tidy or stylish, and Flora has no idea where Lilac's fastidiousness comes from. Lilac's mother, Grace, a hard-working, unfussy woman, was not house proud and spent her spare time in her garden, which was abundant, a place to sit in the shade and cool off, a place to sit and eat popsicles, fudgesicles, snow cones bought from vendors passing by, a place to sit and admire Miss Grace's handiwork, and yes, she did manage to grow lilacs.

When Flora turns off the shower, she hears Lilac telling her to come into her bedroom when she's done. Flora refuses to think about any of the day's events, or her visits to Milton, or her drive round the island with Chang, or who will make up the visiting delegation, or the fact that she can't get any official to investigate Cliff's murder. Instead, she gladly stays in the calm waters of soothing memories.

When Flora's father was professor of tropical agriculture, they lived at the university just a short walk from Lilac's house. Often after school, Lilac would come with Flora to her mother's doctor's office and wait for a ride home. Sometimes May would let them walk home with promises of homework immediately begun upon arriving at either of their houses. Regularly, they'd meet on campus and, depending on the time of year, raid the tamarind, coolie plum, guinep, and mango trees, and then go over to Lilac's and raid whatever was in her yard. Why did she recently hear young parents planning to leave Jamaica to raise their children somewhere else? Did they really think their children were better off in Ft. Lauderdale, Atlanta, Newark, Hartford, Toronto? She would never trade growing up in Jamaica for anywhere in the world.

When she gets into Lilac's room, she's surprised to see her rifling through the contents of an unadorned fragrant cedar chest. Lilac gives her a wistful smile, and Flora sits on the floor beside her. "Have something to show you." She eases the chest out of the way so she can scoot over closer to Flora and shuffles through a pile of photographs that she places beside her. The first one she hands Flora is of Lilac and Liz standing close together, both very pregnant and laughing, Liz with her head thrown back. Liz! Both are gorgeous in the way that pregnant women often are. Liz with her thick curly hair, Lilac with her carefully picked Afro, they make a stunning couple. The next one is of Lilac and Liz with their newborn babies. Of course! Jerome and Shelly are almost the exact same age. Flora's chest is starting to tighten.

Lilac has stopped passing photos, so Flora picks from the pile and finds one of Liz, Ingrid, and Lilac that must have been taken before Lilac got pregnant with her first child, Omar. She studies the photo, comparing Liz to Ingrid. She starts to remember Liz as quiet, very bright, and sort of dreamy and solitary, more likely to be reading or drawing and scribbling in her notebook than interacting with any of the other girls. Ingrid was the highly sociable one, the rascal, the revolutionary, so adored by her teachers that they hated to discipline her and had to find more and more outlandish ways to punish her for her acts of rebellion. Ingrid had detention several times a week, but what she did during detention was anyone's guess. She practically ran the school! Still, when she insisted on dreadlocks more than two decades before it was fashionable, they stripped her of being Head Girl, and Part One of the Ingrid Legend was born.

Flora looks again carefully at Liz, and grasps that Liz is, indeed, Jerome's mother. All this time she's been thinking Jerome has Ingrid's eyes, she's been wrong. He most exactly has his mother's eyes. Flora is afraid to look at Lilac. She has no idea how Lilac can bear this. Flora is starting to get sharp pains in her chest. Lilac passes her another photo. This one is of Ingrid, Tallawah, Omar, Jerome, Shelly, Lilac, and Liz. Flora fights the urge to flee. Omar and Tallawah are about the same age; this photo was taken when they must have been about four, and Jerome and Shelly would have been two. Liz died the following year, Tallawah two years after.

Flora forces herself to look at Lilac. Her face is completely immobile except for the tears that are streaming. Flora scatters the photos out of the way and wraps herself around Lilac, whose face falls onto Flora's shoulder. As she strokes the back of Lilac's head, she tells her repeatedly how sorry she is, that she would do anything for her, just tell her what she can do to take this awful, awful pain away.

Flora has called time out, got Lilac out of the bedroom and away from the cedar chest to lie down on the very comfy couch in the living room, and gone to find Lilac a glass of her favorite red wine. Flora sits on the edge of the couch while Lilac takes small sips of her wine. They say nothing. When Lilac's glass is empty, Flora refills it. More silence.

CHAPTER THIRTY

The silence propels Flora to speak. "Was such a shock to see little Omar. You know, seeing him at that age, the same age as Punky, and equally cute!"

Lilac smiles and continues her slow imbibing.

"He's such a good daddy. When was the last time you saw the twins?"

"In person? It's been two years. Unlike you, me like stay a mi yard. Hate to travel!"

Flora sighs. She's not in the mood to travel at all either. "When I'm on the east coast, I'll go find Omar. Am meeting Mase in New York—won't be hard to see Omar since he's over in Jersey."

"That's nice. How's your boy?"

"Feisty as ever. Writing one rass expose. Me well fraid dem going kill him. But he is determined. So more power to the judge!"

Lilac raises her glass to the judge and drains her wine. "Florita, let's go back in, there's something I need you to do for me."

Flora is dreading whatever Lilac needs for her to do, but she has sworn that she will do anything, so must not do her usual bait and switch! They sit back down by the alarming cedar box, but Lilac is now more relaxed, so Flora stops holding her breath.

"Here's one for the ages!" Lilac hands Flora a photograph of Lilac, Liz, Ingrid, and Flora in Negril. Oh my god, scene of the crime! Why did she think she'd been alone with Ingrid? She had been, but now she remembers that's because Lilac and Liz had gone off further down the beach and left them alone. The four had arrived together. Her ever-protective mother would never have allowed her to travel alone with Ingrid, but she would have let her go just about anywhere with Lilac. And while they were naked in Negril, making love, swimming in the warm, clean water, sleeping on the wide powdery beach that then stretched virtually unspoiled for miles, Ingrid and Liz's miserable youngest sister, Cathy, who had just become "born again," was probably in a river getting baptized. It was an impossible script!

Flora left for Columbia University soon after, Liz and Lilac became inseparable lovers, and Ingrid went off to the wilds of

St. Mary to be in some sort of pagan poly-amorous "marriage" with an Italian woman she had met by chance at a party, who happened to be living with a polygamous Rastaman. Talk about scandalous! The respectable Small family must have been shaken to the core. No wonder Liz married the older, stable, and reputable Harold Fontaine—middle child trying to appease, to bring calm to chaos, to make up for her older sister's transgressions. And Lilac had stupidly gotten pregnant after one night of sex with Omar's father. That must have made Liz feel less than sure of her relationship with I'm-trying-to-be-straight-Lilac. What a fucking mess!

"Tell me something, what ever happen to Cathy Small? I know she migrate to Canada, but I never ever hear she come home."

"Oh Cathy, that's one long ass story."

"Tell me anyway. You know it's weird, Cathy was in our class, but I really don't remember her at all!"

"Well, as you know, Miss Cathy get very religious and don't approve of her two sister. When Ingrid have the accident, and not too long after, Tallawah fall and bruk him neck, she decide seh is God a punish Ingrid for her sinful ways. One whole heap a nonsense. I won't repeat the kind of spiteful shit she said to Ingrid. Was really wicked and hurtful. Anyway, like you seh, she migrate to Canada and never come back. Mussi because her Jezebel sister still deya! But check this out, I hear she coming on one of the big Falmouth cruise ship!"

"We should all go meet the boat sing "Long Time Gal Mi Neva See Ya!" I hear whole heap a diasporics love the cruise ship visits. That way if we natives too rawchaw and uncivilize dem can just get back on the boat!"

Lilac moves to look inside the cedar chest, and Flora starts having difficulties breathing again. Lilac is pulling out piles of what look like letters, cards, writing of various sorts, and without a doubt, all from Liz.

"Flora beg you help me, do! Cyan bring myself to throw any of this out, but cyan bring myself to read again neither."

"You want me to read them for you or throw them out?" Flora, feeling Lilac's desperation, which just feeds into her own, reaches into one of the piles and pulls out a piece of paper, which turns out to be a poem that Liz wrote:

Dawn has come and still I wait
No sound of your steps on the stairs
No sound of your breath in my ears
No sound of your voice calling my name
Dawn has gone but still I wait

Flora cannot read on, she cannot. Has anyone ever written her love poems, love letters? Has she ever written any? Has she ever been in love in a way that wasn't incredibly banal?

"Lilac, listen to me good. Me . . . not . . . going . . . hurt . . . Jerome. I promise. I swear it. Lilac, please believe me, I won't hurt him! I won't do my usual bullshit. I admit it, mi tek one rass long time, but trust me, me finally done grow up. I am now an adult, and I promise I will not hurt Liz's sweet Jerome."

Chapter Thirty-One

Her sixth day of meetings, and Flora questions both her good sense and her ability to physically endure. Why oh why has she taken this on? She must be mad! She IS still trying to save the world, isn't she? Why is she starting a crazy ass institute? She should be retiring. Isn't this the age of less is more, and with no jobs for the youth, isn't it ethical to retire as early as possible? But, isn't this also the age of no pensions, no job security, no health care, no benefits, no social safety net, and you are supposed to work until the day you die? She is convinced she could be a successful latter-day hippy. With her genes and heritage, she must be able to grow her own food, feed herself. Jerome certainly can, as can Ingrid for that matter, so she could piggyback the food self-sufficiency thing with them. And she could take on her own casual uniform that would require buying no clothes. How about just a piece of cloth or a sarong? She could wear it with a bikini top, or nothing at all when at Jerome's/Ingrid's, otherwise she could just wear the sarong and whatever top she has left over from her current wardrobe. She could spend her days with no pressure. It would be idyllic.

Flora is jolted out of her fantasies by a question from one of the Institute's Advisory Board members. Ali Khan, a leader in third-world micro-banking, wants to know how community trust funds will be administered, how to have transparency and accountability (the two gods of neo-neo-liberalism, the third being globalization, the fourth being The Market—the gods not in that order of course), and how to design against corrupt forces simply taking over. Very . . . good . . . question.

She reminds him that the thought of giving extremely impoverished people loans, or even letting them handle money at all, was considered economic anathema, but he had proven that it can be done and has made a substantial improvement in the lives of thousands, even hundreds of thousands, of people. We can't be forever paternalistic. We have to allow people to learn, to make mistakes, to come up with their own organizations and solutions. We have to create opportunities that build capacity, but capacity that will not disappear when the consultants, experts, and middle-class supervisors depart. In other words, we have to allow people to be grown-ups, not dependent appendages waiting for the next load of cargo to drop from out of the sky, always waiting for so much manna from heaven.

Yes, there is no guarantee that there won't be cases of corruption, cases of embezzlement, so we must design with these issues in mind. But you must firstly firmly believe that poor people aren't just a problem to be fixed. You must believe that within communities, no matter how seemingly dysfunctional, there are strengths and functioning arrangements, usually informal and traditional, and you have to work with these capabilities. You have to work with a variety of community members to come up with the processes and structures that will work for them, while always assessing and reassessing and adjusting and readjusting. Even if something works well in the beginning does not mean it will work well forever, and if something doesn't work in the beginning, it does not necessarily mean it is a failure, that there are no options and everyone is to be damned, written off, and discarded.

When Flora, a bit winded, finishes her speech, Ali bows to her and says, "Professor Smith, that is exactly what I wanted to hear." There is an explosion of applause from around the opulent boardroom, and Chang sitting beside her, reaches under the table and squeezes her hand with bone-crushing exuberance. Someone who can hang from a rock face with two fingers should be very careful when he even shakes your hand in greeting, much less squeezing it in excitement!

An ex-World Bank economist asks Chang how his meeting with the World Bank went, and as Chang updates the room, Flora spaces out again. She'll gratefully leave questions of finance to Chang. She will tackle meta-questions of philosophy, ethics, ideology, worldview—The Big Picture, The Approach, The Theoretical Underpinnings to The Model. And she will tackle the minutiae of who, what, where, and when, as it applies to the details of how the Institute will function in Jamaica—The Study Sites, The Community Linkages, The Projects. How will they pay for the Institute? Well, Chang take it away!

Flora had wanted to bring Jerome with her to Boston as part of her "I Am Not A Ditz" campaign, so he could see her in action on the world stage, where she is actually appreciated, taken seriously, and has a large following, where she is a bona fide expert! But he has just been traveling, plus she knew she'd be in meetings for up to fourteen hours a day. There will be other opportunities. He can come with her when she gives the keynote at Columbia University's next commencement ceremonies, and then they can play in New York. She has to confess, all this applause is really quite gratifying, though also a little unsettling since she is used to people flinging rock stones and angry words, questioning her intentions and her motivations, questioning her nationality and her loyalties. But maybe she has been transported into the realm of the fairy tale, and at any moment it will all evaporate. Nonetheless, one standing ovation after another is affirming, and being liked rather than despised feels very good. To be standing as an equal in the company of five Nobel Laureates (she has the photograph to prove it!), to be asked for her opinion without condescension, to be literally At The Table, well, well, any and everyone who has ever treated her with disrespect can go fuck themselves!

The Institute was announced with great fanfare at the glitzy book launch of their anthology, *Rethinking Development: From Failure to a Sustainable Future*, at the conference of the same name, where Flora gave the Plenary: "Science and Environmental Activism: Out of the Lab and into the Streets." Her talk was about the principles underlying the Institute: that scientists cannot continue to hide behind their precious notions of the separation of science from everyday life, struggle, and activism, and they cannot continue to believe that they are an elite, objective, detached group of super humans with special, distinct, and superior knowledge and methods. Instead, they must become active, concerned, contributing participants in the practical needs of the planet and the people who live on it. Not as gods from above but as ordinary citizens working with other ordinary citizens to create sustainable presents that can lead to sustainable futures.

Flora didn't think she was saying anything original, anything groundbreaking, but maybe it was the occasion, the venue, or maybe it was the way she spoke with her usual passionate conviction, or the examples she gave (she again told the story of Environment First and the young man who came in off the street to get help to save his community), or the way she made the Institute sound like there was a way for everyone to contribute, so that all who were listening could imagine themselves playing a role, being useful, when they most often feel useless and helpless. Whatever it was, the response had been rapturous, a ten-minute standing ovation. Chang had led everyone in a hand-clapping, foot-stomping, table-banging chant of Flor-a! Flor-a! Flor-a! Strangers had come up to her weeping, spilling out their deepest regrets and concerns.

She was distraught, then greatly moved, when one of her former professors, a world-renowned chemist, who she hadn't realized was even still alive, came up to her and, trembling, held her hand. He told her that he had wasted his entire career, that he had never ventured beyond the research lab and the classroom, that in his day science was an aesthetic and ascetic thing, abstract, the applied sciences looked down upon, and he had been too cowardly to be different. He said he thought it was also the failure of a monoculture, that science, so male dominated, had created this world of the mind without feeling, without soul, with a disdain for the mundane, the domestic, the everyday. He was so grateful that there were now women like Flora, and he had brought his great-granddaughters with him wishing that they would be inspired. As he introduced them, he said of Flora, "Now this, my dear girls, is a real honest-to-goodness scientist!"

So, not surprisingly, despite six days of meetings—yes, she is physically tired and uncomfortable, yes, she is mentally worn out and distracted and has had moments of questioning her sanity—emotionally and spiritually she is free from the bone-weary exhaustion that constantly haunts her when she's home. Gone is the sense that she is carrying a weight that she cannot bear. Gone is the sensation of overwhelming loneliness and sorrow, her nagging guilt that she can never, ever, ever do enough, her relentless rage and despair. In this setting, she is simply one of many, not an abnormality, no longer a total freak.

Flora has twenty minutes to shower and change, and then it's the last event, the closing dinner hosted by the President of MIT. She is hoping for good food, speedy wrap-up remarks, and no more speeches, lectures, or PowerPoint presentations! Unfortunately, she and Chang must forgo their planned New England nostalgia tour. They won't make it up to Vermont or even Western Massachusetts to see the fall leaves. They will have only the next day together, but he says he's bought her fresh, organic maple syrup and is thinking about what he should make for her to pour it on. So far he's come up with vegan cornbread. They will go down toward the Cape and walk on their favorite beach as they do whenever she is there, no matter the season or weather. One of her favorite moments with Chang was on that same beach walking together in a snowstorm. He had decked her out in the latest mountaineering gear so she wasn't cold. If you can wear it on Everest, a snow-infused stroll on a beach in winter is nothing.

Flora sits at the head table on the right of MIT President Klein; Chang is at his left. First up, the leek, turnip, and sweet potato soup, flavored with just the right amount of rosemary and thyme, is a proper soup for the season. As Flora starts on her kale and beet greens salad, listening to a string quartet playing Brahms, she regrets that she's been in Boston stuck in meetings and done not one cultural thing. Klein is telling her about his first trip to Jamaica as a boy and comparing it with his last trip to Jamaica some twenty-five years later, after which he vowed never to return. He says, despite all that, he is very much looking forward in three weeks to coming back to Jamaica with the Institute team.

Flora doesn't know what to say. She can hear the Tourist Board jingle start up in her head "Come Back to Jamaica and Feel Alright." She doesn't want to apologize; she doesn't think that as a Jamaican it's her duty to say to privileged foreigners, sorry we horrified you and didn't live up to your expectations of paradise. At the same time, she is pretty sure that if she were he, she'd have the same reaction and be telling a similar story.

He had come with his parents and his sister to Portland on a banana boat in the late fifties. They had stayed at a charming guesthouse just outside of Port Antonio and gone rafting on the Rio Grande, gone far into the valley, stopping to frolic in pure springs and cascades and waterfalls, and swam in the exquisite bottomless Blue Hole, and climbed onto the little island nearby in the San San lagoon. He grew up in Brooklyn and had never before been in such a gorgeous place, and though he has traveled since to places of towering grandeur and great beauty—the Grand Canyon, the Na Pali coast of Kauai—still that trip to Jamaica stays with him as his first experience of heaven on earth. They had seen all sorts of wonderful creatures, parrots, humming birds of all types, the amazing doctor birds with their long tails, the speed at which they would whiz by, the sound of their wings. And he had loved best the little goats, skipping along everywhere. He wanted one as a pet and was very upset when he found out they were a favorite food. He had even seen the now-vanished manatee, a mother and calf at the mouth of the river, and once when swimming he had seen close by the reef two turtles in the sea.

Flora doesn't want to hear the bit about what happened to make him swear off ever returning so is grateful for the serving of the main course. On her plate, she has polenta, with a putanesca sauce that is heavily capered just the way she likes it, and assorted grilled vegetables. She looks over to see that Klein and Chang are eating grilled fish. Chang proudly tells her that these fish come from a successful regional conservation project that he is part of. She blows him a kiss, and Klein continues his story.

His last trip to Jamaica was for the wedding of his best friend's little sister. Their wedding party stayed at an all-inclusive hotel, which was surrounded by thick walls with barbed wires and broken glass on top and was guarded by uniformed men with machine guns. They had to wear plastic bands around their wrists to get in and out, and whenever they ventured beyond the compound, they were constantly harassed by hustlers trying to sell them ganja, cocaine, sex, tacky souvenirs, take them on a tour, teach them how to talk Jamaican, insist they go to a certain restaurant or bar, get their hair braided—Flora interrupts and says, yes, she knows the drill; it hasn't changed! That was all bad enough, but what really got him was the night that he saw the police and security guards viciously punching and kicking and gun-butting some young guys. He doesn't know what they did, but when he tried to intervene, it just got very ugly.

Klein says he thought, *I've lost my mind, what am I doing here?* Why am I staying behind barbed wire with machine guns as if I'm in a fucking (excuse my French) war zone, to lounge on a carefully raked fake beach, and swim in a not so clean sea that is mostly dead, so that my buddy's baby sister can have a pretty backdrop for her wedding pictures?

"Flora, I'm sorry but that was it for me. And that's why I am so unreservedly in support of your project. I have seen both sides of Jamaica. I mean, I'm sure there are many more sides, but I mean I have seen heaven and I've seen hell, and I know that your vision is paving the road to heaven, not hell."

Flora, who is trying not to cry, tells him that it means so much to her that he understands and supports what she is trying to do, that he has seen and felt first hand what she is up against, and that she knows with the backing of his eminent institution, and with smart, generous, dedicated people like him on their team, they cannot but succeed. What she doesn't add is that he seems to have forgotten that there is another option to heaven and hell—he has forgotten limbo.

Flora has excused herself and is in the ladies' room. She is the only lady in the room. She wants the evening to end this very second so she can get into bed. She always sleeps well in hotels. A luxury hotel suite has everything you need, just the right amount of space, and is made for sleeping. She knows her colleagues will want to hang out after and have drinks, but she is not going there. Bed, right now that is her nirvana.

After peeing, she sits on a loveseat-sized couch placed facing the basins and remembers that her phone has been off since seven in the morning. As soon as she turns it on it starts beeping repeatedly. She has a slew of missed calls and messages. She stretches out on the couch with her feet dangling over the edge. She knows what the calls are about and doesn't want to listen to them. She puts the phone against her heart, closes her eyes and lies motionless. Two of her colleagues find her like this.

"Flora, honey, you okay? You must be really tuckered out! We are, and we haven't had to sit through all those meetings you've been at." That's Jane Murphy, professor of marine ecology at the Rhode Island Institute for Marine Conservation.

"Thanks sweetie, you're right, am suddenly feeling exhausted. Thought I'd just take a little break before dessert!" The two women smile at her and head into the toilet stalls. Flora gets up; she will not listen to her messages, but she does open a text from Mason. It says very plainly, "Milton gone. Flora I am so very sorry."

Chapter Thirty-Two

The guango tree is lit up with a pastiche of lights that people have pulled out of their cupboards, everything from strings of tiny white lights, to blinking Christmas lights, to lights in the shapes of peppers, fruits, moons, suns, and stars, and around the entire circumference many candles in delicate paper lanterns have been lit. Flora is sorry there are no peeniewallies to join in the celebration. She imagines the tree completely lit by nothing but fireflies and how delighted that would make Milton.

She'd gone to see Milton the night before she left for Boston, but he was not there. Oh, his skeletal, haggard, semblance of a body was lying in the ever-present hospital bed, but he, Milton, was not there. He had left. Danny had come and taken him home. Flora had gone outside and stood under the guango tree watching the twinkling lights of Kingston below, and screamed into the night. And then she dug under one of the roots, and buried a photo of her and Milton, on the back of which she had written, "Thank you, you were my guide and I followed." The guango tree is now her pain tree, the place where her pain has been stored. She had walked over to the tree's rotund trunk, and ran her hands over its rough bark, and then kissed it, and told Milton she'd see him in her dreams.

No funeral for Milton. His daughter has managed to keep his wish to not have a curate of any known religion overseeing the end of his life. Flora is very proud of her, given the severe pressure she has been under by all sort of "well-meaning" people who fear for Milton's heathen soul (but ultimately really are in terror for their own). Ministers, priests, deacons, prophets, clerics from any and every denomination all offered themselves but were not given the opportunity to pray for his departed soul, nor to remind their captive congregation that only through Christ can you be born again and thus saved from the damnation of the eternal fires of hell.

Instead, hundreds of people have been gathering at Milton's home on the hill, coming and going, bringing food and drink, music and song, poems and stories, photos and videos, jokes and remembrances, and at sunset, as the sun dipped into the sea, they walked around the guango tree splashing spirits, scattering petals, flowers, pieces of greenery, and his daughter leading the procession sprinkled some of Milton's ashes as they all sang "Fly Away Home": "One fine morning when my work is over I will fly away home. Fly away home to Glory/Zion, fly away home. One fine morning when my work is over I will fly away home." The rest of the ashes go to Flora, who will take them on a tour of the island, journeys Milton made many times before and will take again on his last lap.

Flora loves the time of day when you look up and see the first star, and then the next pops out, and the next, and then whoosh the sky is stars. She never tires of watching the sky go from day blue, to indigo, to black, which is what it is now. Flora and Lilac sit on the edge of the hill leaning against each other sharing a bottle of Milton's favorite Merlot. They both have had too much to drink, but Jerome is their designated driver, so they have no plans of stopping any time soon.

Flora is telling Lilac stories from her trip: how glad she was to have seen Omar and the twins and to introduce "Uncle" Mason to them. Flora says she did a double-take when she saw Brooke, because she looks exactly like Lilac—precisely like Lilac the first day Flora met her in kindergarten. But Dylan is a replica of Omar, who unfortunately looks nothing like Lilac and just like his father. They laugh over that one, because Omar's father was very good looking and popular with the ladies. During his brief marriage to Lilac, he managed two other relationships in addition to casual dalliances. Flora is revising her opinion of him. Given what she now knows about Lilac, he wasn't as appalling a choice as she had thought at the time.

"If I die, leave the shutters open," Flora stands up, and gesturing into the void, recites one of the poems she had read for Milton. "The stumbling child reaches out startling doves, through open shutters I've seen him." Lilac joins her, "The striding farmer presses plough to earth, through open shutters I've seen him. If I die, leave the shutters open." They give each other a high-five, refill their glasses, clink, then before sipping, pour a libation for Milton.

Lilac, the lover of poetry—Flora is thrilled with the gift she is making for Lilac. Flora has vowed to be a more attentive friend. She's been too self-centered, too flighty, too entitled. It's been crushing to accept that she's been blabbing about any- and everything to Lilac all these years, and as known as anyone is knowable, but Lilac hasn't felt comfortable to be equally forthcoming with her. She hopes that since Lilac shared the contents of the cedar chest with her (Flora actually has it under her bed), she will feel safe enough to tell Flora anything that matters to her. Anyway, she's putting together a book of Liz's poetry, some excerpts from her journals, letters, and writing, with a few photos, some of Liz's drawings and doodles. Espie is helping with the design and is making a cover for the book. She also has specialty paper they can print it on, and she will bind it like an old-fashioned book. A handmade book for Lilac, Ingrid, and Jerome. The more Flora reads of Liz's writing, the more convinced she is that if Liz had lived, she'd be one of Jamaica's best-known writers—such a disastrous loss all around.

Flora, not feeling too steady on her feet, sits back down. "When me die, this exactly what me want, just so, me don't want no funeral, don't want inna no church. Promise me you'll see to it okay?"

"But wait, who seh you dead before me?"

"Well, if you lef before me, den me will see to whatever you did tell me you did want. Come nuh, we make a pact here and now!" Flora sticks out her thumb for Lilac to press, but Lilac ignores it.

"And what if we dead same time?"

"Punky get stuck wid dat one!"

There have been some very humorous stories told about Milton, his love of drinking, dancing, and damsels. And his cursed smoking. But Flora was taken aback by how many of his silent, and she would add cowardly, colleagues from print, radio, and television showed up to pay their sincere respects to Milt the Lion. Many got extremely emotional, and Flora wonders if maybe it is a mixture of guilt and the horror of exposure. Milton isn't there to cover for them anymore. The huge father tree in the forest has been cut down, and the little saplings are shaking in the breeze.

Flora enjoyed hearing Mark McKensie, who was his earnest, charming self, telling stories as a young journalist, starting straight out of high school, how scandalized he had been by Milton when he had been assigned as his assistant. Brought up a good Catholic altar boy, he had to get used to the expansive vocabulary of multi-lingual expletives that would fly out of Milton's mouth. He spoke of traveling with Milton on numerous occasions across the island and realizing both how well known and well loved he was; people would shout out "Milt the Lion" when they recognized him and would stop the car to talk to him. They were late wherever they went because Milton never rushed anyone who wanted to talk with him and listened respectfully to what they had to say. McKensie said that one of the reasons Milton always knew everything that was going on was because he had such good sources.

The man on the street was his source, and that was every street in Jamaica!

But it was Natasha Silo who surprised Flora. Natasha, not silent like the rest of them, but still a nice, respectable lady journalist who knows her place, who, at least in public, is usually deferential and nonconfrontational. Well, Natasha came out punching and kicking. She declared that, yes, admittedly, no one can fill the enormous shoes that Milton has vacated, and, yes, they all feel intimidated and overwhelmed when they look up at the massive mountain that faces them, but when a giant falls, many must rise up to take his place, and she for one intends to have the good duppy of Milton Brown as her companion when she goes into battle.

She encouraged her colleagues to take their work more seriously and not be cowed by the intolerable defamation laws left over from British colonial rule that gags and strangles the press's ability to do their work. She said she is emboldened, not just by the spirit of Milt the Lion that she is taking on as her very own ancestral guide, but also by Flora's institute that will soon be starting up. She, Natasha Silo, will definitely be there from day one to join with Flora and others to see that the rights of Jamaicans are no longer trampled upon and that the Jamaican environment is no longer treated like some inexhaustible gift from Massa God for us to selfishly do with as we please. She will be there to see that journalists' sources are protected, that people who stand up to power are not intimidated, and she will no longer be repeating lies. If that means losing her job, so be it, because she will be gladly working for the Institute.

Her final message to her bredren and sistren was this: Be not dismayed, Milt the Lion is not gone, he will always be here right by our side, holding our hand, looking over our shoulder, making funny faces at us, and we can all follow in the path he has forged for us. And so let all be hereby forewarned, Natasha Silo wants the world to know she is as of today Silo the Lioness! At that, the place broke out into raucous applause, simulated gunshots, shouts of Jah Rastafari, hooting, hollering, and belly laughs.

Chapter Thirty-Three

Flora has Jamaican journeys on her mind. Another poem she read at Milton's memorial is an ode to the now-defunct train that Milton had so enjoyed riding and fervently campaigned first against its demise and then for its return:

Hartlands/Heartlands

The flash of sound across
The city streets, the train
Shunting miles away ——-

Shoulder against the warm wall
I dreamt of trains that crossed
Our little country:
    Bushy Park
    Grange Lane
    Hartlands
        Spanish Town
        Olden Harbour
May Pen
Four Paths
        Kendall....

CHAPTER THIRTY-THREE

After that, the summer stop
For Spauldings,
The stations are not so
Easily recalled
But certainly there
Were also
    Frankfield
    Siloh
        Mount Pellier
            Cambridge
                Mo Bay

The screech the flash
The whistle would wake me.

It was from Milton that she'd learned the railroad's history. In 1845, when construction on the railway started, it was the first in the world to be built outside of Europe and North America, and after Canada the second to be built in the British Empire. In 1992, after decades of decline, public rail came to a complete halt, and despite years of plans, pronouncements, and public relations stunts, there is still no functioning passenger rail system in Jamaica, and entire sections have been sold as scrap metal. But, she heard on the news that a short part of the train system, from Spanish Town to Linstead, had been restored. She's sorry Milton won't be around to ride that train. She will have to ride it for him.

Flora tries to recall details from the only time she took the train. She was about seven. She's quite hazy about the trip, which might have been an outing to some sort of camp with her Brownie troop (she had for a very short time been a Brownie and later even more briefly a Girl Guide). But she knows they took the train to Montego Bay from Kingston, that they left very early in the morning, and at one point stopped because there were cows on the track. She also remembers the train being on a single track and reversing, but maybe she has made it all up.

Whenever Flora passes the once grand wooden station, she glances to see how far into neglect and decrepitude it has sunk. It is a wistful feeling she always has when she wanders through downtown Kingston, registering the historic names, Gold Lane, Rum Lane, Water Lane, Prince of Wales Street, King, Queen, Duke Streets, Tower Street, on and on, each name a repository of way too much. Inhaling the choking smells of sewage, urine, garbage rotting, fires burning, and automobile exhaust, she passes abandoned lots and crumbling buildings and ponders what it is so deeply in us that the only architecture we seem to care for are churches, hotels, mansions, plantation "great houses," bars, malls, and office buildings. We have none of the fetish for maintaining historic structures that so pervades the Spanish, French, and Dutch colonies where there is always the carefully preserved old town, Viejo San Juan, La Habana Vieja, Santo Domingo Viejo. No, in Jamaica, Old Kingston was long ago surrendered to New Kingston.

Flora pores over the map of Jamaica, looking at the places that she will go on the Milton Pilgrimage. She writes down some of her favorite place names: Galleon Harbour, Content Village, Gutters, Scotland Gate, Ginger House, Redlight, Above Rocks, Bog Walk, Ham Walk, Bellas Gate, Buck Up, Milk River, Nine Turns, White Shop, Crooked River, Old England, Bull Savannah, Spur Tree, Pepper, Wait a Bit, Barbecue Bottom, Burnt Savannah, Me no Send - You no Come, Sherwood Content, Silent Hill, Quick Step, Lovely Point, Cashew, Guinea Corn, Macca Tree, Giddy Hall, New Roads, Cash Hill, Rising Sun, Savanna-la-Mar, Fish River. She doubts that Fish River has any fish in it, but maybe she should go investigate!

She thinks of President Klein's story about his idyllic days in Portland. She knows that it leaves out a whole chunk of history, dispossessed people from rural areas migrating to Kingston or abroad, fleeing starvation, low wages, exploitation, and a lack of modern amenities that they were taught are evidence of civilization and when absent, proof of savagery. And she knows that the caller to McKensie's radio show was right, that it is those who already have too much, who have already consumed more than their share, who have the luxury of calling for conservation. Still, Klein's Portland encounter was very close to her own childhood experiences: hiking up by Mill Bank into fertile hills and valleys, sleeping over at the ranger lodge, drinking water straight from springs, seeing the rivers and seas full of life. But in her very own lifetime, she has witnessed this collapse. She knows the land was already compromised from when she was a child; the sugar, coffee, banana plantations, and bauxite and limestone mining have been deforesting and poisoning the place for a very long time. But if ecosystems were in so much better shape when she was a child, imagine how they had been hundred years before she was born, and how unimaginable it will be hundred years after she has died. Not even a hundred years—ten, twenty, fifty. It is this knowledge that has fed her profound sadness, her debilitating grief, and driven her to exhaustion these many years.

Jerome will be their driver as Flora continues her driving strike. The jeep is packed with everything they could possibly need, including tent and sleeping gear. They even have a coal pot to cook on. They also have a cooler full of drinks and prepared food, as well as dry goods. Is it possible to gain weight on a road trip? And, they will have to stop to taste the fare along the way—it's only reasonable to "let off" some money in the communities you traverse, and what would a road trip be without stopping to eat, drink, and chat with the locals, talk with total strangers? Flora smiles at Jerome and thinks, *Well, you said when you heard me on the radio you'd like to travel around the island with me. Let's see how long you stick to that desire!* If ever there is a test of a new relationship, traveling together for the first time in a small jeep crammed with stuff should be it.

According to Flora's travel plan, the first destination is Milton's birthplace just off the road between Wait a Bit and Stettin in South Trelawny, and second is Clark's Town, where he spent the latter part of his childhood. The route they will take is determinedly not straight, direct, or the quickest, neither does it make any particular sense, nor does it closely mirror any of Milton's own trips. That would require they go along the perimeter of the island, and from Negril to past Ocho Rios would mean traversing the tourist corridor, so that is out. Instead, they will primarily stay in the interior of the island, traveling along narrow mountain roads that curve and twist, and go up and down, and half the time, even when you pass a welcome Seventh Day Adventist sign that names the spot you are driving through, you have no idea where you are.

Flora and Jerome depart in the dark at five in the morning, drive through Spanish Town (Flora regretting that it is too dark to see anything, because she has skirted the old capitol ever since the completion of the very expensive Spanish Town bypass toll road, built and owned by the French, that speeds her away from traffic), go north up to Bog Walk, and then veer west off the beaten track into the mountains. Flora has only been to Milton's birthplace once when they were fighting bauxite mining plans for Cockpit Country. They had been to a community meeting in Albert Town, then after the meeting, drove a few miles, parked by the side of the road, and walked up a steep hill on a narrow foot path (Milton huffing and puffing,), but his ancestral little wooden house had been replaced by an equally small concrete house. There were about seven people living in it. Milton thought they might be relatives but wasn't sure.

Flora and Jerome stop at Lookout to stretch and have breakfast: banana porridge kept warm in a thermos and pancakes with some of Chang's maple syrup that Flora has exercised amazing discipline not to have already consumed. They are heading into Cockpit Country via Manchester, not the way she had gone with Chang, which was Accompong to Maroon Town via Mocho. They continue west, hitting the towns of Frankfield, Spaldings, and Christiana, then they turn to the north, and by nine are able to celebrate their arrival in Wait a Bit, where they decide it is as good a time as ever to get out of the car to "rest and be grateful."

As they take a stroll through the small, well-kept town, stopping to take their picture by the Wait a Bit sign outside the tidy, blue and white police station, Flora gets Jerome to talk about his family. He says he can't remember his mother; well, he can't remember what she looked like apart from photos, but he thinks he remembers the sound of her voice, because he sometimes hears her talking to him. She sounds a bit like Ingrid but gentler, more shy. But he always feels her love for him, that he knows. At this, Flora buries her face in Jerome's chest right by his heart. She has read Liz's diaries and knows just how much Jerome meant to her.

When she gives Jerome the Liz book, will it help him or harm him? Will it fill in missing pieces or raise questions about things that have never worried him before? She hadn't thought about this possibility. If he reads about how much his mother loved her little baby boy, will that make him miss her in a way he does not now? Maybe she shouldn't give him the book at all, maybe it should really just be for Lilac and Ingrid, or maybe it's just for Lilac. She has no idea how to decide. She turns the subject to Fontaine, and they joke about trapping him, not letting him leave when he comes in a little over a week. Jerome clearly likes his father and is proud of him. Flora worries about what Fontaine would make of the Liz book. She hadn't thought of that either. It's probably best he doesn't see it.

They leave Wait a Bit, and after about two miles, Flora starts looking out for Milton's home. She's having a hard time remembering where it is, seems like a number of landmarks are gone, wasn't there a big cotton tree on that corner, or is it further? Oh to have a sign that says "Milton Brown Born Here." She's about to tell Jerome she thinks they've gone too far and they'd better turn around when she notices a hedge of red hibiscus flowers that jolts her memory, and then she sees the path, but it's no longer a little goat path, it's been paved. And as they pull to the side and get out, they see a massive retaining wall against the side of the hill and a bright pink mansion almost completed, about three stories high, and like a wedding cake, filled with multiple loops, arches, and columns.

"Bumbaclaat, returning resident!"

Jerome's exclamation would seem to be true. Flora guesses someone, maybe a cousin of Milton's, upon retiring has returned from England, and is letting everyone know that he made something of his life. Yes, he slaved away every day in the filth of the London Underground, or the Sheffield Railroad, or the Liverpool Docks, but he is no longer a "dutty country bwoy." He now drinks Earl Grey, wears socks, and listens to the BBC all day long. They walk up the pathway trying to see if they can glimpse the Milton home that had gone from wood to concrete, but from where they stand they can't see anything but the imposing mansion. They look out and see littered like so many mushrooms after some toxic disaster, a mansion here, a mansion there, in various stages of construction. Flora wishes Milton was with them to make one of his vivid comments—he'd probably use the words *jackasses*, *ninnies*, and *poppyshow*. Flora does her best Milton imitation, and she and Jerome standing precariously half way up the steep hillside, hold on to each other and laugh till their knees buckle.

"Boogie, I really don't think Milton would want to be here, and no point going to Clark's Town neither, but come, me know exactly where would make him happy." And with that, Flora takes Jerome's hand to go back down to the jeep.

They drive north into Cockpit Country along roads by name only. Burnt Hill "road," a hardened one-lane track, precariously hugging the side of the mountain above Barbecue Bottom, the flat floor of the very deep ravine, was built by the British in the nineteenth century from compacted stones that now are mainly covered in grass. Flora is having flashbacks of driving Chang on even worse precipice-taunting roads high up in Rio Grande. They stop frequently to look into the deep valley, the mountains rising on the other side, and everywhere the sinkholes and cockpits that give the landscape its name. The clouds swirl close by and cling to the curves of the limestone mounds. Except for a few patches of cultivation, everything is densely forested. They can hear and see flocks of green parrots with rainbow-colored tails.

From that excitement, they bump onto what might have had asphalt at some point in its history, but now is a rutted, dusty road, with sections that are entirely washed out. They slow down to a crawl whenever encountering people so as not to cover them in dirt. Flora is overjoyed when they reach a paved road, no matter how thin the veneer, because her backside is sore from being pitched about, and her back feels seriously out of alignment. They get as far as Duanvale and then start to circle back south toward Windsor into the depths of Cockpit Country.

They go along a narrow road with rows of trees on both sides, making Flora think it must have been a plantation, then the line of trees end, and there is an open grassy area with a very large poinciana tree covered in bromeliads. At the tree, they turn onto a dirt track at the end of which they alight at the source of the Martha Brae River. Flora never loses her awe at the miracle of how liquid oozes out of a rock to become a pool of emerald green, follows gravity tumbling over stones, first a low, steady flow of water, then becoming a river that, if left alone, not dammed, not diverted, not siphoned off, will flow stronger, deeper, wider all the way to the sea.

Flora wades into the water until it is over her waist and then dives and swims to the deep part of the pool, where a shaft of light breaks through the canopy. She floats on her back looking up through the leaves into the sky. She can hear native woodpeckers going to work on hollow trunks. She and Milton had come here, and he was the one to show her the woodpecker. They were walking along the road, he stopped and shushed her, and there it was with its red head and black body pecking away. She swims back to the shallows, her body grateful for the break from dust, grime, and constant jarring. Jerome is setting up camp for the night. He has the coal pot going so they can heat up their soup for dinner. It will get dark down in the hollow long before the sun sets, so it's best to get as much done while the day is still bright. Flora looks forward to twilight and the swarms of bats that will be flitting up and down the river.

When the camp is set, the soup is warming, and Jerome has found some bush to burn at nightfall to keep the mosquitoes away, they get a bucket, liquid soap, and washrags and take turns washing each other. Standing at a distance from the water's edge so as not to dirty the river, one soaps up while the other hauls the water and pours it. Jerome spills a whole bucket over her head so she can wash her hair. Flora is reminded of her mother bathing her as a child, pretending they were at Dunn's River Falls, using a Rum n Raisin ice cream container to pour water over her, while she splashed in the bath, squealing with delight.

After they bathe, Flora gets some of Milton, and they go to where the pool overflows to become a stream filled with rapids. They walk into the shallow water, trying not to bang their toes or trip on the river rocks, and follow to where the stream narrows, the water now deep enough to look like the Martha Brae River. Flora laughs at the thought of Milton bumping against bamboo rafts piloting tourists down the river, the captain telling tales of Martha Brae, the witch, and what she did to murder the Spanish. "What rubbish, what absolute rot!" is what he would say. "I really wish they wouldn't tell people such crap. Why don't they ever tell them something that matters? Like how many millions of Tainos and Africans lost their lives so you can be lounging on a bloody raft!" Ah Milton, of course that's not what people want to hear. But Flora isn't sure they want to hear about witches and murder either! Flora pours out some of Milton's ashes into a rapid eddy that swirls before plunging down a short waterfall into the river below. "Go Milton, go, make your way to the sea, we'll see you in Falmouth tomorrow!"

Chapter Thirty-Four

In the late afternoon, Flora and Jerome walk through Falmouth holding hands like tourists. They would take a tour if one could be taken, but those are only available when the cruise ships are docked, and despite all development efforts being focused on the new pier—the minister has said only the roads that are needed for the development will get attention—who knows how often ships actually will arrive, once, twice, thrice a week? There jutting out far into the sea, where once had been nothing but seawater, is the brand new Historic Falmouth, a concrete complex of shops, restaurants, and entertainment for cruise-ship visitors—even a replica pirate ship with staged battles. The fishing beach is now a paved parking lot with imported palm trees and trolleys standing ready to transport passengers.

The courthouse is no longer cream-colored, but canary yellow, and has the colors of the Jamaican flag embossed onto its crown. The color choices confuse Flora, but since the original courthouse that was built in 1815 was damaged in a fire in 1926, and this one an inexact replica, why get hung up on verisimilitude? Why not paint it red to keep the duppies away? Don't they know that Cliff and Milton are about to haunt them?

Flora is overjoyed that Mason will be moving home to Jamaica as Director of the Institute's legal division. She pictures him in his Supreme Court wig and robes, looking over his glasses with a steely glare at some official whose memory has suddenly evaporated: "But Mr. X, you seem unable to recall anything pertaining to the murder of Cliff Edwards. Even when I read your very own words to you, you are unable to recognize them. We may need to have you examined by a medic. But for now, let us start with breakfast, sir, can you recall what you had this morning for breakfast?" Flora thinks it would be wonderfully operatic to have Cliff's murder case tried in the Falmouth courthouse.

They drive over to the mouth of the Martha Brae, where the river enters the eastern edge of Falmouth harbor at Glistening Waters, and walk alongside the river, startling herons into flight. The growth is too thick to get very far. They promise each other to come back and kayak up the river, though Flora requests a tow; she'll attach her kayak to Jerome's, and he can pull her up the river. She wonders out loud, "You think Milton reach?" Jerome is emphatic, "Yeah man, long time!"

They drive into the community of Rock to the little dock that holds three fishing canoes. They can't find their friend Monty who will be transporting them. His daughter says he "soon come." They throw sleeping gear (they aren't taking the tent, they figure on the beach, it won't rain like it did in Cockpit Country), snacks, and water into his boat, and then they walk back the way they came, to the corner bar and cook shop, to wait for darkness when they will boat across the phosphorescent lagoon and spend the night near where Cliff's body was dumped.

At Benny's Bar, Flora is recognized as the Environment Lady, and as word spreads, people start congregating. Several also recognize Jerome as the diver who had the fight with the gunman. No kidding, did she hear that right? "The fight with the gunman?" Is that how Jerome hurt his shoulder? Several men come up to Jerome to shake his hand, big him up, and buy him and Flora drinks. Did Jerome kill the gunman, or is he lurking, waiting for revenge? Flora knows she will have to wait for answers to her questions. Several fishermen come in to chat with her about how the "fishning mashing up!" and how much they enjoyed hearing Maas Sam on McKensie's show. The bartender says he has started saving the plastic bottles and not flinging them, and he hears someone is starting up some recycling thing in Mobay. All the fishermen say they're sick and tired of pulling up plastic in their nets.

Monty comes in looking for them and joins in the conversation, which is now raging about the cruise ship pier, the dumping up of the old fishing beach (they are not pleased with the new location of the fishermen's co-op and are now being charged a fee to park their boats), the dredging of the harbor (why would you be stupid enough to choose a shallow harbor prone to silting to park the largest cruise ships in the world?), the damaging wave action now that the reef is gone (has no one noticed that the old seawalls are collapsing?), the loss of the fish nurseries (they need bigger boats with stronger engines so they can go fish in Cuban waters), and they all concur that the luminescent lagoon will be next to go. Since many combine fishing with taking visitors out on tours, they will be financially ruined: no fish, no glow, no money. Their women have to be out in the hot sun under tarpaulin selling, because the Parish Council has mashed down the market and not built the new one that had been promised. They bulldozed the people's homes and dumped them in the hills where they have no water or electricity and have to shit in plastic bags or in the bushes. All so tour buses have a nice pretty place to park. It is with resounding agreement they articulate that development in Jamaica is only for the Big Man, and them, the Little Man, can expect nothing. Without a doubt, Milton is fulminating—Milton is in the room!

At around eight-thirty, a group of about fifteen stumble out of the bar and head over to Monty's, where they start up a dominoes game and continue talking till almost midnight. Jerome and Flora have never played dominoes together, but when they team up and blank Monty and his brother Melville, the place erupts in such pandemonium that Flora knows poor Monty and Melville will never live this loss down. It will become part of Rock's folklore, a tale told over and over.

There is no breeze. Monty says they can row over without any problem, so they move their things over to Monty's father's old rowboat, *Black Power*. Monty and Melville insist on coming with them. The brothers are friends with the security guard at the site and will see that Flora and Jerome are left alone. Despite efforts at boarding up the unfinished hotel villas, several are now occupied (has a roof, has some walls, why not?), and the brothers will sleep in one of those. Monty and Melville row in precise union. As their paddles dip in the water, they glow, the sides of the boat, their wake, her hand in the water, all create a luminescence. Flora slowly opens her palm as she trails her hand on top of the water, and there he is, Milt the Lion, lit up in the dark of night.

The morning light blazes from the east, and Flora is wide awake, but Jerome is sprawled out on the beach fast asleep—he's squirmed his way out of his sleeping bag and has a pillow over his head. Poor thing, he must be exhausted from all the driving, and really they consumed way too much alcohol. Flora can't remember drinking so much rum in her life. Every time someone bought her a rum, she had to find some other thing to mix it with. She knows for sure she will not try rum and cranberry juice ever again.

Flora is pleased with her progress toward neo-hippiedom. She's turned off her phone and spent a significant portion of the day naked, or near naked, by some magical body of water. Jamaica, Jamaica, how beautiful you are! She walks along the shore in the shallows looking for an opening to go in. The sea grass is very thick and healthy; she walks carefully so as not to step on sea urchins. As her feet splash, little fish dart out of the way. She will not think about what will happen if and when construction on the resort starts up again, but she knows that the broken reef and the pollution from the cruise ships will be inescapably bad for this shoreline. As if trying to ward off this knowledge, she makes sure not to look in the direction of Falmouth.

Flora finds a place to submerge. The seawater isn't very deep and, unlike the cold river water she was enjoying the day before, is already starting to get warm. As she doggie paddles in her wet blue world, Flora replays her Falmouth outing and notes that some of the mysteries have been solved. The Welcome to Historic Falmouth sign is still there, even more sun-bleached and ragged than before. The many acres of destroyed wetlands, which for a year she had marveled at what their possible destiny could be, are sewage ponds for the port. The mangroves were to be replanted, but there is no evidence any have, and no, Falmouth will not be connected to the sewage line, and so they can expect more drainage problems for the town, but the port will have the largest sewage capacity outside of a major metropolis. She also saw a new pipe running along the road, she guesses bringing water to the ships and businesses on the pier, but from where, the Martha Brae?

Ignoring the No Trespassing signs, she and Jerome walked onto the dumped up wetlands. Though the sewage ponds aren't anywhere near ready, Jerome thought he'd inaugurate them by taking a piss. As they wandered, he showed her, scattered everywhere, what had recently been live coral and explained that the long, thick metal tubes piled on top of each other alongside the construction staging area were the dredging pipes that had sucked everything up and spat it out onto the land. In addition to uncrushed coral, they found shells of all sorts. The ones that distressed Flora the most were the baby conch shells.

What had been wetlands with streams, ponds, run-off from the Martha Brae, grasses, mangroves, trees, and lots of birds, is now completely naked, the soil cracked, dry, and blowing about, as large trucks keep bringing more dump, and road construction vehicles build a road through the swamp. Past the sewage ponds are big tanks for holding and processing the sewage and, beyond them, the paved staging area for the tour buses. Do they really need so much space? A once- or twice-a-week invasion, then what?

Flora thinks of the rafters out in Port Antonio who mob anyone who comes anywhere near them. Port Antonio was the first of the cruise ports, but the ships don't stop there anymore, and the rafters have no business. When she took Chang on the river, their captain explained there remain the same number of registered raft captains, plus a large number of illegal unregistered rafters and no cruise ships. They have to wait in a queue for their turn. He gets a set of passengers about once a month if he is very lucky. The rest of the time he cultivates his land. Surely, this is an unfeasible way to make a living. What of all the people who will rush to Falmouth to hustle? What are they leaving behind, and what are they bringing?

When Flora gets back, she finds Jerome up. He's stacked all their stuff in a pile and sits leaning against a tree, eating an energy bar. Flora would like to jump him but figures they'd better go find Monty and Melville since they are most likely making them late for work. After kissing hello, Flora rubs Jerome's neck and shoulders. "Boogie you okay? You must be wiped out!" She sits down beside him and takes a bar he offers her.

"Bwoy me feel well mash up! Why me don't love hang wid rummists! Cyan tek di rum."

"Me neither. Go in the sea you'll feel much better."

"Went already. But we should go find M n M—they probably waiting for us."

They gather up their gear, and as they walk toward the aborted villas, Flora broaches the alarming topic. "So Jerome, what is this about you and gunman?" She is sure her neurotic fears were valid after all. But Jerome is very matter of fact, as he tells his account without any embellishments or histrionics. Flora takes this as proof that Lilac must have had a hand in raising him!

"Remember that time when me come to find out who kill Cliff? One gunman drape me up, by Monty where we was, just by the boats, there. Was getting in the canoe with my diving gear and he point a gun at me. Me kick the gun out of him hand and kick him in him face and him fall off the pier. Monty and everyone come running. The eedyat cyan swim. And when him try get back on the dock, them kick him, and use the oars to bang him, and don't let him get out the water. After awhile cyan see him no more, must be drown him drown."

Good old Jamaican justice. Apparently, this gunman had been terrorizing the community for a long time, and they were sick of him. He had raped Melville's fourteen-year-old daughter, and probably other girls as well, but they couldn't retaliate because he was protected by the usual suspects. With gun, Don and Big Man protection he thought he was untouchable—he was that arrogant, that foolish. No one was sorry to see him drown. Jerome isn't certain whether he is the one who shot Cliff, maybe, could be. Flora doesn't see how they can bring Cliff's murderer to justice if he's already suffered his death sentence! This is going to really complicate the case, but wow, Lilac was right when she said Jerome knows how to take care of himself and isn't a little Uptown Boy who will need rescuing.

"Jesus Jerome, so this how you hurt you shoulder?"

"Yeah. When me go fi kick him, mi tank drop and that jar me shoulder. Plus me fall over, lose balance when the tank drop."

"And then with a torn shoulder you get in the boat and go diving for hours, right?"

"Well dunno about hours, but me shoot what, one tape? So was in the water all together about hour and a bit."

"But boogie, you must have been in such pain!"

"Nah man, didn't feel one rass ting."

As they pause at the point where Cliff's body had washed up, Flora is disturbed by the difficulty of truly caring about someone you don't know. Yes, you care, but it's in the abstract, it's theoretical. Soon as Jerome heard Cliff had been murdered, he chose to act, to investigate, to take a moral stand—he immediately showed that he cared. She had no such reaction. She had wanted Jerome to stay with her, sitting together on the couch telling stories while listening to music. Pathetic! No wonder he had cussed her out as a dilettante.

But she had never met Cliff, didn't know him. He was just someone who was supposed to feed her information so she could make her case against everyone who was lying; just another person, multitudes of whom contact her—off record, so as not to lose their job, or be blacklisted, or suffer awful consequences—of some environmental horror, some secret, some government-sanctioned criminality they have witnessed or partaken in, that she, Flora, is to stand up in public and reveal, while they hide safely in the shadows.

But Cliff was flesh and blood to Jerome. They were buddies, literally diving buddies, but also friends outside of diving. Therefore, to Jerome, Cliff was more than a conduit, a conveyer of facts, and certainly not another murder statistic. Flora flushes as she thinks about how differently she would have felt if it had been Milton or Mason, or Lilac, or Jerome, or Maas Sam. She would have been inconsolable; she would mek up whole heap a noise demanding that everyone go to the end of the earth to find the culprit. But, even if it wasn't someone she loved deeply, say it was someone she just knew in passing, like Mousy, or one of the windshield boys she gives money to on occasion, she would still feel something, her tears would have a name attached to them. She watches the way Jerome holds his body, as he stands slightly rocking at the water's edge, his eyes closed. Then she shuts her eyes and tries to imagine Cliff.

Flora had run into Natasha Silo at Environment First's fundraiser and invited her home to meet with Jerome, so they could share hypotheses and findings, and Jerome could show her his footage that backs up his claims. When Natasha showed up that night, she declined food or drink and instead launched into what felt to Flora like a confession.

"Over a year now Cliff contact me. First him email me few times, then him start call me pretty regular. At first he wanted me to write a piece about the coral transplanting. He said they weren't doing it right, and it wasn't going to work." Jerome interjects that he has footage of dead coral that he'll show her that will prove Cliff was correct. "Yeah, that's great, me have some as well. Cliff did send me some video clips and photos. And then him start copy the monitoring reports him was doing and send them to me." Natasha explains that Cliff had double duty as both a diver for the transplantation and a diver monitoring whether the project was proceeding according to permitting requirements and environmental protection standards. So, one day he would dive and break off coral to be transplanted, and then in a month he would be writing a report on whether he and his colleagues had handled that coral properly. Once the coral had been transplanted, there was no further "monitoring."

"Unfuckingbelievable. You really can't make this shit up!" Flora states the obvious, and Natasha continues with her narrative. Cliff had told her that without submission for approval, there were changes in the original dredging plans, and a larger percentage of the reef was destroyed. The acceptable size of corals for removal was arbitrarily lowered so that they could simply use huge portions of the reef as fill for the wetlands. Whole sections were blasted that had not been slated, and dredging proceeded earlier than stated before transplantation was finished.

Apart from his accident, which Cliff always thought was deliberate, the thing that really upset Cliff was the entire month when all monitoring agents for the government were told to stay away and not monitor. That time period made Cliff wonder if all sorts of shady things took place: could there have been dumping of toxic waste, dumping containers that had brought supplies that they couldn't bother to barge back out? And he suspected this was when certain contraband arrived in large quantities, disguised as construction materials and equipment.

Flora, who used the Access to Information Act to get all officially mandated monitoring data, knows from reading pre- and post-blackout reports that some of the issues about the reef destruction and dredging did get documented, but much didn't, and certainly no illicit activities were reported.

Jerome concurs with Natasha's reportage, "Just so, Cliffy did tell me."

Natasha looks stricken. "What is so upsetting is me never help him! Me did try talk to the project Big Man dem, but when them assure me everything was above board and according to proper permitting, me never really pursue it more than so."

Flora thinks of all the upbeat media stories on Falmouth with the Mayor, the Prime Minister, any number of government officials, project supervisors, representatives from the cruise-ship industry, trumpeting the wonderful economic benefits that would rain upon Falmouth and Trelawny. When environmental issues were raised, they claimed that everything humanly possible was being done to make the enormous and complicated project environmentally sound and that the various environmental protection obligations were actually delaying the process by many months and endangering its success. Once again, environmentalists were the enemy, were to blame if Jamaicans did not get jobs, had no money in their pockets!

Natasha is very distressed that she did not write the articles Cliff had wanted her to write. She did not alert the public. She admits it's not a good excuse, but she had been repeatedly told by her editors and publishers that her articles must be balanced, that she always needs to counter one claim with another, and she just didn't see how she could show Cliff to be right and everyone else wrong. Natasha starts to cry, "The ting that really shame me, the ting dat haunt me every day is me feel seh is me kill Cliff."

"But wait, is how you kill Cliff?" Flora doesn't mean to sound callous, but surely not informing the public is not the same thing as shooting someone in the head and tossing him into the sea.

"Well, when me start ask round to try verify what Cliff tell me, don't you tink seh certain people realize Cliff a cause trouble and that mek him born fi dead?"

CHAPTER THIRTY-FOUR

Flora can't think of what to say to make Natasha feel better. Should she say that no one knows for sure who killed Cliff or why and that we are all complicit? This is true, but some are more complicit than others. There is whoever pulled the trigger and shot Cliff at very close range through his left temple. There is whoever hired that person to pull the trigger. There is whoever thought it wise that Cliff no longer walk this earth, and suggested to whomever that maybe they should hire whomever to remove Cliff. And then there are the rest of us: the ones who have become accustomed to this normality, the ones who know what is going on and say nothing, see nothing, hear nothing. The ones who are notified repeatedly in writing, by phone, in person, with substantiating data and documents, and who do nothing, placate, put off with platitudes, hide and destroy the damning facts. The ones who believe that sacrifices must be made and that certain people just have to accept their role in society. Your little house got bulldozed? Your fishing beach got dumped up? Your restaurant got demolished? Your swimming area is no longer available to you? Your market no longer exists? Your wetlands are now dry? Your fish nurseries are now destroyed? Your history has been erased? Your life has been taken? Well, someone has to be sacrificed to the god of progress and so very sorry it happens to be you. Yes, Flora thinks, we are all complicit, but some of us are more complicit than others, and time will tell who will be culpable and if anyone will be held to account.

Chapter Thirty-Five

Flora is trying to not feel depressed by the image that clings to her of Cliff being dumped in the sea to become crab food, his swollen body washing up onto the eroding sand in front of one of the half-built villas and getting stuck in the mesh fence erected by the developers. Nor to feel depressed about the whole specter of people, including Jerome, allowing a man to drown, but really what should they have done? Use his gun and shoot him? Take him to the Don, the police, the Big Man, to have justice meted out?

After hearing his gunman story and seeing him mourning Cliff, Flora feels very tender toward Jerome, for his hard knocks life, for the burden of all he has carried on his not-so-aged shoulders, and so has given up her driving strike and, despite his protests, is driving them to their next destination, an even more depressing place than the one they are leaving. And she's changed her mind; they will go through Milton's Clark's Town after all, and Jerome can discharge some of Milton into the air as they drive across his town! They will drive from Rock through Clark's Town, Stewart Town, out of Trelawny, and into the Dry Harbour mountains, a region Flora knows all too sickeningly well.

CHAPTER THIRTY-FIVE

Almost all of St. Ann has bauxite deposits, and the Dry Harbour mountains are a major source of bauxite mining. Flora has studied the area to death. A third of her dissertation and two chapters of her book focus on mining in these districts, places with strange names: Tobolski, Philadelphia, Alexandria, Iverness. But they are going to just outside of Gibraltar, to a place with the most lovely of names: Lime Tree Garden.

They pass crater after crater, pit after dug-out pit, and mound after piled-up mound; the red earth stains everything so that even something brand new looks decrepit. The degraded soil can't grow anything, so the "reclaimed" lands are just endless grasslands and shrubbery, with the occasional sports and community centers. The bauxite companies are fond of football fields in the land they have hollowed out, so you will be standing looking down into what had once been a hill and find a field with goal posts and sometimes even a small clubhouse. After all, providing males—especially beloved to politicians, "the youths on the corner"—with money and recreational activities is what development is all about.

They drive into what unmistakably had once been a thriving community, homes with yards and fertile soil to grow food. Houses with delicate details of fretting, or carefully placed porches and verandas, that reveal the work of skilled carpenters and builders, but they have been abandoned for decades, windows shattered, paint peeling, walls fractured, roofs leaking. They stroll over to a large yard with a cluster of lime trees; only the foundation of the house remains and steps that lead to what had been the entrances. Flora leads Jerome to three graves that lie side by side. Moss has grown over the stones, and the names are difficult to read, but Flora knows who they are—her mother's family, the Turners, come from Lime Tree Garden—this home belonged to Mrs. Scott, her mother's primary school principal, and the graves are of Mrs. Scott's parents, Douglas and Agatha, and her sister Agnes. What had been the property next door, but is now a crater at the edge of the graves, belonged to Milton's maternal family, the Maises. Flora's mother's family home is up the road a bit, right where they are still extracting bauxite, a gaping chasm where the huge machines dig into the earth and pull out her insides. When the bauxite company bought all the land and they had to relocate, May was sent to Kingston to finish her schooling. She lived there with her maiden aunt Flora; all the rest of May's family migrated to England. Some of the people in the region took plots of land far away in Cockpit Country or moved to towns, but most got on a boat and left, and land that had supplied generations of Jamaicans with food was lost.

She doesn't want to go over to the pit; she doesn't want to look in. She doesn't want to see the machines, hear the jeers of the men at work. But she wants to show Jerome where she comes from, where her mother didn't get to complete her growing up, and why she never talks about her mother's family; they were gone, they were a hole in the ground, she never knew them. Half of herself had been dug up and sent away so that others could land on the moon, could explode rockets in the air, could live the space age, could eat their TV dinners and their fast-food wrapped in aluminum foil, could have modern, clean, convenient lives, so that we all could long for buildings that touch the sky and for fast cars. "Donkey seh world no level," some of us are the sacrificed. Flora is definitely not leaving any of Milton there. She'll keep a little of him for his bench that she's having built to be placed in front of the Hope Gardens office, and the rest of his remains will go into the soil at the ground-breaking for the Milton Brown Archive.

Flora will not linger in the land of bauxite, and she refuses to get into a funk. She wants them to get to Jerome's before dark, very doable since it's just past noon. Jerome is making them sandwiches of pita bread and homemade hummus, an Ingrid special with lots of garlic. They'd managed to finish Lilac's porridge and pancakes, Chang's maple syrup, Jerome's pepper pot soup, stewed peas with spinner dumplings, and all the fruit except a watermelon that

Flora is about to slice. She gives them a high passing grade. She thinks they've done very well together. They can travel anywhere and survive very well, thank you.

"Okay boogie, we not stopping again!" Flora is on a mission and has a goal, and she floors the gas pedal. To keep from dissolving into despair, Flora avoids looking at anything but the road and keeps up a lively conversation. In light of Jerome's encounters with gunmen, she tells him about Chang's wacko mercenary who wants to be her bodyguard. A retired Marine, ex-special-forces in Afghanistan and Iraq, he'd apparently come up to Chang after her plenary and pledged his services for free. According to Chang, he'd taken off his Oakley Razor glasses so he could penetrate deep into Chang's eyes, and said (Flora does her best Clint Eastwood), "Buddy, I want you to know, that if anyone, and I mean anyone, threatens to hurt that gutsy little lady, I personally will hurt them and hurt them real bad." Jerome laughs and doesn't believe a word of it.

Has he ever shot a gun? Yes, but he doesn't too love guns. Flora confesses to having a secret attraction to guns, but she avoids them because she's certain she could easily kill someone, might even be a lurking mass murderer. She's a pretty good shot, having learned from Husband Number Two, the gun enthusiast, and considering his collection of weapons, she's lucky to have come out of that marriage alive. As befits his station in life, he is a serial murderer of many small birds, part of a macho gang of bird shooters. He insisted on dragging her along so he could show off his prowess at killing. If that was supposed to make her swoon with desire, it did quite the opposite. She would have rather fucked a vegan pastry chef any day.

They chat about Punky's upcoming fourth birthday and Espie's sixtieth. When Flora found out that Espie had given her land and guesthouse to Knowledge's two daughters, Pearl and Aisha, she'd been shocked. "But Espie, why?"

"Oh, they should own it. Foreigners should not own land in Jamaica."

"But you're a Jamaican citizen."

"It should be their own. Knowledge would happy his daughters have something. Pearl been running it so long . . . is good this way. Anyway next month me turn sixty. Time to give everything away!"

She is planning an entire year of celebrations all over the world, so they have many options for joining in the merriment. Jerome tells Flora that Espie has always been the funniest person he knows, but since hanging out with her, he thinks she's overtaking Espie in that department. Flora hopes he means funny ha-ha and not funny whacked in the brain.

They get to Bamboo and could easily turn north to Priory to take the North Coast Highway home to Jerome's, but as tempting as that might be, Flora is determined no hotels, so it's the interior all the way. She's heading to Moneague, Guys Hill, Highgate, then they can pick up the last stretch of highway that will take them to Jerome's turn-off. One of the highlights of the trip has been that they have not once gotten lost or had any squabbles over which way to go or how to read a map. Another first for any man she has ever been with! Maybe they really could do rally races together—just get Chang to retrofit the jeep so it can get like a hundred miles to a gallon of coconut oil or whatever bio-diesel-hydro-solar-powered gadgetry he can come up with. And he could get Jerome's cottage running on a tiny wind turbine and a solar panel that he could teach them to make. She will sell her home in Kingston and live in a Bedouin tent, like Chavez did after the floods in Venezuela. She is sorry that Qaddafi is no more and won't be giving away any more of those tents, though of course she doesn't need the presidential edition. She was quite comfy in Jerome's tent for two, which stayed dry in the steady Cockpit Country rain.

So yes, she can sell her home and move onto the land that they will buy in St. Mary near Jerome. Chang has spoken to the owner of the 240 acres, and he is from Boston of all places, has never lived in Jamaica, and thinks their plans for the property are just great. He will look into tax write-offs since the money will be going to a nonprofit, and he's sure they can negotiate a favorable price because he's all for education. The Jamaican owner of the sixty acres that extend along the coast wants an astronomical amount of money and has all sorts of pie-in-the-sky schemes from subdividing into acre lots for luxury housing, to getting an all-inclusive to purchase. But the coastline is mostly cliffs and very rugged, so Flora can't imagine an all-inclusive thinking it a good location. Maybe one of the boutique hotel owners might be tempted, but the road is so bad, it would take too much work to transport guests, unless they helicoptered or boated them in.

If they don't get the shoreline property, that will be a pity, though maybe there is a small lot she can buy for her tent. But the main thing is the land for agriculture and that looks very close to being secured. Lilac has already talked with Livity and Lion about getting a farmer's collective together to grow organics, including what she needs for Janice's sauces. The guesthouse only serves organic produce, and they know no other way to grow food, so it's just a matter of scale and accreditation. Flora wonders what the community will want to do with their trust fund. She starts to worry that there need to be stated restrictions on what you can do with the money: no large gas-guzzling vehicles, no machines that destroy nature, no pyramid schemes, no casinos, no visas, no migrating to foreign . . . damn, the list could get very long!

When they get to their turn-off, Flora pulls over and triumphantly jumps out. She has gotten them almost home in a little over two hours, all in one piece and the jeep without a single dink. They exchange high and low fives, hugs and kisses, and Jerome says, "Prof, you the boss!" Flora doesn't remind him that might one day literally be true, but he hasn't said whether he will or won't work at which or any position with the Institute, and maybe it's best he just sticks to doing his own thing.

Jerome drives the last leg. As they cross the field, Flora sees everything again like the first time: the three horses tethered by the wind-blown trees that all lean in the same direction; the mule guarding them; the little house on the point, looking out onto coral heads and islets in sea water that is calm, clear, and with the shifting light, changes colors from the lightest of green-blues to purple. And, far away, the horizon with its row of clouds marching to where, Cuba? Haiti? And further down the coast, mountain climbing upon mountain, until hidden in the sky. Surely this is the reality, and everything else a dream.

GLOSSARY OF JAMAICAN WORDS AND USAGE

The Jamaican language, popularly known as Patois, linguistically known as Jamaican Creole, and politically known as Nation Language or Jamaican, is a language that developed primarily out of the contact between Africans, predominantly from West Africa, and Europeans, predominantly from Britain, with remnants of the indigenous Arawak language, and adopted vocabulary from later arrivals in Jamaica, such as words of Hindi origin. This novel represents in dialogue a written form of the spoken Jamaican language that represents the language usage of the middle to upper-middle classes, and less frequently the speech of rural and urban working class speakers. There is a continuum in Jamaican language varieties from, on one end, that which is a separate language and mutually incomprehensible to English, and on the other end, Standard Jamaican English, a dialect of English differing in aspects of vocabulary, intonation, pronunciation and other stylistic features. Most Jamaicans code-switch between varieties of Jamaican depending on their linguistic competence and the social context in which they are speaking. There is an orthography of Jamaican that was devised by linguists Frederic Cassidy and Robert LePage, but I have chosen to use English orthography, with spelling that indicates when some variant of the Jamaican language is being spoken, for example, "ting" instead of "thing" and "dem" instead of "them."

Note on monetary exchange rate: There are instances in the novel where Jamaican money is mentioned, for example, "three million JA dollars" or "a hundred dollar bill." The Jamaican dollar devalues continuously in relation to the United States dollar, and this devaluation sometimes happens very quickly. Between writing this novel, and writing this glossary, the Jamaican dollar went from an exchange rate of about 80 to 1, to about 105 to 1. For the purpose of this novel consider a Jamaican $100 bill to be worth about 90 cents. A million Jamaican dollars therefore has much less value than might be suggested by the term million!

Vocabulary and Idioms

ackee: a fruit from West Africa primarily eaten in Jamaica (the word "ackee" is from the Akan language). It is eaten cooked. When combined with salted cod ("salt fish") it is the national dish of Jamaica.

agwan: going on—the "a" prefix makes the action continuous—*tings agwan* can mean something specific is happening/happened, or things in general are happening/happened—*nutin agwan* (nothing is going on) usually means there is no economic or social activity happening for someone or some location.

Bad Man: a term used in admiring ways in Jamaican popular music and culture signifying an ideal of masculinity similar to the admiration for the cowboy/outlaw in the American popular imaginary; a criminal, an outlaw, a trend setter and rule breaker. There is a genre of popular music that lists all the things "bad men" don't do, all which defines hyper masculinity.

bad mind: a person who is evil, malicious, corrupt, deceitful, envious, untrustworthy—a very pervasive and important concept in the Jamaican worldview.

bammy: cassava bread

batty man: male homosexual, a derogative term for a male who is perceived to be effeminate or to have sex with other males. It is also used as a general curse word or expletive much like the word "ass-hole" in the US. Part of violent anti-homosexual campaigns in Africa and the African Diaspora is the notion that no authentic person of African heritage can be a homosexual, that it is a disease and practice introduced by Europeans through colonialism.

Big Man: someone rich, important, powerful, politically, economically and socially connected, someone who controls patronage and who others are dependent upon

board house: wooden house (usually small from the days of chattel slavery)

born fi dead: one whose fate is an early violent death, one who is targeted for assassination.

brawta: bonus, extra, more than expected. For example, when shoppers buy a dozen oranges at the market they expect to get as brawta an extra orange free.

browning: a person of mixed ancestry who has enough African, or other melaninproducing heritage that means she does not appear white but "tanned" or light "brown," who counts as a "browning" is in the eye of the beholder.

bruk him neck: break his neck

Bumbo, Bumbaclaat, Rass, Rassclaat, Bloodclaat: curse words in Jamaica are often used playfully or to express surprise, concern, excitement; they are also of course used negatively to express anger, to genuinely curse someone, in argumentation and can provoke violence. Curse words are often related to parts of the body and bodily functions. In these examples they have to do respectively with buttocks, the ass/anus, and vagina. The word *claat* is the Jamaican word for cloth and signifies that which one uses to wipe one's ass in the case of *bumbaclaat* and *rassclaat*, and in the case of *bloodclaat*, the worst of curse words, refers to the cloth a woman uses when she's having her period.

but mus!: of course!

bwoy: boy—often used as an exclamation showing excitement whether positive or negative

cho: a sound that signals irritation, dissatisfaction, the stating of the obvious, and is akin to a sound made in the mouth called "kiss teeth" in Jamaica, known in other parts of the African Diaspora as "suck teeth" and various spellings of the word *tseups*.

cooya!: an exclamation of excitement—means "look here!", "look at that!"

cyan: cannot

cyan done: forever, without end

dash you weh: abandon you, desert you

dem: them; those people

dem people a bleach: people are bleaching their skin. Around the world, including Jamaica, people with dark skin use various skin lightening cosmetic products, in Jamaica this is called "bleaching" and also "rubbings" *deya:* here

Donkey seh world no level: "The donkey says the ground is not even" a Jamaican saying that means the world is unjust

drug-ists: drug dealers, drug runners, people in the illegal drug business such as transporting cocaine

duppy: ghost, spirit, someone who has died

dutty: dirty. In Jamaican you add the word *dutty* as a prefix describing someone and it is an immediate insult. I.e., *dutty country bwoy* is an epithet meaning hick. *Dutty* is also a Jamaican word derived from Twi meaning *earth, soil, ground*; as in the expression *dutty tough* meaning "the soil is hard," such as when there is drought.

dutchy: a heavy round cooking pot made from cast iron or aluminum pot for cooking

eedyat: an insulting term to call someone, an idiot, a stupid, worthless person; *eedyat ting dat* means ridiculous, absurd, wrong.

eh: ee: nuh: these are discourse markers that appear at the end of Jamaican utterances that turn them into a question, or a request for response of some kind, and indicate the interactional nature of the discourse. In the case of *nuh* and *nuh man,* the request for response is often agitated whether from excited anticipation of a response, or irritation that something is not happening quickly enough.

eh eh: signifies surprise, mild displeasure, skepticism, used to comment on something without being explicit

e'heh: yes; as a discourse marker it signals back channeling, telling your interlocutor that you are listening to them, it can signal agreement, sometimes it signals boredom or avoidance when one does not want to commit to saying anything definite.

feisty and out of order: feisty (pronounced "facety") means rude, disrespectful, improper, as does "out of order." The two together therefore make the meaning more emphatic.

fi: for, to, because

fishning mashing up: "fishing is being destroyed," fishing is no longer a viable livelihood—to "mash up" is to break, damage, destroy

fool fool: foolish, silly, stupid, ridiculous, unwise

foreign: somewhere other than Jamaica, especially places Jamaicans are known to migrate to such as the US, Canada, and the UK

go weh: "go away," "get the (expletive) out of here," "leave me alone"

hereso: here, right here

high high: very high. In Jamaican, repeat a word and it will intensify the meaning such as "clear clear," "big big," "nice nice," "bad bad," etc.

ina: in, into

Ital: in Rastafarianism close attention is paid to language usage and words are changed to express an ideological stance, such as "downpression" for "oppression." The word "I" is substituted to create new words or new understandings of words. Food is very important to Rasta culture. The Rasta ideal is vegetarianism based on natural, whole, living foods that are locally produced. *Ital* is a play on the word vital and is food that meets the Rasta ideal. It is also sometimes food that is cooked without salt, since the belief is that if you eat salt, when you die you will not return home to Africa.

jinal: con artist, trickster, fraud

ketch di breeder: catch spawning marine life

laad: Lord

lef me: "leave me alone," "stop bothering me"

let off: spend money

likle: little, small

likle bwoy: male child, small boy, childish, immature

lingah: linger, tarry, stay

Maas: comes from the word Master but not in the sense of "Massa," the white slave owner, who rules over others, but in the sense of something akin to Mr., it is used usually to refer to an older male of rural background.

Massa God: God—the term Massa (Master) in front of God is to show respect but also that God is master of all things. Father God is also a term used in Jamaica for the Judeo/Christian God.

me/mi: can mean I or my—as in *me no wan' fi go* ("I don't want to go") or *mi dear* (my dear)

mek: make/made

mek a tell you: "I'm telling you! Let me tell you".

Mummy/Nice Lady: as a sign of respect, any female of a certain age will be called "Mummy" or sometimes "Aunty." "Nice Lady" signifies that one is of a class above the speaker and usually the speaker wants something from you.

modda: mother

Mr. Chin: Jamaican's tend to call all Chinese people Chin no matter what their name might actually be

nah; no; *nah man;* emphatically no

nyam: to eat (from the African Fula/Akan languages) *nyam and run weh* means to "eat and run"—considered a rude thing to do.

Obeah woman: a female practitioner of the art and science of Obeah, originally a West African religion, it was outlawed by the British in Jamaica and is still illegal. Obeah is the ability to heal as well as harm through special knowledge of the spiritual, natural, and human worlds. An Obeah woman is someone who can perform "miracles."

one one, two two: a few, some, several

peeniewally: large flying bugs, fireflies

pickney: child/children

pon: on, upon, against

poppyshow: originates from "puppet show," now means something ridiculous

post: to not do what you said you would do, to stand someone up *rahtid:* an exclamation of excitement that can be a mild curse like "damn" and be used positively or negatively. *Rass* can also be used in this way.

Rasta/Ras: Rastafarians—members of a syncretic Jamaican religion that brings together Judeo-Christian and African religious beliefs with Pan-Africanism, Black empowerment, the belief that the Ethiopian Emperor Haile Selassie is divine, the belief in the holiness of the individual and the need to live in harmony with nature.

raw chaw: loud, uncouth, rough, uncivilized

rummists: heavy rum drinkers

Sah: Sir, previously a polite way to call an adult male, now often used playfully: Nah Sah, No Sir, emphatic as in "No way!"

scandal bag: opaque black plastic bags are called "scandal bags." It is also a term used to describe a scandalous person.

seh: say, said, also "that" as in *tell mi seh:* told me that

sell off: sold out

tallawah: strong, tough, resolute. Tallawah is also a proper name. Derived from talala, Ewe (Niger-Congo language spoken in Ghana)

tief: thief; steal

you mussi mad: "Are you crazy?"

you too lie!: "you're not telling the truth"; "you're kidding!"

yout; my yout: adolescent to young adult male; a name one calls young men akin to "my boy"; a young female is called "my girl."

ACKNOWLEDGMENTS

First big thanks goes to my editor Lilly Golden who walked with me the entire way of this oft seemingly endless process and did so with kindness and grace. Second big thanks goes to my friend Paul Lyons, my first reader and editor, a very generous, supportive person, he is greatly responsible for *Limbo* being published. Thanks to my other first reader Diana McCaulay, I have enjoyed our literary friendship. Thanks to friends who read and responded with pleasure to my novel: Liz Deloughrey, Alex Mawyer, Christelle Richter, Heidi Savery, Mimi Sheller, Linda Speth, Terese Svoboda, Sandy Tatham. Special thanks to two poetic geniuses who have kindly let me use excerpts of their works without charge: Kamau Brathwaite and his perfect poem *Limbo*, and David Rudder and his souring song *High Mas*. I have included two poems by my father, John Figueroa, *Goodbye (After Lorca)*, and *Hartlands/Heartlands*, I think he would have enjoyed the intertextuality. I thank Justine Henzell and Keala Kelly for help with lyrics permissions, Cristina Bacchilega for Italian translation and Krista Thompson for the postcard image that is used on the cover. For publishing, contractual, and legal advice, I thank Danielle Andrade, Jennes Anderson, Norma Scogin, Lisa Smith, Dave Taylor, Sherry Quirk. To my family and close friends, thanks always for your love and support without which my life would be empty. This book is dedicated to Diana McCaulay, founder and CEO of Jamaica Environment Trust, deepest thanks for your dedication to Jamaica, and to John Maxwell, Jamaican journalist and environmentalist, John we miss you every day. And to all of us who try in whatever ways we can to care for Jamaica, as my mother would say, God grant us strength!